Graveyard Eyes

David Chacko

Foremost Press
Cedarburg, Wisconsin

David Chacko can be reached at his website at
http://www.davidchacko.com
or by email at david@davidchacko.com

Published by Foremost Press

ISBN 0-9748921-7-3

For Levent Akayli, good friend

Part One:

The Evil Eye

CHAPTER 1

Visualization

He was sure it would go easy. All the lights had gone out in the houses on the street and the blue glow of televisions in dark rooms, too. One streetlight burned half a block away, and several dogs were close by. A hog-neck Rottweiler lived up the street three doors to the right, but even she had surrendered the watch to the breeze rustling through the trees.

He waited until the moon slid behind the clouds before he moved from the stand of mulberry trees and jumped the drainage ditch at the side of the road. He landed on the far side harder than he wanted, sending a message up his spine telling him not to repeat that entry. Without slowing, he walked across the narrow road, stepping around the potholes. Like everything in this country, the road was on the verge of becoming something else, and no one could tell if it was more or less.

He reached the darkness of the seven-foot wall and hugged it as he listened for sounds. There was no wire or glass at the top of the wall and no perimeter sensors inside. He was over the top without trouble, chinning and rolling and dropping onto the ground three long steps from the terrace.

Nothing left but a heat-sensitive PIR on the front door. And that wouldn't matter if he was quick.

The lock on the door was new—a replacement—not the best that could be had, but still a problem. He slid the pack from his back and took the pick gun from the front flap and the tension wrench he had velcroed in. He went twice in the darkness to locate the face of the lock, but slipping the tension wrench into the bottom was easy. Wet pussy was never as easy.

No tension at all. Wet and wild. He felt his way into the keyway with the pick gun. It felt like a brute in his hand, but worked like a ghost. Four snaps set the tumblers so quickly that his time at the door was no factor.

He waited before he pushed the door open, visualizing the interior for the last time. He knew it as well as his own before he had closed the place. There was one long room inside that was really three, but not overcrowded with furniture. A kitchen on the left. A bath.

He knew about the alarm system on the control panel near the bottom of the stairs and knew it was set to silent. That meant no problems with the neighbors. Still, it had to be deactivated within forty-five seconds, or vouched for by phone. Most people set their alarms quicker, but she had problems with her memory when she drank. And she drank. Most nights.

He liked to think he knew the reason. He had watched her for the last three days through the glasses from the car. Her routine did not vary much once she reached the house. If she was alone. When she took strange meat to bed, which she had done twice and each time a different one, there was no accounting for a pattern. The lights usually went on fast in the upstairs bedroom before they went out for good. Both men had left in the morning ahead of the neighbors going to work or to the market. They had their own cars, nice ones, too, parked across the street in the lot.

She had nothing hard to play with tonight. He had waited until he was sure no one would arrive for a late date. One o'clock had been his go.

On a deep breath he went in, whipping the door open and feathering it shut. He could have used a ferrite magnet to disarm the switch, but that was never guaranteed. No, it was a race from this point.

The first floor had metal shutters on the windows that made the darkness inside deeper than the night. Even with his eyes accustomed to low light, he had trouble making his way through the front room without meeting furniture. He bumped the corner of the dining table on the right, but soundlessly.

It was good the alarm system's LED display put out a peep of yellow light when armed. Not much, but a target. The color stood for caution everywhere in the world except Istanbul, where it meant go faster. Beat the red.

That had to happen. He hit the stairs, measuring the height of the risers with the first step and letting it out when he was sure of the reach. Halfway up, the stairs curved to the left sharply. He took the turn without slowing, but his foot bumped on the second step, loud.

He would have stopped another time, giving the sound a chance to mellow in her dreams, but that was not an option for a man working against the clock. He took the last two steps as one, reaching the upstairs hall at a quick walk. He knew he had pushed the time all the way.

Then he knew he had pushed too far. The cell phone rang. Hers. He had a second to get into the bedroom, but that was all.

CHAPTER 2

Byzantium

Levent drove up to the gate of the police chief's residence, where he was stopped by two patrolmen in uniform. Neither recognized him as an Inspector of Homicide or anything else. They took his name and identification, which were the same, and communicated with the interior by a hand-held device. After receiving an answer, they waved Levent through with a degree of respect.

The house was old, but recently restored, with board shutters, jigsaw work, and perhaps gables. At one time, when this area was not part of the city proper, most of the houses looked like this—figured by the imagination, and for most purposes earthquake-proof. There were still some left, set down among the concrete apartment buildings like reminders of a much slower time when the town was known by its Greek name, Saint Stephanos.

The Chief was an urbane man whose features were less Turkish than Byzantine. His face with its brief nose, bright cheeks, and winsome eyelashes, could have been lifted from any of the mosaics at Hagia Sofia without alteration. That meant he was descended from one of the old families of Istanbul. His was a political appointment, leveraged by his ancient name, and not to be trifled with.

He waved from five meters off as Levent entered the sitting room where the Chief did much of his business.

"Inspector, you came quickly."

"On your order, sir."

"It's good you don't live far away, Onur, and unfortunate you should be going back into the city so soon."

"May I know the reason, sir?"

The Chief did not respond as his servant entered the room with the coffee service. Both men sat in deeply creased leather chairs as the middle-aged woman, non-descript but for the size of her breasts, lay the tray on the table between them and quickly withdrew. The Chief took up his small cup of Turkish coffee, leaving the larger cup of filtered coffee for Levent. He had given no order for it. This man knew what his subordinate preferred.

"I called you here to take over a homicide investigation."

"Another man's investigation, sir?"

"That's correct. Inspector Altay, as we know, is a fine investigator, one of the best in the service, but he's not known for his ability to deal with people."

"You mean the press, sir?"

"Among others." The Chief touched his nose with his thumb as if at a bad smell. "This case will generate attention here and abroad. I need someone who can tether these people with kindness."

"It's not a small thing to take over another man's investigation," said Levent. "I'll see resentment from all quarters of the watch."

"I'm sure you're correct," he said. "And I'm just as sure you can handle every problem. I won't mention your obvious competence as an investigator. That goes without saying. I expect you to solve this case—and quickly. You'll have the close cooperation of my office."

That was unusual. This was all quite unusual. It stunk like the sewers of two thousand years that ran under the oldest parts of the city. Not that old shit was worse than the new.

"How much time do I have before the murder becomes public?"

"The vultures will gather soon, if they haven't already," said the Chief. "It was a prominent woman who was murdered in her own home. Her name is Ayla Acheson. She was the founder and proprietor of a tourist agency that specialized in foreign venues for Turks and jaunts in this country by foreigners. AylaTur is the name you might have seen here and there."

"I wasn't aware of her or the firm," said Levent. "Her name doesn't sound Turkish. I mean, the last."

"I understand her father was English. Or English-speaking. In any case, the daughter was multilingual with contacts in many countries. Some, I'm sure, will be coming to call."

Now Levent understood more. He spoke English and had never considered that a flaw in his upbringing until lately. The thought of having to field questions from people who were accustomed to answers did not sit well.

"I imagine I'll be able to handle this case, sir, unless I'm required to hold daily press briefings."

"I don't think that should be necessary, Inspector."

"May I refer the press to your office, sir, for the usual no comment?"

"I'm afraid that isn't a good option," said the Chief. "There are strong overtones to this case."

Levent took a large drink of his coffee, which was not bad, as he waited for the sword to come down. Overtones meant politics. The murder of a tour operator did not usually ascend to a realm that was both higher and lower.

"The lady was a feminist," said the Chief delicately. "A rather prominent one in that respect, too."

"Active?" asked Levent.

"Very."

"Politically active?"

"Yes, indeed."

Levent remembered that when the ancients led their sacrificial lambs to the altar, they sprinkled water over its head before the slaughter began. When the poor beast shook himself to clear the moisture, he seemed to agree to his fate.

"Was Acheson involved in the recent demonstrations, sir?"

"Inspector, why do you think you're here?"

Levent did not follow the logic as well as he could see the facts. The demonstrations that took place on Women's Day began peacefully, but turned ugly when the police charged into the ranks and did what they do best. Photographs of women and men being beaten appeared. Coverage in the foreign press was devastating. A police riot was the most generous thing that was said. The country's accession to the EU, always doubtful, became suddenly more remote.

"Have we changed our position on what happened that day, sir?"

"There have been modifications," said the Chief blandly. "We're no longer saying the provocation was almighty."

"Was there provocation, sir?"

"Of course," he said, waving his hand at the world outside his compound. "We know left-wing elements were involved. Kurdish agitators, too. The problem is that these malcontents cluster together and muddy their own cause. Their numbers are never large enough, and solidarity is thought to be the answer to good sense. And, of course, we don't teach good sense to our recruits."

"No, sir."

"Nor to our politicians," he said, excluding himself by waving his hand wider.

"That would be impossible, sir."

"But the politicians have also modified their position," said the Chief, criticism scratching his words. "Now they're saying that in spite of provocations, and the presence of agitators from within and without the country, those happened to be our mothers and daughters on the street."

"How clever, sir."

"But illogical. I know that must offend you, Inspector. I'm certain you'll discover the perpetrator of this crime, and I know the truth when it emerges will not disturb the body politic more than it has."

Finally, Levent understood why he had been called from his home and the dinner his wife had nearly brought to the table. He was to find the murderer of a political activist, and do it in a way that excluded Turkish society and its politicians. He was to make shit sanitary.

"Has Inspector Altay been informed of his replacement?"

"No," said the Chief. "I thought it best not to disturb the collection of evidence at the scene. We know how important that is at the outset."

"I see," said Levent. "I'm to tell him."

The Chief looked hard at Levent—not the first time he had ever done that, and perhaps not the last. "Since you're already on your way, Inspector, I'll inform Altay of his replacement."

"Thank you, sir."

Levent put the last of the coffee down and got to his feet. "I'll keep your office advised of developments in the case. And the direction it leads."

"Be sure you do."

* * *

As he drove north, Levent no longer wondered how the Chief managed to retain his office through several changes of government, including the current one, which was the most fundamental kind. He was a remarkable creature with brass manners, a silver tongue, and lead in his pants. He was never the first through the door but often the last to leave. The important things were always brought up for discussion after the meeting adjourned.

Levent had once been called to arbitrate at one of those sessions after hours. He was on a case and in the neighborhood when he took a call that brought him to a room on the seventh floor of a seaside hotel. He found the Chief alone in a large suite with four cigars in the lapel pocket of his suit. Throughout the three rooms were the ruins of a major debauch. The smell of alcohol, tobacco, perfume, and sex was so strong it made Levent's eyes water.

At least three men had been present by the evidence, but they were no longer available for questioning. In the bathroom, piled between the toilet and the tub, he found an attractive prostitute. It seemed she had swallowed a condom that somehow lodged in her throat.

It was not Levent's place to ask what so many men had done with a share of the same woman, or how many more women had been invited to the party. It was his job to dispose of the body in a way that attracted no attention to the authors of her fate.

He supposed he would have done that. If the police were not the guardians of morality, they were the ones who absorbed its meaning. Levent thought of heaving the body out the window onto the apron of the swimming pool until he realized the windows were permanently shut in the American fashion. He thought of sending her down the laundry chute for a quieter exit. He was preparing to wrap her in a bed sheet, his hands in her armpits, when he suddenly understood, skin to skin, that she was not dead. Bluish purple, but still alive.

Luckily, a hospital was located two blocks down the same seaside street. With even more luck, the woman survived. What could have been a disaster was now the subject of department jokes that the Chief himself circulated.

The only details that did not come public were the identities of the men who had shared the suite. They were understood to be prominent, but anonymous. Never to be known in any form was the man who by his method in love had caused the complete dysfunction of an experienced whore.

The intervention had not harmed Levent's career as he was afraid it might. The way the event had made its way into folklore was a measure of the Chief's cunning. The threat of blackmail was never an issue, since death did not result. As long as the names of the parties involved were unspoken, the only man who benefited by the silence was the Chief.

And Levent. He was promoted to Inspector later the same year. He knew he had gained the position by merit, as well as he knew the Chief had put in his word. The nature of the incident also gained Levent a reputation as a man who could be trusted for discretion. When a case demanded it, Levent expected a call. He never complained. Not, perhaps, until today.

He had a queasy feeling about this one. Mothers and daughters indeed. When politics and common sense met, the results were always absurd. This time promised to be no different. When he called his wife, Emine, as he sped along the freeway, she had asked: "What's wrong?"

"Nothing," he said, wondering how his words had betrayed him. His work was his mask, and he did not often speak of it to her.

Of course, she might have assumed he would never miss her kirlangich except for an important reason. It was trash fish, as ugly a creature as God ever made, and could not be eaten until its flesh nearly dissolved in a long-simmering pot.

But then it was heaven. And a lesson in life. The really important things, the ones that could not be enjoyed as they came from nature, were the province of women and their subtle alchemy.

CHAPTER 3

Psychopath

Ayla Acheson had been murdered at her summer home in the country, if such a thing existed in Istanbul any longer. What was heavily wooded land not long ago now looked like a suburb in patchy leaf. As he drove in, Levent had passed two new housing developments with swimming pools and tennis courts. Levent had never met a Turk who played tennis, but thought his innocence might not last much longer.

The victim's two-story house, painted a strange but comfortable shade of gold, stood alone and fenced all around, with several neighbors a few meters distant. Levent parked his car across from the house in a small lot scratched out at the side of the road. The house had a short driveway and garage, but it was completely filled with police vehicles, including the technician's van.

It was an unwritten law in the department that the more prominent the victim, the more homage paid in personnel. Already, the front lawn had been trampled, cigarette butts embedded in recent footprints. So much for outdoor forensics.

Levent made his way through five patrolmen standing on the terrace without making comments or losing his temper. Plenty of time for that. Dealing with Inspector Altay came first.

He was a grim stocky man whose coat had not been buttoned since it left the lowest rack at the discount store. He came to meet Levent at the doorway, his heavy eyelids almost closing at what he did not want to see. Lighting a Samsun in his mouth off the one in his hand, he blew smoke at his colleague, speaking in the gruff voice that intimidated many men.

"You don't need to worry, Onur. The Chief called."

"I'm sorry about this, Deniz. You have to believe it was not my doing."

"I don't have to believe it," he said. "I have a right to be pissed off, and I don't want you or that sex kitten taking it away."

What a strange way to refer to the Chief. But appropriate. Altay was never far off target. "Who found the body?"

"We did." Altay's eyebrows went up halfway to his brow. "Anonymous call to the authorities, don't you know?"

That was as bad as it came to the table. Someone who knew enough to alert the police to murder knew enough to have done it. Or who had done it. And wasn't telling.

"Don't worry," said Altay. "You and the Chief believe in angels. You just don't believe in wings."

"Go home, Deniz. Make love to your wife, but be sure to call first. She might have to move someone out the back door in a hurry."

He smiled, biting his overhung lip. "If you're thinking it's going to be as easy with this one, you're mistaken. When they analyze the semen in her bed, you'll have to stand for a roll call."

"That busy?"

He took the cigarette from his mouth and pointed it at Levent. "According to the neighbors, this is a whorehouse without apology. I sent them home for now because the numbers they gave me were preposterous. AylaTur, one called her. That's supposed to be a joke."

Levent should be sorry to hear that. An investigation could drown in too much information. But a lottery of suspects meant a range of choice. That was better than none.

"How long have the technicians been here?"

"An hour before you," he said.

"Good," said Levent. "I'll get them out the door as quick as I can."

"I can take a hint, Onur. I'll leave a copy of my notes on the table as soon as I make sense of them."

"Thanks, Deniz. I owe you."

"Your balls," he said. "That's what you'll lose this time if you don't give that pussy what he wants."

"What does he want?"

"A psychopath would be best," said Altay. "Mindless, of course."

Altay moved onto the terrace and displaced the crowd of patrolmen. He sat in a chair before a glass-topped table under an electronic insect-machine that snapped every time it made a kill.

Levent could not help wondering why anyone would leave such devices and fine furniture where they might be stolen. The chairs were paper-wrapped a thousand-fold to look like snug wicker. Indestructible by the elements and eight hundred dollars apiece. Four of them.

She would have put them inside unless she was living here more than not. Still careless, though perhaps not for the rich and promiscuous.

The interior of the house was as expensive. Levent had seldom seen furnishings like these except at a showroom in one of the best parts of the city. He always wondered who bought things with fabric so colorful, angles so sudden, made with bright metal fittings, and, yes, daring. The only things that seemed traditionally Turkish were the carpets and kilims scattered about. Even these were done in seldom seen shades of orange and blue and all the variations of gold. Very cool. Earth tones, if the earth had ever been so fashionable.

The murder had been done on the second floor by the traffic that passed up and down the staircase. Levent noticed the security system mounted on a panel at the bottom of the stairs. A lot of good it had done the victim.

"Are you finished up there yet?"

"Soon," said the man coming down the stairs. His name was Tavshan, and he was a fingerprint technician.

"Find anything?"

"How would I know? There're lots of prints in the bedroom from lots of people. And the rest of the house, too."

"Your report in a week?"

"I'm sure we can do better."

"Try."

Tavshan muttered something unheard. A good thing, but Levent did not discard technicians' work like some detectives. It was not impossible for fingerprints to match up with a murderer.

That happened once three years ago. It would happen again in 2009 unless the averages lied. Every killer, or burglar, knew enough to wear gloves. Levent thought he had a chance with science if he dealt with an amateur or a madman, though an angry lover might be both.

When Levent reached the top of the stairs, he met Derya Silme coming down the hall. The medical officer, grossly fat and triple-chinned, was the best man for guesswork until the autopsy came in.

"What do you have for me, Bones?"

Silme smiled with teeth that had been made and others that were unfortunately natural. He was a science fiction addict who reveled in blood, which only seemed like a contradiction. Turning around in the hallway barely wider than his frame, he led Levent to the second room on the right.

"I've seen worse, Onur, though not lately and not from star-crossed lovers. He used a knife for the work, and probably not from the kitchen. It looks like a double-edge with a serrated back."

"A hunter."

"Of bipeds," he said, as they entered the room.

Not a bedroom. A study, and as modern as the rest of the house. A writing desk stood in the center of the room with little clutter except for the laptop computer. Directly ahead was a television set large enough to present life-sized images. A tall built-in bookcase sat on the right with two filing cabinets opposite. All of it—every piece in the room—had been disturbed, including its occupant.

She was a woman of about thirty-five who sat in her night-gown in an office chair on wheels with her hands behind her back. Her throat had been cut, and other parts of her body seemed mangled, too. The garment was ripped down the front, so most of the blood skirted the nightclothes, painting her breasts and settling like slush in the chair. Its fabric had always been red, but a difference could be seen now.

Levent tried to discover what she looked like before her death. He had little success. Her left eye—the one that was turned away—

had been plucked from its socket in a rage of blood and transferred to the printer stand at the side of the desk, which she faced. Look at me, it said, and think of the other. Levent looked at the other. It was blue and wide open.

"I'd like to see the autopsy results quickly," said Levent. "Tomorrow would be late."

"You're dreaming."

"The Chief doesn't dream. I think he'd be normal if he did."

"Then I'd better get her out of here before she starts to melt," said Silme. "I'd have done it already if they hadn't said you were on the way. I know you like to shake hands with the dead."

Levent liked to know them, true. That was the best way to find out who wanted them dead. Somewhere he would put a hand on a lever that would prove a killer as human as his victim. She was very much that.

"When did it happen?"

"Less than a day. I'd say last night late until we know more. We should be able to narrow it down."

"No evidence of rape?"

"None that shows," said Silme. "Unless he had a liking for half-blind women, I'd be surprised."

So the Chief might have his psychopath after all. Levent did not often see torture in his work, and never such a mutilation of a woman. The man who did this was deliberate and absorbed in his work. Unless the victim had deactivated her security system downstairs, he bypassed it. He had taken the time to bind and terrorize her, so he probably wanted something.

What?

Levent noticed a fingerprint, oval and dirt red, implanted on top of the printer. Bald with no whorls, a gloved hand had made it. The print was probably useless if the blood was the victim's. It had been left behind as if the killer was careless. Or as an advertisement.

When he moved around the desk to the back of the chair, Levent saw her hands were cuffed. Unless she liked sexual games, the killer brought them. Standard black and cheap, they could be found without much trouble. Still, it was unusual. This man came well prepared.

On both her hands were fine rings. One was a diamond set among smaller, more colorful stones. The other, as big as a Napoleon cherry, had been carved from a single piece of stone. It looked like a bird in flight, and no doubt was expensive. So this did not appear to be a robbery—not the ordinary kind.

On her back, about eight centimeters below the beginning of her neck, was an incision too precise to be called random. Or mayhem. Levent could not tell more because of the blood.

"There's a cut here," he said. "The garment was pulled away to make it."

"Yes, I saw that," said Silme. "Rather neat. He could have put some pressure there to tell her that he was serious. At a glance, the wound doesn't look deep enough to sever the spinal cord."

"But the cut extends below the skin," said Levent. "Would he know how far to go before she wouldn't be able to help him any longer?"

"A surgeon would. A man off the street—no. If there's a half-way place between those two, I haven't seen it."

"An experienced torturer might know."

"Come across many of those?"

"Not yet."

Levent was afraid he would never know if the man was as good at his trade as he seemed. Experience like this set him apart from ninety-nine percent of suspects. Unless Ayla Acheson kept mean company, the killer could have been hired. And that meant someone had hired him.

"Anything else?"

Silme pointed to the floor. "She had six toes on her left foot."

Levent looked. He saw nothing unsightly about the foot, but even among the carnage, he felt a shock. Something primeval had crept into an investigation where so much was incomprehensible.

"I noticed because her slipper was missing," said Silme. "The surgery wasn't done last night. She had the extra one removed some time ago. Better for the beach. And at the haberdasher."

"In some places, you know, that makes her a witch."

Silme's laugh was like the wheeze of a wounded giant. "I wasn't aware you were superstitious, Onur."

That was a joke. All Turks were superstitious. They learned that, if nothing else, at their mother's knee.

CHAPTER 4

Time of Death

In the bedroom, Levent found the lost slipper half hidden by the duvet that lapped onto the floor. Had she been surprised while asleep?

Obviously, she had time to put on the slippers. The killer might have given her that time, but it seemed more reasonable to assume that she had awakened and put on both of them, possibly at the moment she was taken. And lost one before leaving the room?

There were no other signs of struggle, but a double-edged knife at the throat gathered attention instantly. It would be in character for the killer to carry another weapon, like a gun. This man came equipped.

Except for the heavy work he had done in the study, Levent found no trace of the killer. He had left no cigarette butts or dropped anything he had not picked up. No sign of forced entry, though the front door had probably been used. A lock pick sometimes left tracks. The techs might be able to tell if the tumblers were scarred.

One thing bothered Levent. He found no cell phone. A woman in business, let alone a Turkish woman, would never be without one. As necessary as makeup, at least one would be in the house and close at hand. If she hadn't wanted to be bothered, she could easily have switched it off.

An inconsistency. When Levent got over being bothered by them, he liked them for the questions they brought up. Could the killer have been in her phone directory and not wanted to leave a trace of himself behind? That seemed unlikely, but Levent had known stranger things that psychopaths overlooked. Think in those terms. The Chief's terms, as it were.

Levent went on a hunt for the cell phone. He did not find one in the spare bedroom. Nothing in the bathroom either, which was overused in most respects. He saw things he had rarely seen before, including a bidet and cosmetics from every part of Europe and America.

Levent did not know why he found himself staring at the object hung by a chain on the back of the door. It was a *gozboncu*. A glass bead. They were usually blue, and almost always round with a definite center, like an eye. They could be big or small and were to be found in every home in the country in almost every room. Levent had noticed several at strategic places in the victim's rooms.

The gozboncu was said to ward off the Evil Eye, which resulted when jealousy was directed at the inhabitants of the house. In theory—and it could not be otherwise—the glass bead attracted negative power and deflected it from its target. Sometimes, when the jealousy was directed in a powerful way, the glass cracked.

Now Levent realized why he looked so intently at this little blue bead described in descending circles of yellow and white.

It was cracked.

* * *

There was more than enough to envy in all the rooms of the house. Levent made a list as he went down the flight of stairs that turned a complete one-eighty. The kitchen that lay directly ahead was what he expected. A bright fall of brushed metal with counter space in granite. The appliances were German with digital displays, and the cabinets Italian, blood red, elegantly forbidding.

All these things seemed a lot for the mind of a maid—and there must be one. She would come round in the morning unless tomorrow was her day off. Levent might still be here when she arrived if he was unlucky. He looked forward to meeting the woman who could tell the most about her mistress' home.

One question he would ask concerned the alarm system on the wall between the kitchen and the stairs. It had been deactivated by Altay or someone, but seemed to be physically intact. Levent was not well versed on this system. Was it armed at all times? Could it be disarmed by the owner—or anyone else? How many people were on the OK list?

Usually, the alarm worked on a timer. Thirty seconds from the door without entering the codes alerted the security firm. If they received an unsatisfactory reply, they contacted the police. Levent looked at Altay's notes, because he was sure the inspector had noted that. One of the first said: "Call BSS."

Levent dialed the number Altay had written. Without much trouble, he located the supervisor for the district, who asked for his bona fides and was not too easily satisfied. That was fine and competent, if slow.

"All right, Inspector," he said with a long sigh into the receiver. "I believe you're with Homicide, and I imagine there was a murder. We hate to lose customers. What can I do for you?"

"First, tell me if you had any reports from here last night?"

"Just a moment."

It was more than a moment before the voice returned. "We had two calls to that location last night," he said. "Both verified."

"How were they verified?"

"By the contact person," he said. "Ayla Acheson."

"You're sure it was she who answered?"

"We require our customers to verify our calls by a password they choose," he said. "And we instruct them not to share the password with anyone. If she shared it, that might be the reason she's dead."

So the victim—or someone who knew her password—provided the verifications. That was clear, but not foolproof.

"When were these things done?"

"The first was at 8:43," he said, quickly now. "I don't know the reason for the alarm. We get a lot of this sort of thing. Usually, they forget to punch the codes into the box, or don't do it quick enough. From what I see in the records from that number, the lady malfunctioned now and then."

"Careless?"

"I didn't say that."

"How loud does the alarm sound?"

"That depends," he said. "They can set it as loud as they like. They can set it to silent as well."

She might have done the latter. And possibly that was the reason she was dead. "How do I tell?"

"Set the alarm off yourself," he said. "It won't matter because I'll know you're there. You'll know when your ears begin to scream."

"So the alarm is loud?"

"Depending on the level they set, the answer should be somewhere between yes and God almighty," he said. "We've had dogs that were left in the house go insane from the noise."

Levent would set off the alarm next. Now, he had other questions. "How long did she have to input the codes?"

"Forty-five seconds in this case. That varies from client to client. It's what they ask for that determines the interval."

"And she asked you to call her directly?" said Levent. "Not the police?"

"Yes. That's another option they have."

A confident woman. Alone out here, but apparently unworried. Levent guessed there were not many like that. She was accustomed to dealing with problems, and she probably came across many in her business.

"What about the second call?"

"It came in at 1:12 a.m.," he said. "Another false alarm. The client answered with the password and did *not* ask for assistance."

Levent was interested in a call that came in late last night. Silme, who was usually accurate in his guesses, thought that was the approximate time of death.

"Who took the call?"

"The man on duty."

"His name?"

"That would be Tahsin Turkler."

"I'd like to speak to him."

"He's at home, Inspector. This is his day off."

"Did I ask for anything but his number?"

"Just a moment."

* * *

Tahsin Turkler was at home, but slow to respond, saying he would be with the police in "just a minute." Assuming the minute would grow, Levent stepped to the box set in the wall at the base of the stairs, activated the alarm system, and set off the intruder alert.

Nothing. Not a sound.

Careless. A silent alarm was very careless. The killer could have entered with nothing to fear if he knew he had nothing to fear. And he might. He seemed to know everything he needed to know about the house. All he had to worry about was the call that came from the security firm. From Turkler.

When he came back to the phone, his voice was abrupt, as if he had been disturbed at something important, like watching a football match. "You're not showing much respect for me. What did you say your name was?"

"Inspector Levent. I'm the man who's going to drag you out of your home in the next fifteen minutes if you don't straighten up."

"No need for that," he said, backing off instantly. "What do you want to know about this woman?"

"You took a call from her last night just after one o'clock. Tell me everything you remember."

"Not much," he said. "I had an alert from her house and called to see if anything was wrong. She told me she forgot to hit the box when she went out of the house."

"At 1:12, she went out of the house?"

"I don't argue with them. If they say there's no problem, that's how it stands."

Levent was sure of that. If Turkler was all that stood between the victim and her fate, she had been in trouble from the day she signed up for the service.

"The contact number was her cell phone, is that correct?"

"It always is if they have one," he said. "It's better that way. They might be anywhere in the house or even on the toilet. They could be gone from the house if it wasn't them that set off the alarm."

Levent did not know why the victim's cell phone was missing, but she had used it to take the call from security. It was on the loose now.

"Did you often have to call her late at night?"

"It happened. Earlier for the most part, I'd say."

"Did you notice anything in her manner that seemed strained last night?"

"I don't think so. She was one of my regulars. About once a week she couldn't find the codes in her head or anywhere else. It's not unusual. Sometimes I think they do it—or don't do it— because they need someone to talk to."

"Is that what you thought last night?"

"No," he said after a pause. "She didn't run on. Just said goodnight and thank you."

"Did she usually thank you?"

"I don't think so," he said.

"So *that* was unusual."

"I'll have to think about it."

"Please."

Levent heard Turkler's breathing in the phone. If that was his protest, or his way of thinking, it needed work. "I'm going through my mind," he said, "and I don't think she ever was polite. I usually got a 'no problem' from her and a quick goodbye. A couple times she was drunk and fooled around, but I can't say she was passing out invitations. Or tripping over herself to be polite."

"Based on your previous contacts, would you say she seemed under stress last night?"

"I can't guarantee it, Inspector. She seemed in a hurry to get off the phone, if that helps."

Levent was thinking the killer might have made his way to the victim before she answered the call. That made him the fastest break-in artist in the country. And a gambler. Did that make him a psychopath?

"Was she quick to answer the phone?"

"Not at all," he said. "I remember that. It was six or eight rings. I was ready to hang up and try again."

"Was that unusual, too?"

"I can't say it was, Inspector. People forget about the system. They fumble in the dark trying to find their cell phone. Sometimes they have it shut off, so it buzzes in their pants. Those are the worst ones. I have to call your people then. When they come to the house and find nothing wrong, they're unhappy."

No surprise. But a guaranteed police presence put a premium on answering the phone with a positive response. That happened last night at an awkward hour during an intrusion that turned deadly. Levent hoped that what he had found was a reasonably exact time of death.

CHAPTER 5

Contacts

Just as the body was being removed, Detective Erol Akbay, Levent's best man, arrived in his dusty BMW. Before entering the house, he took a long look at the body as it was loaded into the van. Akbay never trusted photographs or reports. He smoked most of a cigarette as he examined the corpse, holding it by the left hand that was one finger short of a fist.

"Sorry I'm late," he said as he came up to Levent. "I was on the Other Side taking care of my father's things when I got the call. Forty minutes to the bridge, forty on the bridge, and the rest here."

Nothing was ever to be done about traffic in Istanbul in Europe or Asia. Akbay was on leave because of the death of his father and had a good excuse not to show at all.

Levent spent some time filling Akbay in—longer than he thought. When he finished, he said, "I'm going upstairs to look at her study again. I'd like you to visit the neighbors. Inspector Altay didn't get much from them."

"I'm sure Altay was happy about being relieved."

"A little less than us, Erol. We're on the front burner again. This one comes from the Chief."

"From his mind or his asshole?"

"Both."

"Some day you'll let me know how to tell the difference."

"Some day you'll know yourself. Meanwhile, get as many of these bystanders out of the way as you can."

Akbay set to work clearing out the uniforms that were still milling about. Some of the technicians, who liked to extend their time outside the lab, had already started out the door as Levent climbed the stairs again.

The study seemed more unquiet after the body had been removed. It was often that way, as if death left a residue that increased when the flesh was elsewhere. Levent, who was minimally superstitious, never failed to note the phenomenon. Ayla Acheson was gone, but in some form she still wandered.

In the first drawer of the desk, Levent found an address book with a golden cover. These were once the *sine qua non* of police work, but now everyone kept their numbers electronically and often failed to correct the print. Still, it should be useful in tracing her contacts. The book was filled, and the margins crammed with additions, so it might be up-to-date.

The filing cabinets were filled with commercial papers that Levent would look over more closely later. For now, they confirmed that the victim was a successful entrepreneur with contacts worldwide. The Middle East, Europe—and Russia if it was European—were her main areas of concentration. The trend followed closely the main lines of Turkish tourism.

The computer was more interesting. Devoted to business, it also kept her personal correspondence. One directory held letters to women's groups all over the world. A second was for friends. Levent made notes of those. She had several acquaintances in North America and Russia.

She had an active online presence through her DSL connection. Her email contacts were substantial, and Levent printed those. She also used ICQ, a communications module. Her online handle was Hera, the goddess of Heaven. Wife of Zeus. Or, in other incarnations, Mother Earth.

In the time that Levent cruised her files, Hera was buzzed twice by her ICQ contacts, one named Dilek (Wish) and another named Blue Cruise. The second name related to sailing excursions along the southern coast of Turkey, unless it had another meaning in English that Levent did not quite comprehend.

He did not list the ICQ contacts, who used fictitious names. The real ones should be on the company's books, but would take some doing to discover. He did not spend time looking at her library either. There were as many books in English as Turkish. A lot dealt with her business, guidebooks and atlases, but the fiction was revealing. She liked thrillers, American mostly. He did not see any feminist tracts, but probably would not have known them anyway.

Akbay had not returned, so Levent called the number he had been given for continuous updates to the Chief. He had little to say to the man who answered the phone, but said it at length, so the Chief would think he had done his job. It was like that when reporting to the clouds. By the minute, not relevance.

When Levent heard a call from Akbay downstairs, he left the study and tramped down the steps again. He wondered how anyone could have made a fast trip up the steep winding staircase. A young man, probably. An athlete was more like it.

Except for two uniforms on the terrace, the downstairs was nearly empty. The supersonic furniture, the fantastic colors, and the gewgaws placed exactly where the eye could find them, looked like the deck of a cruise ship headed for an unknown destination. Say, the stars.

None of the neighbors, of course, had been in bed. Akbay could have conducted interviews in their houses, but knew it was best to have witnesses test their memories in neutral surroundings.

It was too bad the house was not more neutral. Three of the four neighbors had never been inside the place, and the first occasion turned their minds to awe. They were all happy to finally gain a view of the interior and tattle on its owner, although they had little more than tattle to give.

Not until the last couple entered the room did things change for the better. Temel and Meral Buhar were proof that a long-married couple did not have to come to look like each other. He was dark, slim and taciturn, his wife gruesomely fat, maliciously blonde, and talkative. As a division of labor, the arrangement seemed to work as broken mirrors functioned when their purpose is gone.

"At least three bottles of raki a week, every week, and sometimes more," said Meral, turning toward her husband vengefully. "If you drank like that, you'd be up all night pissing."

Temel seemed to shudder at the thought, but said nothing. Clearly, he did not share his wife's opinion of their neighbor. But if he felt the need to revise, he could not bring himself to it.

"Mrs. Buhar," said Levent. "How do you determine things such as the alcohol consumption of this house?"

"I talk to the maid now and then. She's as friendly as the other one was stuck up."

"Her name?"

"Fatma. She lives a good way from here, but I don't remember where. She takes the bus three times a week to work."

"You're a keen observer," said Levent. "That's always helpful to an investigation. What we'd like to know is if you saw anything unusual in the last week around this house?"

"I can't say I saw anything like that," she said. "The normal was bad enough. In fact, there were two in this week, though that isn't worth remarking for her."

"Two?" said Levent.

"*Visitors*," she said venomously. "You know the kind. They come late and leave early. You can tell by the way they walk to their cars that they had enough to last them a while."

"They were men?" asked Akbay. "Strangers?"

"As strange as two moons in the sky," she said, drawing her hand across her face. "But if you mean have I seen them before, the answer is no to the first, and yes to the second. He was the Thursday night for lack of a better way of putting it. He drives a white Mercedes, and you'd better get out of his way."

"This man came every Thursday night?"

"Not on a clock, but often. Leave out vacations, then it was pretty much Thursday night on the hoof."

"Do you know anything more about him?" asked Levent.

"Married for sure," she said like a war cry. "He's got this one night a week out of the house to visit his sister with cancer. She lives where his cell phone finds him."

"Where does he live the rest of the time?"

"Istanbul by the license plates," she said. "But you're talking about a citizen of the world in that one."

"Do you have any idea what he does for a living?"

"They don't work when they look like that," she said. "We pay them to visit the common folk in style."

Meral looked at her husband as she spoke, as if he was a gigolo, too. Although nothing seemed more unlikely, Temel used the occasion to speak for the first time.

"He works for the city municipality."

Temel immediately shrank back, aware that he had interrupted his wife's tale with fact. Levent would not allow him to hide again.

"Mister Buhar. Sir. Can you tell us how you know this man works for the municipality?"

"I saw him downtown one day last year when I went about my Social Security," he said. "He works for the tourist bureau. That's her business, too, but on the other side. The private side, I mean."

"Do you know his name?"

"No, but I can tell you where to find him."

* * *

Levent didn't make too much of the connection between the victim and her visitor. Thursday nights for a quiet dip was not the same as torture and murder, but it should be profitable to talk to someone who knew the victim and her habits in a very personal way. It was early to predict how the investigation would turn, but Akbay was excited by the new direction.

"He'll be easy to shake loose if the husband knows what he's talking about. A married man working for the city. With those covered heads and their lords and masters around, we won't have to make a scene."

It was true that fundamentalists were always most concerned with the sins of others. That kept them from looking too closely at themselves, where the view was twice as boring.

"We could make our pay for the year if we were that kind," said Levent. "But we're not, and we have to tread carefully on this one."

"If that's the way you want to play it."

"That's the way we will play it," said Levent. "Why don't you go upstairs and check for things I missed. Another pair of eyes should be useful."

When Akbay left to make his sweep, Levent did the same downstairs, looking for anything he had overlooked in his scan. He found nothing in the front room, which was so orderly it had obviously seen the services of a maid on a steady basis.

He went into the kitchen next. He found several carving knives, but none that were missing from their holders. Silme was probably right. The killer brought his own tools, and they were professional weight.

On the sink top stood one empty raki glass with pale liquid at the bottom. She hadn't had company last night by that measure. Levent searched all the drawers, finding nothing until he gave up and came to the notes hung by magnets on the refrigerator door. There were several names and phone numbers, all for local services, he thought. One said Fatma—672-9380.

The maid, probably. Although it was midnight, Levent thought of calling her when he heard Erol's voice from upstairs. "Onur, I think you should see this."

Akbay's tone pushed Levent up the stairs fast. He turned into the study to see Erol at the desk looking intently at the computer screen. Now Levent remembered he had left the machine on.

"Come and look," said Akbay. "This name means too much to be a mistake."

Levent sat down in the chair that Akbay vacated. A small window was open on the screen. An ICQ window. In it was one line of text.

KARANLIK: Hi.

Karanlik meant darkness, or perhaps shadow. The Shadow? Whoever he was, he must have been OK'd by Hera, so she had talked to him before.

"When did the window come up, Erol?"

"Just now. I was sitting at the desk when the icon lit up. I didn't say anything, but let him enter because of the name."

Levent took a moment to switch the keyboard from Turkish to English, which was the language Karanlik liked. Levent was still wondering what he would say when he hit the first keys.

HERA: Hello yourself.

For a long moment, Karanlik gave no answer. He must have been waiting for a response, but loosely. Having a smoke and not paying attention? Thinking of what he would say? His first words were pertinent, and perhaps impertinent. They assumed too much.

KARANLIK: Who am I talking to?

HERA: If you don't know, I'll have to end this conversation.

KARANLIK: I don't think you will.

In spite of what Levent knew of this night and any other, he felt a chill pass over his back. He could not swear it began with the hair on the back of his neck.

HERA: Your confidence is misplaced. Tell me what you want, or I'll sign off right now.

KARANLIK: You won't sign off, cop.

That said a lot. That said everything, but who would have the nerve to call this house at this time. Karanlik had obviously gone online and seen that Hera's ICQ was active. The program came up automatically when the machine was turned on. And he might have been waiting for a while. He must have been.

HERA: I'm listening.

KARANLIK: That's good. The next thing to obedient. Now tell me your name. First and last.

HERA: Police Inspector Onur Levent. I should know yours.

KARANLIK: You can look it up in the directory later.

Levent was sure he would find the alias of an alias there, but he was determined to please this dark man. He knew the police were in the house. Had he called them to report the murder as he was calling now, anonymously?

HERA: I'm at a disadvantage. I'm not used to that.

KARANLIK: You'll have to alter your ways, Inspector. I've had to all my life.

HERA: That makes you sound like an old man.

KARANLIK: That makes me sound experienced. I've lived a long time in bad places. When it was different, I don't recall, but I never got proper compensation. Not like the pigs do now.

HERA: I'm sure you know best about that. I'll accept it for now.

KARANLIK: Now is forever, Inspector. Pay attention, or you won't know what you need to know.

HERA: You mean the information you have to give me?

KARANLIK: It's better than any you'll get. You can be sure anything I say comes from the source.

HERA: Are you saying you killed Ayla Acheson?

For the first time, Karanlik's response did not swarm across the screen. He seemed to be thinking about the question, or which answer served him best.

KARANLIK: Did you look at the back of her neck, Inspector? I left a souvenir for you to find.

Many people knew about the murder by now, but Levent thought only Silme, and possibly Altay, had noted the cut-like incision at the back of her neck. Did Levent mention it to the Chief's assistant? No.

HERA: I found the mark on her back. Is that your signature?

KARANLIK: Let's say it's a token for my new friend.

HERA: That's a strange way for a man to be known.

KARANLIK: I'm sure that's what you think.

Levent thought he was talking to a lunatic. Although he had done that in the past from time to time, this one seemed very different.

HERA: I suppose you'll tell me why you called. If it's to go on about your conquest, I don't have time. I should be following your trail right now. And I will be.

KARANLIK: There is no trail, Inspector. Who do you think you're dealing with? You have nothing to follow, and you don't even know which direction to go. I'm going to tell you now, so listen closely. Go up, Inspector. Go up until you see the sky.

The sky? The moon and stars? A fast plane leaving the country? Levent had no idea except the obvious.

HERA: Is that your way of telling me you're God?

KARANLIK: That's poor, Inspector. Very disappointing. I'm afraid you'll find this will be a long time in the wilderness for you. We won't be talking again, so keep a sharp eye out. There's a lot to see in the life of that woman.

HERA: Is that what you found so fascinating?

KARANLIK: Let's say yes for now. You'll see all that and more before you're done.

HERA: Are you planning more events for us to admire?

KARANLIK: You'll see if I do. Believe me, I wouldn't want to surrender to anyone but a pen pal.

HERA: I'm glad to hear your mind works the same way as mine. I'd like to accept your surrender.

KARANLIK: Not yet, Inspector. We'll play the game of Keep Away. You run in circles, chasing what you can't reach. It's a children's game, but that's where it all starts, doesn't it?

HERA: If you say so. Some of us grow up.

Levent waited for a reply to crawl across in the window, when instead a large open mouth with grinning teeth appeared. The symbol for laughter. Karanlik was having fun with his new friends, the police.

KARANLIK: I'll say goodbye. Be sure to look everywhere, even the places that don't seem likely. If you find where I've been, you might know where I'm going. If you find where she's been, you'll know everything.

And he vanished.

CHAPTER 6

Stars

Levent stared at the screen and the white space below the final words, until his surprise and a lingering sense of achievement made a hard turn back to reality. What had happened? A lot, yet nothing. Levent had been contacted by a killer in a completely anonymous way. The man had given no information beyond teases that were probably meant to obscure his traces.

Then why had he called? What kind of lunatic killed piece by piece only to insist that the pieces meant something more? Look into this woman's life, he said. And don't forget, to the sky.

Levent became so angry, he nearly clicked the ICQ screen away. He probably would have done that if Akbay had not tapped his arm and said, "Don't forget to save the chat."

Levent did not know that was possible. He vacated the chair to Akbay, who set about saving and printing the session. Like most young men these days, he was computer literate, if only as a way to play the dating game. He probably had not understood many of the English words that passed, but was that important?

Levent stepped to the French doors that were tucked between the filing cabinets. He opened them onto a useless balcony that overlooked the brevity of the front of the house and the more ample space with the swimming pool at the left side.

The air was crisp and country cool. Looking up at the stars overhead seemed to open him to a draft of even cooler air. A lot of stars were out tonight. Millions? Did they all have names?

The names people chose for themselves, replacing the imaginations of their mothers and fathers, were revealing. Sometimes, they whispered like a secret wish. Or became another way to hide.

Hera. Queen of Heaven. What did she want to be, or what did she lack, to make her choose that name? Did she crave the power of a throne? Did she know she was incomplete without Zeus? It was all harmless, but suggestive.

Karanlik.

A man from the darkness. The shadow had chosen a Turkish name to pair with his fluent English. He had not hesitated as he typed the words in the window, as Levent did. He was in no way hesitant. Bold to the point of insanity, but stopping short of it. That's what Levent thought. And that's what he felt.

"Onur," said Akbay, who was still at the computer. "I found his biography on ICQ. But it's not what it's supposed to be."

Levent turned back into the room to the desk, where he stood behind the computer as Akbay ran the cursor over a page of information.

NAME: George Bush.

ADDRESS: White House, 1300 Pennsylvania Avenue.

CITY: Washington, D.C.

No postal code. He probably didn't know it.

"Is he telling us something?" asked Akbay. "He calls himself Bush. If we follow the logic, he's a murderer without a conscience who thinks he's justified in everything he does."

"Powerful, too," said Levent. "He rules the world he made for himself. And for us."

"This bastard could have called himself Milky Way for all the good it does," said Akbay, waving his hand at the screen to dismiss it. "I don't understand why he gave us that much. I don't understand any of this. He may be trying to get to our nerves so we don't think straight."

"Let's say he's a psychopath who wants to talk," said Levent. "Or he's one of us with a very bad sense of humor."

"A lot of people on the force would do it for a joke," said Akbay. "But I don't know anyone who has the ass for this kind of thing. Not even Altay."

"I agree," said Levent. "I'd like to hear what Meryem has to say when she reads the printout."

"She'll love it. It's the first time she'll have an excuse to justify her pay."

Not quite. Meryem was a psychologist the department had hired to work out the denominators of the criminal mind. The Chief had probably read the same thrillers as Ayla Acheson had when he hired his profiler, though it was more likely he had gotten the idea from television.

"I'll let you deal with the computer people, Erol. I'm sure they'll find it hard to trace that call."

"For them, impossible."

"We have to narrow the search. If we get lucky, we might be able to find out if he's still in the country."

"You don't seem to think we'll come across him in the usual places."

"No. But I'd like to be surprised."

"I'll run for pattern through the files, and see if we come up with any unsolveds or any of the old pardons."

Levent did not think Akbay would find a torturer/murderer in the cold cases. Pardons were a better place to look. Several years ago, the government granted them to violent criminals as well as others, emptying out the jails. All the departments, especially robbery and homicide, still dealt with the aftermath.

"Did you have time to look around the rest of the upstairs rooms, Erol?"

"Yes," he said. "I could do more."

"Now tell me what you found that everyone else missed."

Akbay ran his fingers through his curly hair that was longer than anyone, including Levent, liked. "It's what I didn't find that bothers me."

"What's that?"

"Her purse," he said. "I mean a working purse. I found two hanging in her closet—nice, expensive, and large. But they were empty, except for the tissue and breath mints she wouldn't miss if she didn't transfer them. I found another purse in the third dresser drawer. It was nice and expensive, too, but smaller. Nothing much in it except the stub for a ticket to a concert at Aya Irini almost two years old. I don't think she used it in quite a while."

"So you're wondering where the *real* purse is."

"That fucker took it," said Akbay. "We don't have enough purse snatchers in this town. Hell, they'll take your arm with the purse if you don't let go fast enough. This one took an eye, but he's the same kind of maggot."

"If he's wandering around with the victim's purse, that might make him easier to find."

"It can be confusing," said Akbay, taking a step toward the door with a mincing gait. "It's gotten to be the fashion for a man to carry one. I'll admit it takes some balls, though. No one outside society circles would dare."

"This is already a society murder, Erol. There's no reason why it can't go all the way to the top."

"We'll see about that when we find the purse."

"Let's hope we do it quickly," said Levent. "I'm going home to clear my head of this filth. Murder's bad enough without having it rubbed in our noses."

"I'll look around one last time," said Akbay. "There's got to be something more we're not seeing."

"Just get some rest. I have a feeling tomorrow will be one of our busy days."

"I'll see you in the morning, boss."

It was already morning.

* * *

Levent awoke smelling the kirlangich from the night before. His wife would never have left the smell of fish linger in the house, but he had found the shrink-wrapped bowl in the refrigerator when he returned. Reheating it in the microwave, Levent meant to have just a taste.

He had overeaten. When he thought he should stop, he ate more. When he was full to the point of discomfort, he sipped the broth, savoring the deep flavor that had been absorbed to saturation.

"Just coffee?"

"Yes," he said to his wife.

Emine poured a tall cup from the German machine and brought it to him as if he were an invalid. That was the way their marriage had evolved. Levent was the man of extremely odd hours whom she cared for in lieu of children. She had yearned for them, of course, and they had tried, God knows. A wanting seed, the doctors said, never explaining how that could happen.

"This is a bad one," she said. "Worse, I mean."

"Yes," he said. "The son of your aunt's second cousin gave me the assignment by his own filthy hand."

"Don't put him off on me," she said. "He may be the chief of your police, but no one wants to claim him until they need a favor."

Why was it the other way around with Levent? He knew the call he had received that put him at the end of a hotel orgy was due to his relationship—by marriage—with the Chief. A Turk never created an obligation outside the family if there was a way to keep it within. Barter was barter, but blood at any remove was better.

"Do you know anyone who's active in the women's movement?"

She looked at him, surprised. She knew he had opened his investigation to her, and in doing so, breached what was normal.

"A feminist?"

"Yes."

"In *this* country?"

"There are such things."

"And should be more," she said. "There isn't an intelligent woman in this country who'll bear ten children. Or even five. If we had enough educated women on this earth, its greatest problem would be solved automatically. In case you haven't looked out the window lately, it's the one from which all the others flow."

Looking out the window did not work in Istanbul. What Levent saw when he turned his eyes from his twelfth story apartment was a panorama that did not end in any direction, including the vertical. He and his wife had been born into a city of two or three million with only a few hundred who mattered in the count.

The few hundred still ran most things even as the population moved in a logarithmic progression to five, ten, then fifteen million. The numbers were probably beyond that now. They were exciting as a blizzard is exciting.

"You can't even find me one feminist in all this city?"

"I didn't say that, Onur. I'll ask some friends. You should be aware that you're apt to come up with a communist."

"I'll take that if I have to."

"Or a student."

"I might prefer the communist."

"This *is* a bad one," she said. "Desperate."

"It will seem that way until I solve the case."

"And you will," she said. "You always do."

* * *

Levent filled his wife in, telling her who had been murdered but not exactly how. If in her gallivanting she ran across someone who had known the victim, it was better to have the basic facts. That might save time and create opportunity. Levent's work was all about opportunity. Knowing how to exploit was the last part.

Levent was into his car and onto E-5 in unusually light traffic when the first call came in on his cellular. The crime scene. It seemed that the media had come to exercise their right of obstruction. They had been kept away from Acheson's house last night, but first thing in the morning the men on duty were put upon by the herd. They had already called for reinforcements to handle the crowd. Even a television van had appeared with plans to broadcast from the street.

Levent gave instructions to the uniforms that he would address the media at five o'clock at headquarters. He did not know if he believed that. It depended on whether he had anything to say, and if he could say it to them.

As he moved off the highway toward downtown, Levent went to the cell phone again to check in with Akbay, who should have something.

"I got a good line on one thing last night," he said. "I stopped at the neighbor's house when I saw their light on—you know, the wife and the mouse. Their kid was still up with all the excitement. He says he saw a man around the neighborhood the other day. A stranger in a blue Volvo that was less than new. Turkish plates. Istanbul, he thinks."

"That's all?"

"I know it isn't much," he said. "We could spend days going through the records to match. I'll get Turgut on the job."

"As long as it's not you doing it."

"Don't worry about that," he said. "And just for curiosity, I ran the victim's name through our files. She's a traffic monster apparently—one violation for speeding, which is pretty hard to do in Istanbul. Another for not wearing a seat belt and refusing to put it on when she was told to."

"She seems normal."

"Yes, but the second thing is more interesting," said Akbay. "I took the report from Shishli district. It's a complaint filed by one of the neighbors at Acheson's apartment in the city. She was having an argument—a loud argument they say—with a man, that was accompanied by some breakage. The man was gone when our people got there, but she gave them hell for abuse. Drunk and belligerent. They could have run her in if they'd been bored that night."

"What night?"

"It was February 17th this year."

"What night of the week, Erol?"

Akbay went silent for several seconds until he found something like a calendar. "It was a Thursday," he said. "Yes, I see what you mean. It could be our oversexed tourist official."

The man who drove to the country for his entertainment could easier stay in the city where he worked. With a white Mercedes, he might have GPS to find his way.

"Have you spoken to the maid?"

"Just hung up," he said. "She worked at both the victim's places—the country house and the apartment—so she should be a source. She'd been to the house the day before the murder and saw nothing wrong. She was on the bus going to the apartment when we spoke. Do you want to meet us there?"

"You'd better get to that apartment fast and keep her from cleaning up the place. I'm stopping at the Tourist Bureau first."

"Okay," he said. "But I don't think she'll be busy unless that's how she works out her grief. She was broken up at losing her employer. Incoherent over the phone. I'll hold her hand until you get there."

"Try to keep it to that."

Keeping his hands off women was Akbay's only flaw, which he shared with most men, including government officials. As Levent turned off the expressway into city traffic, he made his way down the back side of Shishli to the complex that housed the Bureau of Tourism. The department's headquarters was in Ankara, the capital, but no one visited that place without a summons. Istanbul was the center of tourism as it was the center of everything but meat-wagon politics.

The Bureau was in a sprawling group of modular offices that seemed smaller due to the usual overstaffing in government departments. Fortunately, only one white Mercedes was parked in the lot. Levent discovered that his man was a supervisor whose job was to liaise with tour groups and conventions. His office was relatively private on the second floor.

Emre Oz was on the phone. He did not put it down or look at his visitor when Levent stopped at the door. Turning in his chair to face the blank wall behind him, he continued the conversation. He said "of course" three times. He said "okay" twice. Levent wondered when he put his finger down on the nipples of the cradle of the phone, cutting Oz's connection to the outside, if he would really notice.

Yes, he did. When he turned around, his face with its perfectly made nose and perfectly shaven cheeks turned the color he probably turned on his subordinates. His perfectly ironed shirt, handmade and silk, had suspenders he clasped like weapons. But he was unsure of his visitor, so he did not shout.

"Do I know you?"

"Inspector Levent. Homicide."

"And this is concerning—"

"Your relationship with Ayla Acheson, recently deceased."

He knew about it and might have been talking to his lawyer. His right hand ran up his suspenders to his chin, while the other stayed in place, as if he knew he had lost half his support.

"Yes, Ayla," he said, putting concern in his voice like another gear. "We were acquainted. In fact, we were friends."

"Good friends," said Levent as he sat in a chair at the side of his desk and drew it closer to his man.

Oz rolled himself back in his chair, recalibrating the distance. He looked at the phone as if willing it to ring. Next, he looked at his laptop computer. It was the same make and model as the victim's.

"I've known Ayla nearly five years," he said. "First through the business she had with this office, then on a more informal basis."

"I'm comfortable with calling it informal," said Levent. "I'm not sure everyone else, including the press, will agree when they find out."

"And you're sure they will?"

He spoke in a level businesslike tone that meant he had started to bargain. First, it would be for his name. The other things would arrive in time.

"I'm sure the news will travel fast," said Levent. "What the press does with the information I can't say. That will depend on where it leads them."

"What control do you have over the direction, Inspector?"

Levent shrugged expansively. "I might be persuaded to misdirect matters if I think it's wise. You're a married man, I assume."

"Very much so."

"I can't guarantee anything. I won't bother to try unless you cooperate. The first thing I want to know is where you were the night before last."

Oz put his hands on the desk as if holding it down. "I was here that evening until I went to dinner. With two friends. They'll tell you the same."

"Their names?"

He gave them quickly, one man, one woman, and not the wife. Levent put the names in his notebook as if he had put them away. He was sure they would check. This man's phone had been busy all morning.

Levent referred again to the notebook, and a different page, as he spoke. "On the night of February 17th, you had an argument with the victim at her apartment. What was the subject of the discussion?"

Oz sunk in his chair with the effort of recall. "February 17th, you say?"

"I imagine you remember that night, unless you had violent arguments with Miss Acheson on a regular basis."

"No," he said. "That, to the best of my recollection, was the only one."

"Then you should have no problem sharing your recollection."

He answered after a pause. "This is personal. I mean, the subject."

"I can't be shocked," said Levent. "There's nothing worse than homicide. You should want to see her murderer pay."

"I do," he said. "More than you know. We were close. Very close. We shared almost everything, including certain aspects of . . . revenue."

"So you argued about money on the night of February 17th."

"Distribution," he said quietly.

"Let me ease your mind," said Levent. "It's not my job to police your department, and I'm not sure that's possible. How much did she turn back to you?"

"There were certain fees due to the department," he said in a greater hush. "They could be understated without much problem by me. There also were some favors she asked. These were usually things she found convenient to have overlooked."

"Did you argue about the fees?"

"No," he said. "They were strictly based on percentages, and Ayla was honest in disbursing my share."

Honest. Yes. When the figures could be checked by the man who kept them, that made for the greatest honesty imaginable.

"Then the issue between you that night concerned the things you were paid to overlook."

"In a manner of speaking, yes."

"Speak to the manner, sir. Do it without dancing."

He looked at Levent with a weak plea. His right hand went out as if to offer it to a friend. "I was asked from time to time to have a word with customs inspectors in Istanbul, and occasionally Antalya."

Levent was nearly sure of the reason, but wanted to hear it. "What did you say to the customs officials?"

"They were to let things pass," he said. "Put simply, they were not to open the baggage or look closely at passports."

"What was in the baggage?"

He wagged his head as if everything in him wanted to know. "I have no idea of what Ayla was bringing into the country. You have to believe me. It's the truth."

"You never asked?"

"Of course I did," he said. "It was one of the things we argued about that night. I told her I wouldn't continue if she refused to tell me everything."

"And she wouldn't?"

"Repeatedly."

Levent tried to imagine what would be so valuable that she would involve Oz in the scheme. He found no answers. There had been an international forgery ring that produced good copies of old precious Korans, but they were shut down two years ago. They had dealt in small millions for the bogus goods. This smuggling venture could have been more substantial.

"Suppose I believe you," said Levent. "How much money was involved? And what was your share?"

"I don't know what Ayla took out for herself," he said. "But I had fifty thousand dollars."

Not bad. But his Mercedes cost more. "How many times were you paid to guarantee that customs would look away?"

"Usually not more than four times a year," he said. "The first year it was less. Twice."

So it had taken Emre and Ayla a while to become acquainted, but when they did, that meant weekly meetings and two hundred thousand per year on average for Oz. If he had been in business with her several years, he might have made a million or thereabout. This man had no need for his government pension. What came into the country had to be quite valuable, but Levent would give a lot to know the schedule of the things that were overlooked.

"I want you to tell me the dates when you performed these services for Acheson," he said. "Also the airlines or shipping lines that were involved. And anything else you think is pertinent."

"I can't do that from my head, Inspector. It's impossible."

"Then consult your records."

"I will," he said. "But that will take some doing. Perhaps by tomorrow."

He was stalling. With computerized records, he should be able to gather the information in hours, if not minutes. But the records might not all be computerized.

"I imagine you have plenty of money," said Levent. "And I imagine you moved a lot of it out of the country. But don't think of leaving to join your graft. You'll be caught, and you'll be prosecuted on multiple counts."

"I understand, Inspector. I promise."

"Tomorrow morning then," said Levent. "Let's say I'll have the information on my desk by ten o'clock."

He nodded and relaxed, and it showed in the slow roll of his shoulders. Levent thought he might have given the man too much leeway. This man's best was far from perfect, if the past could be trusted.

"One more thing," said Levent. "Do you use ICQ?"

Oz was surprised by a question that veered suddenly, but recovered fast. "Yes. Sometimes, but not often."

"What's your handle?"

"Wonderland."

Oz. Alice. The Tin Man. It made sense, Levent supposed, though not in Turkish. "Have you ever met a person called Karanlik on ICQ?"

He shook his head slowly. "The name means nothing to me. I wouldn't say it was impossible, but I simply have no recollection."

"Ayla Acheson knew him."

Oz shrugged. "I don't mean to sound flippant, but Ayla got around in her way. Cyberspace could be one of them."

"But you'll research the matter, and let me know when you find an answer that differs."

"You have my promise, Inspector."

Part Two:

Pictures at an
Exhibition

CHAPTER 7

Fatma

The victim's maid was called Fatma. She had no last name, because maids could not afford them. Levent heard her sobbing as soon as the elevator opened onto the landing of the fourth-floor apartment in Nishantashi. His thought was that it was better to deal with thieves like Oz, rather than people whose hearts were truly touched by murder. Better, meaning easier.

Fatma could not even answer the door, leaving that job to Erol Akbay. He ushered Levent into another designer room with hectic modern paintings on the walls and carpets of striking Far Eastern design. Fatma sat on the sofa described in lavender and green gyres. She looked up at Levent as if he was the latest enigma in her life, of which there had previously been only one.

She did not stop weeping. She held a washcloth balled in her hands, woofing into it in spasms. Levent, who carried smelling salts at all times, broke the capsule and put it under her nose. When she inhaled, she jolted upright, her eyes agog.

"There, you'll be fine in a moment."

"What?" she said. "What was that?"

"Medication," he said. "My name is Inspector Levent, and I can see you loved your mistress very much. What we must do now is turn our minds to finding her killer."

"I'd help if I could," she said, threatening to devolve into mania again. "There was never a kinder or more generous person than Miss Acheson. No one knows that better than me. Two years ago, when my daughter fell sick, she had me take her to the best doctors in the city. They told me she had a tumor on her spine, and the best place to have an operation was Zurich. The mistress sent both my daughter and me there, paying all the expenses. After the operation, the mistress came herself to see that everything was put right. You tell me who would do that for a poor working woman."

Not many, Levent thought. None that he had heard of. "How long have you worked for her?"

"Three years," she said, counting behind her dark brown eyes. "It could be a bit more now that I think of it. It was right after she bought the country house."

So Fatma was here for the glory days of head counts and contraband. A vacuum cleaner, imported and motorized, stood in front of the television, so she must have arrived planning to clean the place. When Akbay showed up, Fatma found an audience to witness her grief.

"Tell me, did Miss Acheson seem herself lately? In the last few days, that is. Did you notice any unusual behavior?"

Furiously, her hands worked the cloth she held to her bosom, though it was hard to tell where that might be. Her dress was shapeless and strangely colorless. Normal for a maid, though hardly for a city woman. Her face was as plain, but for the wart alongside her nose.

"She was mostly out to the house for the last ten days," said Fatma. "We had that turn of good weather last week, and she wanted to get out in the sun and share it with her guests."

"Guests? Last week?"

"On the weekend," she said.

"Did you meet them?" Levent corrected himself. "Did you see them?"

"I was there when three of them came on Friday," she said. "The Turkish man brought his bags, but the others didn't."

"The others were foreigners?"

"They didn't speak Turkish."

"What language did they use?"

"English," she said. "But I can't be sure if they were English. Miss Acheson said she couldn't understand half of what they said either. She told me to have them point to what they wanted."

Interesting that they were not native speakers. English was the language of business, and almost everyone had some. All the European countries and many of the Asian, even if badly.

"But they were European, these two?"

"They were a couple," she said as if that pleased her. "As white as you or me. The woman was blonde, too. Her name was Lise."

"The man?"

"He was accustomed to being served, if you know what I mean. He pointed a lot and drained half the liquor cabinet before I left. Vodka at first, then he moved onto rum. He kept asking me to squeeze more lemon juice for the rum drinks, whatever he called them. And when he ran out of cigarettes, he took to smoking mine."

At the mention of her vice, Fatma put down her washcloth, reached into the side pocket of her dress and took out a package of Murats. Levent waited as she lit one, thinking it might keep her from hysteria and sharpen her memory.

"He said he'd pay me back, but I wouldn't smoke those things he was putting in his face," she said. "They were as black as coal and smelled worse."

"Filtered?"

"Yes."

"Blue package?" asked Levent. "With a swirl on it?"

She nodded. The cigarettes were Sobranies. Not many people cultivated the taste unless they learned to love it at home. That probably meant the man was Russian or from one of the satellite countries that were once Russian. That made a list.

"The Turkish man who stayed over," said Levent. "Had you seen him before?"

"Once," she said. "He came both times with baggage to stay over."

"Was his name Emre?"

"It wasn't Mister Oz," she said. "I know him."

Levent didn't think he would get lucky. Oz was the Thursday night. This was the weekend, which might mean he was new. But Fatma would know more about a Turk she had seen twice.

"What can you tell me about the countryman? What was his name?"

"Metin," she said. "I'm sorry, but I never knew his last. I think it was written on his baggage."

But she could not read to pass on the information. That was another reason why she was a maid. "Do you know anything more about this man?"

"He said he was from Antalya."

That was the second mention of Antalya today. On the Mediterranean Coast and a popular resort, it was the fastest growing city in Turkey—a primary destination for Russian and German tourists. Millions every year.

"How long did Metin stay each time he visited?"

"I can't say about the second time, because I didn't work Saturday or Sunday. I remember he didn't stay at all the first time."

"He came with bags but didn't stay over?"

"Yes," she said, nodding with suspicion. "He brought them into the house. He didn't have me do it, even though I offered to. So he didn't use them for what you'd expect. That's odd, isn't it?"

"It could be," said Levent. "Did you happen to overhear any conversations between Metin and your mistress? Accidentally, that is."

"They didn't say much when I was about," said Fatma. "Once I heard them talk about icons. You know, the little things the Russians make so well."

Once made, if Levent was any judge. These days the icons were probably counterfeit. But if they were trafficking in Christian goods, Turkey was an odd place to bring them—unless it was not the final destination.

"I didn't see religious icons at Miss Acheson's house," said Levent. "Nor here at a glance. Have you?"

"Never," she said. "And I would have."

"Did she keep valuables at the house?" asked Levent. "Or here?"

"Not that I know of," said Fatma. "She has a safe at her office. I've never seen it, but she mentioned it once."

"How did she mention it?"

"When she forgot something in it and was angry at herself," said Fatma. "One day, she came to the house meaning to stay, but when she saw what she was missing, she turned around and went back into the city."

"You have no idea what it was?"

"I went home as soon as she left," said Fatma. "But I think it had something to do with a Black Cruise. She had one coming in the next day."

"Black Cruise?"

"Cruise ships come down from the north by the Black Sea," she said, happy to explain. "Mistress started the cruises is what she told me. Those people up there don't see the sun often, and they liked to see it as long as they had the money. And now they do, some of them."

"Where do the ships sail from?"

"Well, I wouldn't know," she said. "There's lot of places up there."

And they all believed in free trade, which meant smuggling in every language. Levent saw many possibilities for contraband goods. Too many, at least until Oz came in with his list.

"I understand Miss Acheson had any number of male guests," said Levent. "They sometimes stayed overnight. Would you know their names?"

"You must have been talking to the neighbors out at the house," she said. "Those fools. Miss Acheson never let them in the place, and I wouldn't either. Jealousy is what makes them carry on like that. The mistress had several good friends. All fine gentlemen. Mister Emre was one, and Mister Suleyman another, and, of course, Mister Samuel and Mister Giovanni."

Levent waited for her to finish, and he was glad Akbay took the notes. Four good friends and who knew how many others? Perhaps they could meet and exchange cards at the funeral.

"Detective Akbay will take the names and what you remember about these men," said Levent. "Tell him all you know. I'm going to look around the apartment now."

Plainly, Fatma didn't like strangers roaming in her mistress' private things, but she nodded her permission before Levent walked away. Passing down the long hallway with two full baths, he moved toward the bedrooms at the end to verify that the victim did not have a safe on the premises. Or other surprising items.

Levent had never seen a woman's boudoir paneled in wood dyed the color of new plums. She also had a king-sized bed with a duvet in a complementing shade of purple. The effect was intimidating, though he could see how it might lend the proper feeling in the evening after a drink. Make that two and make it whiskey.

In the main closet filled with expensive clothing, Levent did not find a safe or anything that worked for concealment. Plunging necklines and dresses with erratic hemlines were more the case. The closet drawers were filled with undergarments, all so brief that they looked incomplete. And that included the back holster.

A surprise. There was no weapon in the holster, but it was big enough to carry anything up to a nine millimeter handgun. He wondered where the gun was and spent some time migrating from the drawers to the shelves atop the closet and into the chest across from the foot of the bed. He found nothing much.

Nothing but a purple cell phone. Because it was one of the newer models, Levent expected the directory to be current. There was nothing in it. Not a single name or number. The phone did have a camera, however.

When Levent called the photographs up, he was surprised to find four. A gallery. No, an exhibition. He found himself lingering too long as he passed through the shots. That was unprofessional, but given the circumstances, understandable. Pornography always was, he supposed.

The first photograph showed two men naked from the waist down, and a woman, naked in the same way, which he supposed was the victim. No way of telling, but those looked like her thighs.

Or perhaps not. The next shot showed the faces of the two men, and a woman who was definitely not Ayla Acheson. All were strangers to Levent, but not to each other. They looked quite relaxed, each with a glass of milk-white raki in hand and bare-chested. They did not look as if they knew they were posing, even the woman whose breasts were quite large.

The third shot was much different. It was a progression in every way. Now four people inhabited the king-sized bed, including the victim, and they knew they were being photographed. In fact, they were performing for the camera.

Ayla Acheson's image was closest, so close that it was distorted, as if she had held the camera at arm's length to take the shot. The other three were visible, too, in athletic poses. The second woman had been mounted by the first man, and the second man used what was left of her orifices to complete the cycle. Amazing. Who would want to be captured in a photograph like that?

The last of the four was simply a blowjob. Levent recognized the man's member by referencing the first photograph. He had no need to cross-reference the woman. She was his victim, and this was how she enjoyed herself.

CHAPTER 8

The Safe

Levent liked to think he was not cruel. Of the four pictures, he showed only one to Fatma—the group with three bare, and for that moment, nearly decent people. Even so, the maid was deeply abashed, her face flushing as bright as the colors that looked back at her from the cell phone.

"Yes," she said, taking up the washcloth once more. "I do recognize these people. I gave a service for the mistress at a dinner party about three months ago. Perhaps it was less. Twelve guests came. Ten for dinner, and the others came later. These three came late. It was nearly my time to leave."

"Do you know their names?"

She looked at Akbay as if his question was indecent. "Not at all. Except to recognize them for you."

"Had you seen any of these people before?" asked Levent, flicking the phone.

"No," she said, staring at the picture like the genii of sin. "I would remember."

"Nor at the house?"

"Not there either."

Levent had been hoping for a break, but he did not think Fatma lied to protect her mistress. The group might have formed as an extension of the party. How strangers could become so intensely intimate so quickly was a puzzle—or a revelation. Even without clothing, these visitors did not look like they had been gathered off the street. Off a cruise? From an escort service?

Impossible to say for now. The event may not have taken place that evening. It could have been an office party gone rank. Or a node of friends that the maid knew nothing about.

Levent felt a flurry of deja vu. It was as if the Chief had inserted his presence into the investigation, calling for assistance from a seaside hotel. Levent put the phone deep in his pocket. Discretion was called for, and he was the man who provided it.

* * *

They left the victim's apartment twenty minutes later for the offices of Ayla Tur in Sultanahmet. They had gotten what they could from Fatma. If more was in the pipeline, she would cooperate in delivering it.

"Why do you think she kept pictures like that?"

"I don't know," said Levent, watching the numbered floors pass in the elevator. "She might want a remembrance of a wild night. Something to keep her interested when she was alone."

"It's easy enough to print them up," said Akbay. "She could have done that and kept them in a drawer by the bed when she wanted to beat off. She could have made them poster size, too."

"Other people see pictures and posters," said Levent. "People don't look at your cell phone if it's in a drawer. Most people, that is. You could have asked Fatma if she peeked."

"No, thanks," said Akbay as they passed from the elevator through the lobby. "I feel sorry for her. The poor woman won't sleep tonight. Instead of smelling salts, you should have given her tranquilizers."

"Remind me to carry a medicine bag," said Levent. "For the good ones, anti-depressants, for the bad, truth serum."

"There isn't any such thing," said Akbay. "There's just us and God for the killers. That's why I like this job."

And that's why Levent liked Akbay. He had a nose for the work that came from total absorption. He could be put off the scent, but not off his passion. In every case he had worked with Levent, Akbay always found something others had left behind. He had lost his left ring finger when he refused to leave behind a suspect who meant to, and did, chew it off.

"Whatever you say, this is strange shit," said Akbay, as they reached their cars. "It's blackmail waiting to happen. You don't think she kept the shots with that in mind?"

"I'll tell you if it's in character when we know more of her character," said Levent. "For now, let's say she was forgetful. Or sentimental."

"Sentimental. I like that. I was thinking of a dog in heat. That's not a good way to think of our victim."

"What we think of her doesn't matter."

"Well, I did manage one thing," he said. "I asked Fatma about Madame's purse. She said there was one that seemed to be the favorite of the last few weeks. An Yves St. Laurent. Not a knock-off, mind you. Leather with golden clasps, dyed green, about the color of a twenty-lira bill. I think that's significant."

"So when we see it, we'll know it."

"I'll be looking for it, Onur. Somewhere, I'll find it."

"I'm glad you're optimistic," said Levent. "Now see if you can find Mahir to open the safe in the office at AylaTur. Some-one there may have the combination, but it would be better not to rely on them."

"I'll get on it."

* * *

As Levent moved across the city toward Sultanahmet, fight-ing traffic like a counter puncher, he felt distracted and unaccountably annoyed. The feeling increased when he took a call from the Chief while stopped at the light at the bottom of the hill on the seaside road. He wanted to know what progress was being made on the case. Several of the victim's relatives had been in touch with him, wanting very much to know the same thing.

"They're *concerned*," he said. "It's always like that when a rich relative dies. I'd like to know how rich she really is."

"We may find out," said Levent. "I'm on my way to her office now to talk to the people there."

"Talk to the accountant," said the Chief. "It would be nice if I could tell these people she was secretly poor. That might keep them quiet."

"Yes, sir. I'll see if we can look into her books."

"Be sure you do something, Levent. And quickly. Or we'll be shuffling inspectors again."

The son of Emine's second cousin hung up abruptly, leaving Levent with nothing in his ear but the sound of a vegetable truck passing so close that it brushed his side mirror, collapsing the image of what was behind and showing Levent a sliver of himself. The streets leading toward the main tourist district of Istanbul were narrow and always crowded. Here the remains of the Ottoman Empire sat atop the remains of the Byzantine Empire, which was itself a remnant of the Roman Empire. History. In the end, it was a river of shit.

The greatest civilizations had devised the best methods of carrying it away. All the vast subterranean arteries of the cities spoke of their genius. To this day, Byzantine cisterns ran under the streets of Sultanahmet. Fish swam in them. And tourists were fish to be baited and caught. That was AylaTur's business.

The office sat on the first floor of a restored building not far from the hilltop palace of Topkapi. Its logo was a flight of cranes streamlined in a cobalt sky. Folklore said anyone who saw that formation would soon be going on a trip. All Turks believed in folklore and did not think it superstitious. Levent believed in it now, because Karanlik had told him to look to the sky.

It should be said that the bustle inside the office was far from funereal. AylaTur apparently carried on its business without a pause. At three desks, travel agents sat talking busily on their phones. One had a transceiver attached to his head. He looked like a monster in a half-mask, but his hands were kept free while he worked.

Levent walked all the way across the room to what was obviously the manager's office in the rear. No one stopped him. One of the women on the telephones looked up, but did not once close her mouth.

A well-dressed man of forty-five years or so sat in the chair at Ayla Acheson's desk, looking through a stack of papers with period reading glasses. On top of the desk was her nameplate in brass or gold. Lack of respect for the dead, Levent supposed. Wish fulfillment?

"May I help you?"

"I'm sure you can. I'm Inspector Levent, and I'm directing the investigation into the murder of Ayla Acheson." He paused like a sports announcer. "You do know that your employer is dead."

"My partner, yes." He lowered his eyes.

Another surprise. Here was a man who knew everything about AylaTur's business, but given the twists in the business that Levent had come to understand, he was also the man who should have something—possibly the most—to hide. His manner was so polished it seemed like he must be a screen for some sort of clandestine actions. Levent had seen better suits and ties today, and better cufflinks, but only on Emre Oz.

"My name is Faruk Duran, Inspector," he said, removing his glasses and offering his hand. "I must tell you we're not what we seem here today. It was a terrible shock to all of us when we heard the news this morning. We should have shut down for the week, but no one can afford to shut down in this business. Tourists don't stop for death or holidays. In fact, that's when they come alive."

"Like the police."

Duran opened his hands in hospitality. "Will you have coffee?"

"Filter, please."

While he dialed up his service, Levent sat in a sculpted plastic chair that was less comfortable than it looked, and much harder. He waited until Duran placed the order before beginning his questions.

"Were you a full partner with Miss Acheson?"

"She held the largest share of the company," said Duran. "Fifty-five percent. The rest was divided evenly between her family and me."

"Were you privy to all the things that went on in the company?"

"I like to think so."

"Does that mean you are not in some way?"

Duran blinked, as if he was not sure that the question led in an unfortunate direction. And he had to be. This was a gentleman's interview, because gentlemen were usually smarter than barbarians.

"I shared in the profits and losses," he said, stressing the last word. "I'm familiar with nearly every part of the business. But there are some things I suspect Ayla kept to herself."

Neatly done. "Were there any major concerns you think Miss Acheson did *not* share with you?"

"There would be nothing on the books of that kind," he said, creating room for himself again. "But Ayla could be secretive. I didn't know until last year that we had a man in Tehran. I didn't know until today that we owed him money. At least that's what he claims."

"He called this morning?"

"Twice," said Duran. "It's amazing how fast bad news travels, though I think in his case the news might be good. If I die tomorrow, he's sure to be rich. He certainly is planning to be."

"I didn't think it was possible for an Iranian to get the better of a Turk."

Duran smiled. His teeth were excellent. His medium length brown hair had been cut within the day, including the lashes above the pale blue eyes. Levent thought he might have to wait a long time to see the record of AylaTur's losses.

"You build your profit into the first two payments in that part of the Middle East," he said. "In many parts, I'm afraid. You do it because you know you'll never see the last payment. If you're stupid enough to ask for it, you'll find the company no longer exists under a name you recognize."

"Do you have the same problem everywhere?"

"Not in the same way," he said. "Most Western agents remit promptly at the same stall for years. That's not the same as saying they can be trusted. They bargain hard and squeeze out the last drop of profit. Our margins are tighter than you think."

"But the company *is* profitable."

"For the last three years or so, yes. There was a time when it seemed we'd go the way of the dinosaur. That is, until Ayla thought of making the cranes our symbol. Since then we've done well."

The last three years approximately. That was about the time when Oz joined the scheme to bypass customs for selected events. That was also the time when the victim hired a full-time maid to serve at two locations. A boom time.

"Was the pressure on the firm intense four years ago?"

"That was at the beginning of the Crisis," he said, referring to the breakdown of the economy in the earliest years of the century. "There weren't many firms in any business that survived without strict economy measures—or filing for bankruptcy. We barely avoided that ourselves."

"It must have been more than three birds that pulled you through."

"It took a tremendous effort," said Duran, running his hand through his thick hair. "I put up some of my money, and Ayla sold some of her share to her uncle in England. The rest was scrambling for every lira we could find. And you know what the lira was worth then. We were bringing vacation tours into Antalya and clearing fifty pounds on a hundred heads, but at least we were paid in hard currency. The hotels cleared less. They covered their costs if they were lucky. Some lived to see another day."

"And you did this through tours only?"

"What else? I mean, I could have sent our bus drivers to Iraq to work for the Americans, but I do have a conscience. And, of course, we tried everything we could think of to bring in revenue. We didn't supply pillows on the charter flights when we could rent them. We drove out into the parched lands on our bus tours, and when they were dying of thirst, sold them bottled water at triple the price. We did everything but make up lotteries for the prostitutes at the conventions."

"I thought you did that, too."

"Well, sometimes." Duran laughed and waved his hand. "You can believe we did anything at all to make a go of it."

He spoke as if expecting nothing to follow. Levent thought Duran might have been heedless, or innocent, which was sometimes the same. Or he might have lost his brains when Acheson lost her life.

"I'm interested in any extreme measures the firm might have employed," said Levent. "Can you think of anything in your operations that could supply a reason for your partner's death?"

Duran looked at Levent with slack eyes. "I thought Ayla was murdered by a psychopath."

"How do you know that?"

He seemed to stumble for a moment, but surrendered quickly. "Why, I was told by your Chief."

Levent silently cursed that man again. "Someone might want us to think it was the work of a psychopath, but they're not common in this country. Turks prefer love or money—and sometimes both—when they come to kill."

"I see," he said. "I was misinformed perhaps."

"In any event, this investigation will proceed in every direction," said Levent. "What revenue do you know of that did *not* hit your books?"

"You're speaking of significant amounts?"

"Yes."

"None that I know of."

"But there must be some money you suspect passing through the company. I've talked to people who tell me that's true."

Duran's eyes blinked rapidly. "Who said that?"

"Business associates of yours," said Levent. "They tell me your partner sometimes brought contraband through customs."

Duran knew he was walking a fine line that might vanish if he was not careful to give something to Levent. The dark eyes that had been surprised narrowed like agates—or any stone formed under great pressure.

"Inspector—"

"Please don't tell me you're going to call the Chief, your good friend, again. He's everyone's good friend until it comes time to pay. Then he goes to Antalya for the vacation he missed."

"I wasn't trying to threaten you." Duran made his first response in a prissy tone. "I want to see Ayla's murderer caught as much as anyone. Do you know what a disaster this has been in my life? In everyone's life?"

"I'd like to know exactly what kind," said Levent. "What did your partner bring into the country, and who was involved in transporting the goods?"

At that moment, the coffee came through the door on a teetering tray carried by a big-headed dwarf. Although Levent craved caffeine, he did not welcome anything that gave Duran time to regroup. If the man used the break to decide to cooperate, that was best. It happened sometimes.

"I'm afraid you're not going to like what I have to tell you, Inspector. I wish I could do better."

Levent drank the first sip of hot coffee from the Ataturk mug and did not disagree. He usually thought any coffee was better than none, but would have to revise that opinion. Dwarf coffee was poison for taste.

"If you say it like that, Mister Duran, I'm sure I won't like the answer. But you'll have to find something."

"I'll tell you straight out that I don't know what was being smuggled," he said, using the proper word. "I had no part in it."

"I can believe that," said Levent as if he wanted to. "But did you never ask where all this new money came from?"

"I wasn't aware of it at first," he said, turning away from Levent in the chair and looking toward the low cabinet that probably held the safe. "Ayla quite naturally kept the money off the books. But I came to know of it as she began expanding our operations. She told me when we went into luxury junkets to Dubai that she would put up the money to get the project off the ground."

"You believed she could?"

"I thought it was her uncle supplying the funds, as he had before. He was a partner in our firm at that point."

"He must be a wealthy man."

"Quite well off," said Duran, as if he had corrected the impression upward. "He had his own consulting firm that specialized in developing countries. He gave—sold—his advice to governments and NGOs. Ayla told me his position put him on the ground early in several ventures that turned out to be very profitable. Dubai, for instance, was one of those places. He bought several parcels of land twenty or thirty years ago, using a local partner as his front. At least one hotel was later built on that land. I believe he may even have gotten a piece of one. When I was there two years ago to check our arrangements in Dubai, the hotel cost nearly a thousand dollars per night. I didn't pay. Ayla took care of that."

"When did you become aware that this new money came from a different revenue stream?"

"Last year," he said, turning back full face to Levent. "I spoke with her uncle by phone one day. During the conversation, I thanked him for all the help he'd given us. I believe I said the help he'd given us lately. I could tell he was surprised by that."

"Did you pursue the matter further?"

"Not at the time," said Duran. "Ayla was off on a trip to Moscow, and when she returned she was off again immediately. Two days later, she called from Izmir and asked me to stand in for her at the airport. I said yes. I met a man there, an Iranian who got off a plane from Kiev with a hundred other people. I walked him through customs, going to the booth where I was told to go. I was surprised when no one looked at his papers. They waved him through and didn't even wave. They didn't look at his carry-on either."

"Did he have other luggage?"

"Nothing," he said. "We didn't stop at the caravel. I took him to a hotel at Taksim where Ayla told me to go. It's one we never use, but there was a reservation in the company name. I was surprised by that, too. It was like seeing a hidden layer of my own firm that I knew nothing about."

"You didn't want to find out what was going on behind your back?" said Levent. "Even if it was profitable not knowing?"

"I decided to look into it," he said. "I gave the desk clerk at the hotel some lira and told him to call me when the man went out—or had visitors. I had lunch at a place down the street where I could see the entrance. And three coffees, if I recall. About four o'clock, I got a call from the desk. The man had just had a visitor. It was Ayla, though I didn't know it then. Apparently, she'd flown up from Izmir on the first flight. I hadn't seen her enter the hotel. The man at the desk said she wore a full length coat and a headscarf when she arrived."

That was ironic. The headscarf was the symbol of Islamic fundamentalism in Turkey and other places. Most of the mothers and daughters of the current government wore them to announce their dependence. But it would be a good disguise for someone like Acheson.

"Do they make fashion-conscious headscarves for liberated women?"

"I'm afraid I'm not up on that," he said. "I'd never seen Ayla with one, even in the wind and rain."

"But for this man she wore it."

"If you think that was his concern," said Duran ironically. "I doubt it. He didn't seem like one who would care. He was a Westerner, or as Western as they're made in Iran. Not a thug or a backpacker either. He was somewhere in his forties or late thirties, and dressed for casual travel. A windbreaker and jogging shoes. But he wore sunglasses on a dull day."

"Did you go up to the room then?"

"No," he said as if he regretted it. "That didn't seem like the time for confrontation. I waited outside the hotel for nearly twenty minutes. When Ayla came out alone, I followed her to her car."

"Did she have the carry-on?"

"No," he said. "A large briefcase."

"Where did she go from there?"

"Nowhere," he said softly. "I caught up with her in the parking garage. We had our discussion there."

Duran had said no three times. At the crucial moment of confrontation, he wanted Levent to believe he backed out of solving the mystery that vexed but augmented his life so well. And perhaps he had. This man was not made for confrontation. A salesman of the more refined type.

"What did you discuss with Ayla Acheson in the parking garage?"

"We made a scene there," said Duran, moving his hands like oars on the arms of his chair. "The lights are so bad in the place that I wasn't sure it was really Ayla under all that cloth. But I looked closely and probably embarrassed her. She never had any doubt it was me and became very angry. You should understand that Ayla never backed down from anything. There was Turkish for the fire and English for the stubbornness. It was a combination you don't see every day, and you were better off not being on its bad side. If you dared to challenge her, you'd to be prepared for body blows. And she gave her best that day."

"What did she say she was doing at the hotel?"

"I asked her, and she told me it was none of my business," said Duran. "When I told her it was exactly that, she wanted to know where I was when everything was going to hell with the economy. It was *she* who had to find a way to keep the company afloat. And *she* did that."

"How?"

"By getting in bed with the devil, she said." Duran closed his eyes as if the idea was too much for him even now. "Actually, she said it was the devil she knew."

"I don't understand."

"It's an expression," he said. "I don't know where it comes from, or the poor fool who thought of it first. It means you're dealing with the devil you know rather than the one you don't know."

"So this was a familiar devil. Who?"

"She wouldn't give me a name. The problem, she said, was that after we were solvent, she couldn't get out of that bed." Duran held up his hand as if he had nearly had the demon in it. "I didn't press her hard. Hard enough. If this man had put a scare into Ayla, he could put it into anyone."

"Do you expect me to believe that?" said Levent. "Even of you?"

"You'll have to," he said. "It's true."

"So you never knew whom she dealt with? Or for what?"

"I never had any idea of the ways and means, or what could be so valuable," he said. "I ask you, what could be smuggled *into* this country at a great profit? But I knew what the end product was."

"That should be helpful."

"It was money," said Duran. "Hard currency. She picked it up at the hotel to make the conversion to lira. And she said her next stop was Tahtakale."

"So she was laundering money for someone."

"That seems clear."

"Whom was she dealing with at Tahtakale?"

"I don't know."

Levent did not believe Duran, but he would find out what was being hidden. He waited until Akbay arrived with Mahir the locksmith to open the safe, only to find that his services were unnecessary. Duran knew the combination. When he dialed in the numbers, of course they found nothing.

CHAPTER 9

Atilla

Levent did not leave at once for Tahtakale. He had questions to follow up with Duran, starting with devils and ending with the victim's personal contacts, like the Russians who visited her house, and the man from Antalya called Metin. The Russians were unknown to Duran, but Metin was the firm's representative on the Mediterranean Coast, and reliable it was said. He had been with them a long time, almost eight years. The company had been founded about then, three years after Ayla completed her schooling and moved back to Turkey to stay.

She had graduated from a university in London and later worked for an English tour company before deciding to go on her own. Duran had met her at a convention in Amsterdam, where they struck it off at once. She guaranteed him that she could deliver virtually unlimited tours to the south of Turkey from England.

Something about her made him believe in the young woman, or her dynamic, and Duran never regretted that instinct. Over the next couple of years, she fulfilled the promise better than anyone in the business, packing the palefaces in from Bodrum to Fethiye until every hotel on their list was at capacity, and every day trip, too. AylaTur had been profitable almost from the first—not Mafia-rich but doing well—until the Crisis.

Everything seemed to implode at that point, as it had for many people. Duran spoke of it like a scratch burial with hungry wolves circling in the distance. Levent had to agree, but he still was not sure if pursuing that line was helpful. The end leading back to the source of the money should matter more. Finding the source did not have to lead to the killer, but the victim had known whom she was dealing with for the money. A solution that brought the connection in view was all that mattered.

It was Akbay who moved the flow in a more productive direction. While Levent was talking again to Duran about his partnership, trying to explore all the things the man was hiding, Akbay called Levent over and walked him toward the door to the outer office.

"Do you recognize that young stud there on the street? I say he's one of our digital boys."

Levent looked at the young man Akbay had spotted. He was enjoying a break, smoking a cigarette as he stood in a furtive patch of sun. Yes, he looked like one of the men from the victim's photo gallery, and this was the second time Levent had seen him. He had been sitting at a desk, wearing a headset that made him look like an astronaut when Levent entered the office.

Levent called Faruk Duran over. "Who's that man?"

"Atilla Kocaman."

He had answered briefly without offering to expand. Levent thought it was a bit strange that Duran did not seem relieved to have reached safe ground. He should have been eager to direct attention from himself, and especially what had once been in the office safe, but he acted uneasy as he spoke.

"Tell me more about Atilla."

"He's been with us for the last five weeks and done a good job," said Duran. "Our best commission salesman since he was taken on."

"Who hired him?"

"Ayla did," he said. "She made most of the personnel decisions."

Levent would have guessed that even without the photos in the cell phone. The length of Atilla's service for AylaTur might match the length of his member. Had he been hired on the basis of a single performance?

"I'd like to talk to him."

"Of course."

"Privately."

Duran shrugged nonchalantly, trying not to indicate interest. "As you wish, Inspector."

The young man with curly black hair, a primitive jaw, and the bright eyes of a bird of prey stepped on his cigarette when Levent and Akbay came from the office into the street. He noticed them with a smile, moving aside to let them pass. Good shoulders. Big feet in square-toed shoes. What they said about big feet was apparently true.

Levent found it disconcerting to question a man he knew best from the waist down, but Akbay had no problem. When he held out his hand for the cell phone, Levent quickly filled it.

"I've always wanted to meet a real gigolo," said Akbay. "A successful one, that is. I understand your name is Atilla."

The young man did not take Akbay's hand. He stared at it. "What do you want with me?"

"We're going through a list of prostitutes in the city," said Akbay very seriously. "Your name came in near the top of the stallions for hire. That's interesting, but what we're really interested in is if you go both ways? There's a premium on a fellow who can service women *and* men."

"I don't have any idea what you're talking about." Atilla knew that he was speaking to the police and for his manhood, and that they were different. "You have me confused with someone in your family."

"Are you telling me you got this job because of your language skills?" asked Akbay. "How many do you speak?"

"Turkish," he said. "And some English. Enough to tell you what I think of you in both."

"You should be careful how you talk to the police," said Akbay, holding the cell phone playfully and showing its face to Atilla. "What I have in my hand is an improvement over the techniques we had to work with in the past. It's called an electronic lineup. If you can tell me how you found yourself in it, we might agree to leave you in peace."

Akbay snapped on the phone and rolled to the photo that showed two men and a woman, bare-chested, holding up raki glasses. He kept rolling. Atilla's face went from surprise to bloody grim, blanching when Akbay stopped the slideshow at the display of four people in states of fornication on a king-sized bed.

"Atilla, if I'm not mistaken, that's your ass I'm looking at. I'd say the pimple on that hairy ass belongs to you, too. It isn't a good thing to go to an orgy without proper grooming."

The young man stared at the sun-dulled photograph as if it were of someone he knew and had always hated. "You should have some respect for the dead. Even a cop should have that."

"We do," said Levent, taking the cell phone from Akbay. "We're the only chance that Ayla Acheson has to see her killer in jail. You should cooperate with us. There won't be consequences if all you did was what we see here. It may be a sin, but as far as homicide goes, it's not a crime."

He looked at Levent as the way out, nodding before he spoke. "It wasn't even a sin," he said. "You had to know her."

"Think how it looks to us," said Levent. "You found your way into a job as a reward for services rendered. Six weeks later, the woman who hired you from her bed was murdered in her home. It doesn't look good, Atilla. Was she disappointed? Did she find you with another woman?"

"I have a girl in Atakoy if you really want to know," he said. "And I've never been with her like that. This happened after a party. We were all drinking, as you can see. And one thing led to the next. It happened only once."

"Once?" said Akbay.

"Twice," he said, spitting the words. "And the second time was the last. She said if I was to work for her there couldn't be any more . . . excursions. And she kept to that no matter what I might want."

"I say we take this one down to the station," said Akbay. "He'll be confessing to a lot more in a little while."

"Do you want that?" asked Levent.

"No, sir. I haven't done any killing."

"But you weren't surprised to hear she'd been murdered."

Atilla looked at Levent as if to ask how anyone could know what he thought. But he now believed someone did. That man would become his confidant for the balance of the conversation.

"She was like two people," he said in a softer voice. "At work and socially, at night and during the day. I never met anyone like her, and I don't think there were any. She'd give orders like someone in military service. 'Get me a capacity tour to Side and make it Germans in good euro. Talk that cheap Turk on board with his Lions Clubs.' But then she turned around and was understanding even if you didn't bring them in. She'd tell us what we did wrong and how we should make it right the next day. And she'd buy us all dinner. At the Four Seasons once."

"You can see her doing something wrong, though," said Levent. "And making it up later. But she couldn't make it up with one man. He wouldn't let her. He went into anger, and yet remained cold-blooded in the things he did. He enjoyed doing them. And they were terrible things. Tell me if you know anyone like that?"

Atilla listened as if the details he was being told, but not shown, made them more real. "You're saying he took his time."

"They like to think they have all of it," said Levent. "It's because their victims have so little."

"I'd help you if I could," he said. "God knows I would. But we're not in that kind of business. The Mafia owns TekirTur, but they leave us alone unless we steal too much of their trade."

"Did you?"

"Once before I knew better," he said. "Never again."

"Who made you aware of the problem?"

"Miss Acheson," he said. "She wasn't angry that day, I remember. She just said I couldn't take any more of their business. Another company, fine, but these people paid off their competition in blood."

"Was that a frequent problem with your firm?"

"No," he said. "We don't have to be told to leave the Mafia alone. None of us in there is crazy."

"Had you ever seen Miss Acheson with a weapon of her own?"

"A *weapon*?"

"Let's say a handgun."

For the first time, Atilla seemed to doubt Levent's secret connection to his psyche. "I think you must be joking."

"She had one, you know," said Levent. "At her apartment. I'm sure you remember that place."

"Yes."

"And her country home."

"No," he said. "I was never there. She went there to get away from all of us."

He might be telling the truth. The maid said she had never seen him before, and she probably would have at the house. Levent was on the point of believing Atilla, if he passed one more test.

"Tell us about the others in the photos," said Levent. "Be honest—or it will go badly for you."

"The man is Mehmet Kaya," he said, shrugging off any loyalty he owed. "He's one of our guides on tours that go to the East. He's out on one now, if you really want to know."

"When will he return?"

"Tomorrow at the earliest," he said. "It could be the next day before he shows up for another job. Possibly more."

"Get in touch with him," said Akbay. "Tell him he has to come to this office the moment he gets in. Your second call is to us."

"I doubt if he can tell you much," said Atilla. "He's just a good-looking man who got his invitation to the party when he dropped by the office the day before."

"Now tell us about the other woman in the photographs," said Akbay. "We want to know who she is—or you lose your chance at the police freedom medal."

"She was Miss Acheson's friend," said Atilla. "We called her Hello Dolly that night. I didn't know her real name until I saw it in the papers. She's a high society lady and not one you'll be able to push around. Her name is Tara Gunduz."

Levent hoped no one heard the breath he let out slowly. That name was very well known in the upper reaches of society, but unlikely to stay that way. Simply knowing it in this context was unhealthy.

"Thank you, Atilla. You can go back to work now, but stay close where we can reach you."

* * *

They took a late lunch along the same street at a restaurant that catered to tourists, as nearly all the places did in Sultanahmet. This was not Homicide's usual beat, and the owner did not recognize his guests as the police. The food came without being ordered in large quantities and automatically. The check would be automatic, jacked up to inflated prices that only tourists could afford.

Levent said nothing to the waiter. He accepted the dolma and the fava and had begun to work on the plate of doner and rice, when Akbay finally found his tongue in the place he had put it for safe keeping.

"Is this woman who I think she is?" he asked with a smile. "The one that does all the work with brain-damaged orphans."

"Yes."

"And cleaning the filth out of the Bosporus?"

"Yes."

"And screaming about the women who get beaten by their husbands, like it was something rare?"

"Yes."

"While she's fucking the clerks in Sultanahmet?"

"The last time I looked, women had the same rights as men, including the right to go to bed with a man they like."

Akbay shrugged on the short side of approval. Like most men, he did not like the expansion of women's rights in that area, though he knew little could be done to alter the course. Women had had the vote in Turkey and the protection of the law for a long time. Longer than almost any Western nation, thanks to Ataturk's reforms. In spite of the current fundamentalist government, those rights had recently expanded. That was something for the politicians to wave in the face of the EU, as they did at every opportunity through wide-smiling Islamic teeth.

"How are we going to interrogate this woman?" asked Akbay. "Do we submit our questions to her secretary?"

"Questioning her will be your job, Erol. We'll call it the unfortunate end of a promising career."

Akbay laughed, but warily. "We can always say she was just having fun. I mean, it looked like she was. You don't really think she did those things to our victim. Hell, this one wouldn't know how to handle a knife. She's probably never been in a kitchen except to herd the servants."

"Now you're thinking, Erol. I'm sure you'll find yourself on the same track as the Chief when he learns her name."

"You're going to tell him?"

"I haven't decided."

"I'm glad you're the one to do it, Onur. You don't think Gunduz could be mixed up in the scheme with the money, too?"

"That's a question for her bankers," said Levent. "Society women are always wealthy unless their lifestyle is too grand for their credit cards. I'll try to find out if anyone's heard rumors about her finances."

"Your wife's nose to the ground again?"

"We'll see how sensitive it is. I can't go barging into a situation like this until I have some idea of how the land lies."

Akbay touched his nose. "But what if the money is hot? And they're putting it through the laundry to cool off. I don't know how seriously anyone up the line will take it. From what I've heard, the politicians looked the other way during the Crisis, and afterward, too. If you brought hard money into the country, you found yourself invited to all the receptions in Ankara. You might even expect honors to fall your way. It's not the first time criminals got to be heroes in this country."

"The EU's taken the place of hot money in every politician's mind," said Levent. "Our friends in the West keep saying criminals are criminals."

"They don't understand us, do they?"

"I'm very much afraid they do."

The bad feelings Levent had about this case were right from the start. What kind of dunce would pursue a crime no one thought was wrong? What would happen if he found that Tara Gunduz was a partner in money laundering, too? He could not imagine putting a woman like her through hard questioning, knowing that every response moved him closer to retirement.

Levent took his bad humor out on the owner of the restaurant. When the man came to deliver the check, Levent put his wallet on the table, open to display his badge. It was big enough for anyone in the tourist business to choke on.

"Of course we're always ready to do our best for the police," he said with a smile that nearly failed. "Will you have more coffee, sir?"

CHAPTER 10

The Money Market

The money changers were not found in Tahtakale but further down the hill from Sultanahmet in the Covered Bazaar. Walking distance, if anyone walked in Istanbul. The money market had migrated from the streets where it was born to turn indoors under the vast roofs of one of the prime tourist attractions in the city. Any goods could be found in the Bazaar for a price, and the price was fair to those who knew how to bargain. Jammed with fantasy shops, it seemed proper that the state of mind pushed the real aside at every turn.

"I've got a man here on Altin Street," said Akbay, after they had parked their cars and moved inside the Bazaar along one of its widest streets. "He's a counterfeiter who went as straight as they ever do. I've used him several times, and he hasn't screwed me yet. But we'll see."

Akbay turned into a shop a few steps up the way that may have been twelve meters square. Called Heaven for the Bride, it was filled with all the dreams in jewelry that any woman could want.

"Where's Zeki?" asked Akbay of the old man with a brush mustache behind the counter. "I need him now."

"He's out. But I can have him here soon enough."

"Do it."

The old man picked up his cell phone and punched the button for Zeki. He did not wait more than two rings and did not speak except to say, "Central."

That was what they called it. Tahtakale had begun as an illegal money market that in time became as legal as any. With the arrival of the cell phone, or *cep*, it became much more fluid. Inside the Nurosmaniye Gate, transactions took place in shoebox shops that never saw their product until the last minute. Negotiations were conducted by cep with other parties on ceps, and when a price was struck, it was inviolate. An honor system that worked, it was unique as far as Levent knew.

It was not much more than five minutes until Zeki entered the shop, stepping inside to a depth where he would not be seen with the police. He had pursued his original career in ATM cards, forged for one-time raids, which made him hard but not impossible to catch. Now he looked like most of the traders in the Bazaar, half-shaven, with eyes that seemed to watch each other. Dressed not to call attention to himself or his product, he wore black pants, a black shirt, and a black leather jacket with a silver cep dangling by a chain from his neck.

"Erol, so good to see you. Will you have coffee or tea?"

"Apple tea and filter coffee," said Akbay, not wanting to refuse. "But we're in a hurry and looking for a man who might be hard to find. That probably means homework for you."

"Always ready for a challenge," he said, sitting on a divan where customers sat. "Who's the man?"

"We don't know his name. But he's here, and he dealt in money with a woman who stopped by from time to time. Ayla Acheson was the head of AylaTur in Sultanahmet. She was a blonde, tall, with blue eyes and tits that might be missed at a glance. You might be reading about her in the paper."

"I don't read anything but the financial page," he said with a gap in his smile. "And most of what they say, I already know. You don't have any idea where she came in the Bazaar?"

"No, but she would have been converting dollars or euro to lira," said Akbay. "She didn't like taking it directly to a bank."

"I see."

Levent could see that Zeki had already narrowed the list of money traders in his mind. While any one of them might make the transactions, a man who did large volume was more uncommon.

"It could be a dozen people," he said. "Give me an hour, and I should be able to come up with the right name."

"It would be best if you did it in ten minutes," said Levent. "You'd earn yourself credit with God and the police."

"How much credit?"

"Future consideration," said Levent. "That should mean a lot to a man who needs it. My name is Inspector Levent."

"An inspector," he said. "That's as close to God as it comes in this place. You should have that coffee and tea. Take a look at the stock. We'll guarantee you the best price on earth, if not in heaven."

As they waited for the refreshments, Levent checked his cep. He had silenced it when they went out in the street to question Atilla and forgot to turn it back on. Three calls had come in.

The first was from Derya Silme, who must have something from the body. Levent rang him back. "Tell me something that gives me a lead."

"Onur, have I ever done less?" Silme usually laughed at his own jokes, which always concerned the dead, and Levent had gotten used to it. "This time I brought in the case at a single stroke. You know that incision at the back of her neck? The neat one? We speculated some knowledge of anatomy might be required."

"We did."

"Well, this animal has the knowledge, Onur. I was wrong about the spinal cord. He severed it neatly. To the proper depth and no more. Under the circumstances, which were stressful, he must be a professional."

"Well, that is good news. I suppose it means we should be looking for a killer who's a doctor."

"A surgeon," said Silme. "I'll do some asking around at the hospitals and the other sort of butcher shops. The only thing that's puzzling is what he was really trying to do."

"Besides torturing her."

"That's up in the air now," he said. "With her spinal cord severed, she might not have felt much pain."

"Are you telling me he anesthetized her?"

"In a way. You could call him a gentleman torturer if nothing better meets your mind."

"Then he couldn't have gotten much information," said Levent. "If she wasn't able to feel or talk."

"Possible," he said. "Hadn't thought of it like that."

"I don't want to think about it either," said Levent. "It doesn't seem to make a lot of sense."

"I have to admit you're right, Onur. At least until we figure it out."

"Let me know if you do."

Levent closed the cep in disgust at so much confusion. A kindly torturer? That was worse than confusing. It was contradictory. He didn't even want to talk to Akbay about the news. A case that advanced one step forward and three back was too much on a full stomach.

The second call had come from the computer department at the lab. They were new and more than useless considering their pay. Levent had never known one helpful thing to come from them, but he was willing to listen.

"This is Levent."

"Karanfil Chichek here, Inspector. I have something I thought you'd want to know."

Although Levent did not recognize the voice on the line, the fact that it was a woman calmed him. Her first name meant carnation and her last, flower. Did competence smell as sweet?

"I'd like to hear something that points forward, yes."

"We haven't been able to do anything tracing the origin of the call," she said. "But I did get in touch with a man at ICQ. I dealt with him once before, and he's human for a techie. Usually, they won't let out information about their subscribers, but he told me the person who goes by the handle Karanlik used an ISP in Holland when he signed on. That should be accurate."

"A name and address would be better."

"I don't think we'll get anything like it," she said. "They're wary of giving information even if what they have is correct. And I doubt it's correct if this person was careful. He could have used a public computer to sign up. That's what I'd do."

"You'll keep trying, though."

"Yes, sir. You can be sure."

Levent wished he was. An address in Holland made the case international, but it had been like that from the start. Could

Karanlik live in Holland, land of the free and easy? Could he be a Turk living in Holland? Plenty were there. Levent had never heard of one who could stitch his own trousers, let alone perform midnight surgery on a body, but he would like to be wrong.

The last call had come from one of the Chief's assistants, a new man with a snotty voice who was called Donmez. "I'm glad we could finally get together," he said without hiding his annoyance. "We have a new man on board—a foreigner who just got off the plane. He's demanding to speak to the head of the investigation. The Chief insists that's you."

"That seems like something you could handle," said Levent. "I have nothing to tell him now. Or the Chief."

"I don't think that works for us at this end," he said as if his words made sense. "The man is a relative of the victim. An uncle."

"From England?"

"Exactly."

"I changed my mind," said Levent. "Make an appointment for six o'clock at his hotel—or anywhere downtown."

"That would be the Ritz-Carleton."

"Fine."

Levent hung up thinking not everything that came from the Chief's office was useless. He would like to speak to the uncle—the silent partner in AylaTur and its family banker. Possibly, he held keys as well as money.

Five minutes later, at the same time as the coffee and tea arrived, Zeki returned to the shop with a moneychanger on his arm. The man looked much like Zeki except that his leather coat was brown and his cep blue. His name was Selim Tam, and his widely set eyes refused to meet Levent's on the first two passes. On the third, he put out the clammiest hand in Istanbul and kept it in place too long.

"I'm glad to help the police, Inspector."

"The first time is usually the hardest," said Levent. "But relationships grow faster than we think."

"That's what I wanted to hear," he said. "My son—my first son—found some trouble at school. They say he took someone's car for a drive. He says the car was lent. It's a dispute the police have joined, so much the worse for him."

"I'll look into it," said Levent. "Something might be done."

"His name is Kerim."

"Noted," said Levent. "Now tell me of your relationship with Ayla Acheson in as much detail as you remember."

When he blinked, surprised, Levent realized he shouldn't have phrased the question like that, knowing what he did of the victim. Tam was not a bad-looking man if your taste ran to dark and sloe-eyed. And who knew what she didn't like?

"What passed between us was strictly business, Inspector. We exchanged money. Like traders do. Even the banks have offices and representatives here. There's nothing under the rug."

"Then why didn't she go to her bank for the exchange? I imagine she has more than one account."

Tam demurred with a shrug. "Sometimes clients like to change large amounts of foreign currency so it remains completely silent. If the amounts are too large over a period of time, there might be questions."

"But not from you."

"Part of my job is to spread the money—and its origin—in thinner quantities about the market."

"That makes it almost impossible to gain notice."

"Correct."

They were getting somewhere slowly. Tam had not mentioned the name of Ayla Acheson, but that was unnecessary. He did not want his professional discretion compromised. Levent understood.

"Let's say this person came regularly to you to exchange money. What quantity are we speaking of?"

"An average?"

"Your best."

"In the area of a half million dollars, let's say."

The conversion had to be that big to justify the payments to Emre Oz, and who knew how many others in the scheme. Probably not many others. Security was also a concern.

"The transactions were always in cash?"

"Almost always," he said. "Twice I took drafts on a bank in Belize. That's in Central America."

"Their name?"

"First Fifth Trust."

"The drafts were good?"

"Good enough is perfect," he said. "Anything less is a problem. Thieves have gotten very clever at counterfeiting bank drafts, especially ones written on foreign banks. You might ask Zeki about that."

"Later," said Levent. "How much were the drafts made out for?"

"Once for two hundred thousand in dollars," said Tam. "The second time, one hundred and fifty. In dollars."

"You have a keen memory."

"That's my job," he said. "Of course, I called to verify the drafts. That makes it easier to remember."

"So your client brought this money to you in cash or bank drafts. She always brought them here?"

"Each time."

"Was she always alone?"

"Yes," he said, and quickly amended his words. "All but once. A man was with her. I'd say about a year ago. If I recall, it was near The Children's Holiday—or a day or two after."

As recollection went, that was better than good. "Who was he? Did he give a name?"

Tam pursed his lips and nodded. "It would be impossible for me to recall his name, except it was so odd. It was Delir. I'd never heard the name before. At least not on a Turk."

Tam's turn of memory was curious. Levent had never heard the name either, but a verb in Turkish had the same spelling. *Delir* meant to go mad. That was a reasonable description of this case.

"Did you think he was Turkish?"

"Not that I could tell," said Tam. "He spoke a bit, but I didn't think he was a countryman."

"You think he was a foreigner who learned the language?"

"If I have to say so, yes."

"Describe him."

"Younger than me," said Tam, searching his memory with a hand in his hair. "In his early forties, I'd say. He was well preserved, so it's hard to guess the age. About my height. His hair was dark brown, but gray at the temples, and he had a scar under his left eye. A crescent scar. The teeth were younger and the body, too. Not badly dressed. A suit with an open blue shirt."

"Was anything else unusual about the transaction that day?"

He shook his head slowly. "The money was in the normal range. The arrangements for dispersal were nothing out of the ordinary. Her bank twice removed." Tam focused the glitter in his eyes. "I can tell you she seemed to defer to him. It was something in her manner. And his."

"As if he was important."

"To her, yes."

"Do you remember anything he said?"

Tam fingered his cep as men did their worry beads, playing with the numbers as he called up the past. "Not much, I'm afraid. He said he was staying at the Marmara Hotel. And he made some comment about Tehran."

"Do you think he was Iranian?"

"Possibly. But he didn't say more about it. He might be an Iranian if he was educated."

"And you never saw him again?"

"No, Inspector. I asked her about him the next time we met, but she said he was out of the country."

The stranger should have plenty of money to spend on his journey to or from. He was intimately involved in the victim's affairs, and large amounts of money were among the most intimate.

"When was the last time you saw Miss Acheson?"

"Three days ago."

The day before she was murdered. "For the usual transaction?"

"It was unusual in one way," said Tam in a tone that emphasized nothing. "The size of the conversion was larger. In the area of eight hundred thousand dollars."

"Where was the money deposited?"

Tam shook his head as if he had finally said too much. "It wasn't. She walked out the door with the cash in a leather bag."

That was a shock. A woman might walk into this place with large amounts of cash in a bag, but Levent knew of no one— man or woman—who would walk away like that. It should not have happened here or anywhere without a bodyguard.

"I imagine she trusted you by then, Tam."

"Why not?" he asked. "She'd always been satisfied with my services. Nothing was ever left in doubt."

Tam did not sound concerned, though he was in the best position to have hired someone to question the victim about the cash. A day, however, was a long time to let pass with the money at risk. That gave her time to put it away. The funds could have been transferred to any bank in the country. Or on earth.

"You'll be sure not to leave the city for the next few days," said Levent. "We may have further questions for you."

"I don't go anywhere unless it's a long holiday," he said. "I can't afford the short ones at this job."

That was to tell the police he was a simple worker in the fields of money. Levent would believe it until he knew better.

CHAPTER 11

The Uncle

Levent seldom stopped by his office when the time was better spent on the move. Unfortunately, he had reports to file and trash to confront, which included the press and its watchdog, a former subordinate of Levent's named Besh.

Besh was a fundamentalist who had been inserted onto the force to make Homicide's life miserable. Only by deft maneuvering had Levent arranged for Besh to be promoted to press liaison officer, a position that until that time had not existed. In the flow of recent history, it must be said, press conferences hardly existed.

"They're rabid," said Besh as they entered the conference room on the second floor. "She was a woman, you know. A foreigner."

"Thank you, Besh. I'll include that in my case summary."

"Just a warning, Inspector."

Half a dozen reporters and a television camera were gathered around the conference table that had once been the Chief's desk. Everything in the room seemed misplaced, including Levent's memory. He thought he recognized the reporters except for two, a man and a woman who were obviously foreign. That problem was partly solved by conducting the briefing in Turkish, as it should be.

"As you know, Ayla Acheson, the owner of AylaTur, was murdered at her country home." Levent looked out at the crowd as if taking attendance. "The investigation is proceeding along converging lines. In the meantime, we await the results from our forensics examinations and should have them soon." Levent paused for the gravity of science that even the press respected. "I'm sure we'll have more for you tomorrow."

"Any suspects?" said a voice from the rear.

"None that can be put forward at this time," said Levent. "You'll know them when we do."

"No suspects," said another voice.

"We heard the killing was done with maximum blood and gore," said the first voice as its master stepped forward. Mehmet Siyah was a reporter for the largest circulation daily and a bad specimen of his kind. "They tell me you had to wade through a river of blood, body parts, etcetera. It was like Baghdad, they say."

"If I knew who *they* were, I could respond," said Levent. "Let's say most murders are bloody and this one worse than usual."

Siyah made a show of writing in his notebook. "As bloody as Baghdad," he announced to his colleagues.

A female reporter for the intellectuals of the city had her pen in the air as if marking a spot. "Do you have any idea of the reason for her murder?" she asked. "Or should I say, have you ruled anything out?"

"We've ruled out suicide," said Levent.

"How about a traffic accident?" asked Siyah. "From what I heard, you could have put a cop in the street in front of her house and saved the city the expense of a stoplight."

Not a lot of laughter in the room, but more than seemed appropriate. The hounds had been talking to the neighbors, of course. There was no way to get around that except with an appropriate lie.

"Miss Acheson was an enterprising and busy woman who often conducted her business from home," said Levent. "It was a worldwide business that kept her going at all hours, and by every means."

"That's good, Inspector," said Siyah. "I'm going to quote you."

"Always glad to help."

"That would be a first."

"Inspector," said a woman's voice from the back of the room. "Melanie Goshen here. Do you have any indication that Miss Acheson's work for the Women's Movement played a part in her death?"

Stepping away from the two male reporters beside her, Goshen emerged as raw as a saddlebag, her notebook in her hand and her red hair in spiky ringlets that were all airborne.

"English," said Besh in Levent's ear. "The Guardian. Radicals. Not our friends."

Levent did not know how to find friends on a battlefield. As he waited for the translation from English that he did not need, he put on his NBA game face. The playoffs, which he loved, had begun this week.

"We've found nothing to indicate Miss Acheson's work with her causes has anything to do with the murder," he said. "We're looking at that angle as well as others. Any motivation is possible until we find the correct one."

"Real is a concept," said Goshen. "What I should ask is if you're taking this investigation seriously?"

"We're not used to taking murder less than seriously here," said Levent. "My last unsolved crime went to the books two years ago. I'll put that record against the police in your country. Or anywhere else."

"We hear the victim was tortured," said Goshen quickly. "Do you plan to use similar interrogation techniques?"

"That would be against civilized behavior," said Levent. "To say nothing of EU standards. This case will be solved by patient investigation. When I find the killer, he won't have the need to confess."

"Inspector," said a man with two notebooks. "Andrew Blyleven from America. Are you telling us that you never use torture in your work?"

Besh was in Levent's ear again as the translation passed. "*The New York Times*. They're worse."

"I understand these issues are in the air," said Levent. "Most of all in your own country. In my opinion, torture happens for two reasons. At the ground level, subordinates are given inadequate training that allows them to substitute their instincts. On a higher level, these techniques are condoned by superiors who feel themselves under pressure to produce. Those conditions do not apply here."

"So it's a walk in the park for you."

Levent answered quickly, betraying his knowledge of English. "It's my job and I'm good at it. You can be the judge."

"Let's say we are," said Siyah in a loud voice. "And the only one you're likely to get, Levent."

* * *

"How did it go?" asked Akbay, who seemed amused as he sat with his feet on the desk. "The press conference, that is."

"Grim. But the Chief will be happy that nothing can be used against us."

"That's good." Akbay took his feet down, stood up, and put his cigarette out on the floor. "We're having some luck tracking the Volvo that was seen near the victim's house. Less than a hundred blue ones turned up. That can be taken down to about twenty if we allow that the car is more than four years old. If we don't count the Other Side, we have only twelve."

"I'm not sure we can exclude the Asian Side. Nothing says a murderer can't cross a bridge. He's not a lazy one, we know."

"Not a stupid one either," said Akbay. "I was thinking that if he's foreign, or one of us living abroad, he'd stay on this side to hold down his commuting time."

"That's reasonable. We can go with this side first. Get a couple of men on the move and see how it goes."

"They're on their way already," said Akbay with a smile. "I told them not to get too close. If they find anything promising, they're to call. I'll be ready to cover all night. I'm going up to the Marmara now to try to get a line on our visitor Mister Delir. It's apt to be a long haul there."

"Did you call them first?"

"Sure," said Akbay. "But I want to look around for myself. That's what I was taught, Inspector."

Levent said nothing about Akbay's teacher, who would remain nameless and good. He checked the messages on his desk phone. In the end, only one call seemed to be worth returning.

It had come from his wife, probably to report on her social reconnaissance.

"Yes, my dear."

"You never call me 'dear' except when you don't want to hear what I'm saying." She gave a slow pause for his objection. "Why did you ask me to do your work if that's how you feel?"

"It has nothing to do with you," said Levent. "It's been a long day that will grow longer. I hope you have something cheerful to say."

"I have a report on your victim's good works," said Emine as if the list was long. "She was a member and one of the founders of the Women's Action Group in Turkey. There's a name and a number for them if you want it. She was also on the board of the Mothers Against Domestic Violence and helped fund the Rape Victims' Shelter. I have numbers for them, too."

"I'll take them all."

Emine gave them, but as if she was disappointed. He waited until they were in his notebook before he asked what he really wanted to know.

"What sort of gossip did you gather?"

"About Ayla Acheson?"

"You're being obtuse, my dear."

"Everyone gossips a bit about the dead, Onur, but no one has much to say about a saint."

"Which she was."

"Apparently," said Emine. "She gave her time and a lot of money to her favorite causes. The only negative note comes from cousin Sema, who says no one ever gave out that much money unless it came from the sewer."

"What sewer?"

"The same one everyone talks about," she said. "You know those two big office buildings that went up off TEM? They're some kind of Mafia, no surprise. Cousin Sema says Ayla Acheson was one of the movers behind the scene."

"Our Mafia," he said. "The local sort."

"Who else has the need to wash their filthy money in a project that big?"

It was a very big one. Levent had heard the rumors, too, but no one seemed to know which Mafia had underwritten the two gigantic towers. Was it possible none of the local families was involved?

"I don't know who's behind that project," he said. "I'm not sure anyone around here knows, but I'll ask. Meanwhile, did you hear anything in your virtual travels that connects with Tara Gunduz?"

"*The* Tara Gunduz?"

"If that's what they call her."

"How did her name come up?"

"Second hand," he said. "She and the victim were friends. Whatever you can dig up on her would be grand. Especially of the second kind."

"The gossip kind."

"Well, yes. I'll be very keen to hear what you have to say."

"Does that mean you'll be home for dinner?"

"You know I always try."

"Yes, Onur. You'll call."

* * *

Levent would have liked to talk to the contacts at the victim's list of charitable organizations, but he put that aside for the moment. He barely had time to make the meeting with the victim's uncle at his hotel. Akbay waited patiently at the door he held open.

"When you talk to me the way you talk to your wife, Onur, I'll know I've finally arrived."

"You could hasten that day, Erol, but you're not respectable. When are you going to get married again?"

"When I find a willing woman," he said. "Trying them out beforehand is a must. That eliminates a lot of candidates with proper parents."

"You don't want to go with your mother's choice this time?"

"She means well," said Akbay. "But she wants them to be like her. I watched my father suffer all those years, and I won't repeat the mistake."

"I can ask Emine to scout the current crop, if you like."

"Thanks for playing the uncle, Onur. But I'm sure I can come up with something. If I don't, I'll sort through your cousins afterward. There's sure to be one with six toes in the bunch."

Levent waited until they had found their cars in the lot before coming back to the subject. "Six," he said. "That number's playing at your mind. The witch factor."

"The pussy factor is more like it," said Akbay. "Our victim didn't seem to have to beat the drums to find a partner. I should have been the one to catch that domestic disturbance back in February."

"I don't think her behavior would draw much comment in England," said Levent. "They're more relaxed."

"Do you think her uncle is?"

"I think he's her uncle."

* * *

Levent took the sweeping turn around Dolmabache Stadium to the parking lot of the Ritz-Carleton. A monstrous building of grandiose size set on the first hill back from the Bosporus, it was known as The Dagger in the Heart of Istanbul. How something as ungainly and ill-made could be compared to a shapely blade remained unknown. It was simply a blunt forty-story mass of concrete and glass that had blighted a handsome part of the city.

But it had a view from the parking lot, and from any room near the top what arrived in the eye was sublime. The mighty Bosporus churned underfoot like a rug. The sudden hills of the Asian side turned painterly and naive. All this diminution could be purchased by the night for a staggering fee that the man who answered the door to 3714 would hardly miss.

"Inspector Levent," he said in a tone that sounded friendly. "I've been expecting you. My name's Samuel Wilding."

"Pleased to meet you, sir."

"I'm pleased to meet any man who speaks good English."

He opened the door to a room that was as much as Levent expected. Its occupant was more. A tall man with skin the color of his fair hair, Wilding had been constructed of angles rarely found on the far side of the continent. His bones were like daggers and nearly as prominent. His eyes were a thin blue and his mouth small, the words given at American speed. He had dressed for dinner in a dark coat with a gray vest that made his slender frame look more substantial.

"Drink?" he said.

"No, thank you."

"I brought my own," he said. "Twenty years old. The last nineteen in an earthen pot."

"In that case."

"Good man."

He poured two glasses as if he would wash in them, filling both to the brim without ice and passing one to Levent. "Please, have a seat."

Wilding waited for Levent to take a seat in an opposite chair of a similar make and apply the welcome sip of the whiskey, which was very good. It was the best Levent had ever tasted.

"So," he said after he had taken his own measure of whiskey. "Do I ask the awkward questions a relative asks, or will you tell me what you know without the usual nonsense?"

"I'm afraid I don't have anything to say. The investigation is still in its beginning phase. We're gathering the facts, questioning people who can give us an idea of who might strike out at her. It's all incomplete now. Tomorrow should be different."

"But you were there at the house to see," he said, as if he could not say what. "Give me your assessment as it stands."

Levent knew he should not say anything. He knew he had to say something to satisfy protocol as it came from the top. That was a pity unless it could be turned into an opportunity.

"It was a violent crime that found your niece, Mister Wilding. By that, I mean a crime of special violence. I'm uncomfortable talking to you about it."

"Don't be," he said with something like menace. "What's the difference if I hear about it now or later? I'll know soon in any case."

That was to tell Levent a shortfall would mean a call to the Chief. Or someone of higher rank. This man was accustomed to dealing from a position of strength with Third World civil servants.

"Her throat was cut," said Levent, matching Wilding's tone exactly. "But her eye was plucked out first."

He took another pass at his drink. It was more than a sip, and he seemed to chew the whiskey down in long swallows. When he took the drink away from his face, it was almost drained.

"Torture," he said.

"It looks that way." Levent used his hands as he did with people who never used theirs. "But her spinal cord was severed high on her back. She may not have felt much, depending on when it was done."

"For Christ's sake, you're telling me it *was* a psychopath. That there was no purpose in it."

So the Chief's theory had made the rounds. Unfortunately, it was still the most useful approach for a man who wanted to keep his mouth shut.

"That is what it looks like now, yes."

Levent had spoken as if he didn't quite finish his sentence. Wilding picked up on it immediately. "But you don't think so, Inspector. Do you?"

"I can't be sure at this point," said Levent. "We have indications that the killer may be motivated by money. But it wasn't the usual burglary. Large amounts of cash seem to be involved."

"Cash?" he said. "In the house?"

"We don't know where the money was then or where it is now," said Levent. "Three days ago, your niece exchanged eight hundred thousand dollars in the Bazaar in Istanbul. According to the man who arranged the transaction, she walked into the street with the money in a valise with no one to accompany her."

Wilding pulled his glass before his face again, but did not drink from it. He used the glass to massage his right cheek. The action might be typical if he was alone, but was distinctly absentminded in the presence of another.

"I see," he said finally.

"Exactly what do you see, sir? It would be helpful to have your reading of the situation. I assume you knew your niece well. Does this seem like something she would do without a very good reason?"

"Hell, no," he said.

"In your opinion, what would make her behave that way?"

"I have no idea," he said. "None."

"Was she having any financial problems you're aware of?"

"I don't think so."

"Then had she come across financial opportunities that could account for the size of the transaction?"

"Again, I'm not aware of any." Wilding waved his hand. "She was in business, of course. She was doing well with it."

"How well, sir? Being a partner in the firm, you should be in a position to know."

Wilding crossed his legs and folded his hands across the legs with the whiskey still in place. "They told me you were good," he said in a tone that was confidential and aggressive. "When I asked if money would help things along, they said that wouldn't be necessary in this case. I'd never heard that said before in the Middle East. The man who doesn't have his hand out is the one who had it chopped off for stealing. Or has it behind his back to hide his knife. Isn't that the way it goes?"

Levent did not answer. He rarely answered a question when he had one of his pending, especially if the question was rude.

Wilding went on with reluctance. "Somehow I was hoping— this is stupid, I know—that a man so competent might find it proper to investigate the crime rather than the victim." He paused for his point. "Tell me you've made some progress there, and we'd have something to discuss."

"We have made progress," said Levent. "If you can tell me what happened to that money, it will move matters along."

"I told you I don't know."

"Will you find out?" asked Levent. "I'm sure you're in the best position to do so. If I knew where to look, I'd have located it already."

Wilding put his glass on the table beside him. He was done with whiskey and nearly with the meeting. Clearly, his money was his business and not to be shared.

"My partnership in the company was largely silent," he said. "But I'm aware of two accounts Ayla kept. One in this country and one offshore. It's not impossible she had more."

"If she found them necessary," said Levent. "But why would she have the need to hide so much money away?"

"You're asking me?" he said as a challenge. "I can tell you this country is one very good reason. It wasn't long ago I was advising Ayla to pull all her money out of Turkey. The lira was crippled. The stock market was the best place to lose all the money you had. There was a real risk the government might freeze everyone's accounts. And that wasn't all they might do."

"But they didn't," said Levent. "The economy is doing well for a change. And the lira is stable. You must know that, too."

He nodded. "I keep informed."

"How closely?" asked Levent without waiting for an answer. "According to my information, your niece exchanged large amounts of foreign currency on a regular basis under the counter. She'd been doing so for the last several years. The money came from outside the country. I'd like to know where it originated."

"The firm had offices in several different cities in Europe," he said. "I imagine they would be remitting."

"Those things can be easily done by wire," said Levent. "These things were not. The money came in dollars and euro by courier. We don't have a clear idea of where these couriers originated, but

I'm sure we'll track all the sources in time. You can shrink that time if you choose."

"Suppose I look into it," he said. "That would ease your mind and redirect it in the proper way."

"If you promise me answers."

"You'll have them," he said. "And you'll have my heartfelt thanks if you find the answer I want."

He was lying. Levent was lying. Everything was understood except the things that were hidden.

CHAPTER 12

The Marmara Hotel

Levent was on the way home when his cep rang. He did not want to take the call in traffic, but he flipped open the Motorola, holding it in his hand as the electronic tones returned to their matrix. The bright but nearly unreadable screen said the caller had been Erol Akbay.

He had something to say, and as usual it could not wait. Levent let Akbay wait, thinking as he drove on the feeder road to the highway that he did not have to answer. If he declined, he might still make dinner at home.

"Yes, Erol."

"Where are you?"

"On the road," he said.

"I'm at the Marmara," he said. "I found something and thought you might want to know."

"Go ahead."

"It's better if you come here. Senior assistance will be useful."

"Fifteen minutes."

Levent was there in twelve, doing things he did not like to do in Istanbul traffic. The Marmara was a large hotel at Taksim, the central meeting place of the city, dominating the eastern side of the square with a gorgeous view over the Golden Horn and the many mosques lit up at night. The management was local—as local as corporations were found these days—and cooperative when in the mood.

Akbay looked as if he had spent some time on public relations. He seemed at home at the manager's desk, sitting before the computers that were somewhat less than a firmament. He rose when Levent entered the office, rolling his hand.

"We should have systems like this," he said. "Click the mouse and you can call up the history of the place for the last five years."

Levent sat at the desk before the computer, thinking these things were always uniform but never quite the same. He always had to think about what he saw.

"What am I looking at?"

"Occupancy for the week of the last Children's Holiday on this one," he said, tapping the first computer. "I found this man Delir without trouble."

Levent saw the name Delir Rasfar highlighted among the hotel's occupants approximately one year ago. He had stayed three days at rates that should be stiff if he did not receive the discount extended to travel firms. And probably stiff if he had.

"When you see a bullet," said Akbay, "it means the occupant presented his passport at the desk."

"In this case?"

"Moldavian."

That was promising. Several facts pointed toward old Russia and its independent offshoots. Moldavia was the most tenuous of those republics, run by ex-communists and businessmen who combined to make it one of the more corrupt places on earth. Its enterprising citizens, some of whom spoke a Turkish dialect, moved on gladly. Levent had handled two cases in the last year that ended in the arrest of Moldavians who had come to Turkey. One was a live-in housekeeper, the other a chauffeur, and both had fleeced their employers before murdering them.

"It looks like you found the heart of darkness, Erol. But the man's name doesn't sound Moldavian."

"The manager remembers him because he was a repeater," said Akbay, pointing to the fields on the second computer screen. "Says he's about as Moldavian as he is Cuban. Iranian, possibly, though he's not sure. Could be Azerbaijani or something in that area. The name says as much."

Levent looked at the second computer that tied into the same system at another click of the mouse. The readout said Delir Rasfar had stayed at the Marmara four times in the last four years. The length of time ran from one to four days with the four being done on his third visit to the city. The dates were not at exact intervals, but came in close to yearly.

"What does this asterisk mean after the four day visit?"

"He rented a Conference Room."

"For a *conference?*"

"It was the Small Conference Room," said Akbay, as if that mattered. "It seats eight around a long table, or maybe ten if they're Chinese. Of course, he didn't have to fill it up, and from what the manager recalls, he may not have. Our friend had the meeting catered, and the bill is here on the machine. About two hundred and twenty lira for coffee, tea and cakes."

"I wonder where we'd be if he had rented the Large Conference Room?" said Levent. "In the middle of a revolution?"

"I don't think we can call it that," said Akbay. "From what I hear, the Mafia runs all of Moldavia. They don't call it Mafia, though. They can't when it's actually the government."

"It's too bad we don't have an address for this man south of the Black Sea," said Levent. "He speaks some Turkish, he comes from a country where they kill for their morning exercise, and he knows the victim well enough to accompany her when she exchanges large amounts of currency."

"Are you thinking Karanlik?"

"I don't know, but he seems like a dark shadow. He's standing behind her just like one."

"We can run the name through the Moldavian authorities, but I don't think there are any we can trust."

"Hold off on that for now," said Levent. "Check the name and what we have for a description through Interpol first."

"I doubt if he used his real name. And I hate to think what a Moldavian passport costs these days. It must be like getting one of those glasses free when you buy a carton of Coke at Migros."

"But we might get lucky with a man who has a crescent scar under his left eye and gray at his temples."

"And if he lives in Holland?"

"That would be more than luck," said Levent. "That might mean a promotion for Detective Akbay."

"I'm working on it harder than you know," he said. "There's one old man who's been with the hotel since Ataturk was a boy. He was in the crew that serviced that conference—that's what the manager says. The old man lives not far away and the manager promised to get him here as soon as he can."

"You mean tonight?"

"I can handle this, Onur. Go home for dinner."

"You really are working hard for that promotion," said Levent. "I can tell you already have a woman to share the wealth. A live one, and respectable, too. Instead of that nonsense you've been giving me."

"You must be a detective," he said.

* * *

When the old man came, Levent did not doubt he had been a hotel worker when Taksim Square was a pasture for farm animals. His hair was platinum, not white, and his mustache dyed jet black. For his audience, he had dressed in the hotel uniform he wore during the day. It hung like dried meat. The tie clamped to his neck must have cut off circulation to his lower parts. Pulling the coat tight over his body, he stood to attention as he entered the office.

"Alican Sonmez," he said with a practiced bow. "I was told you'd like to speak to me."

"Inspector Onur Levent. Please sit down. Take my chair."

He would no more accept Levent's chair than he would burn it. Levent moved to the side and took him by the arm to lower him to glory. Which the old man did, slowly and carefully.

"We need some information that may difficult to retrieve," said Levent, as he sat on the edge of the desk at a conversational distance. "It concerns a meeting in the Small Conference Room that took place last year. There were a number of men present. We don't know who they were or what their purpose was. That's all the help I can give except to say it was about the time of the Children's Holiday. The man who reserved the room was a

foreigner who spoke decent Turkish. He had a scar under his left
eye in the shape of a crescent."

"Oh, yes. Mister Rasfar."

Levent looked at Akbay, whose mouth had fallen open in a
smile. "So you know him," said Levent.

"He's a good tipper," said Sonmez. "The bags up and the
bags down. Himself at the table and into his cab. And in the
Small Conference Room as well. Of course, he waited until
afterward to do it. Like a gentleman."

"Was he?"

"He tried, sir."

"I'm glad you remember Mister Rasfar so well. Your help could
be important to our investigation."

"Of Mister Rasfar?"

"Indirectly," said Levent, not wanting to condemn a good
tipper to jail just yet. "We'd like to know all you remember of
that meeting, since you served the beverages and snacks."

Sonmez did not spend much time in the memory bank. He
cocked his head as if the past was off his shoulder, and spoke to
the point. "He ordered petit four and chocolate cheesecake with
the refreshments. I remember that. He wanted to impress his
guests with the hotel's savories."

"He said that to you."

"Yes, sir. I was in charge of the service that day."

"How many men were present at the meeting?"

"I can't be certain," he said, shaking his head. "I remember I
entered the room and noticed it was nearly full in the chairs.
Perhaps eight chairs were occupied. Not less, I think."

"Eight men?"

"I believe so. I would have noted women and children. That
did not seem like a place where they would be welcome."

"A serious meeting."

"It was obvious, sir. There was so much smoke in the air I
thought the table had caught fire. It's ventilated, the conference
room, but the devices worked to little effect."

"How long had they been in the room?"

"For half an hour, sir. When they rang, I came in with the service as requested."

"Did you speak to Mister Rasfar?"

"No, sir. Except as he said thank you."

"Did anyone else speak to you?"

"No, sir. They spoke some words among themselves. In a foreign language for the most part."

"English?"

"Unlikely, sir. I have some myself, and that was not it."

"Russian?"

"Perhaps. The sounds seemed harsh to me. I think it should be so to them."

Ataturk would be proud of this man. He did not hesitate when he spoke, and he did it with authority. Levent did not think what question he should ask Sonmez next, but what he could not.

"Had you seen any of the men before that day?"

"Only one, sir. He was a guest of the hotel from time to time. And he frequented the coffee shop more often than he was a guest."

"Local?"

"Yes, sir."

"And yet he stayed at the hotel in an expensive room?"

"It's not so odd, sir. I'd say it was common among a certain class of clientele. They can afford the rooms, and this man could afford it more than most. When he stayed with us, it was in company with several women—usually different women. I did notice it was the same woman once or twice."

"You're telling me that none of them was his wife?"

"I doubt they were." He smiled for the first time, displaying teeth that had been remade several times. "They were all younger—much younger than him. And attractive, if you like taking a chance. They looked pretty much the same, dressed to kill in all the bright colors. But I recognized one of them."

"How so?"

"She's a whore. A high priced one, but a whore."

"Her name?"

"Pepper," he said. "Parmak may be her last name, though my memory could be faulty. In truth, the name seems too obvious."

Whores were too often obvious, and parmak meant finger. She would have five. They would be busy in every direction of the compass.

"When did you see the woman last?"

"Sir, I haven't seen her around here in some time, and the last time was with him. If I had to guess, I'd say she attracted the attention of your people. That happens if they aren't careful."

Levent made a note to call Vice. They might have a line on Pepper Parmak. If not, they might have her in jail.

"Do you know the man's name?"

For the first time, Sonmez did not want to answer. He squinted as if looking past Levent to an uncertain future. "It was Mister Gunduz, sir. Mister Ahmet Gunduz."

Now Levent understood Sonmez's reluctance to speak. Ahmet Gunduz was the husband of Tara Gunduz, whose image occupied a discreet place in Levent's left pocket. If this husband and wife cheated on each other, it was more like a competition. At their level of society, it was exactly that and no less.

"You say you didn't speak to Mister Gunduz at all that day?"

"No, sir. I recognized him. I believe he recognized me, but only in the way servants are recognized."

"I understand."

CHAPTER 13

Mine or Yours

Levent did not frequent discothèques for pleasure or the job. This one, called Mine or Yours, sat at the top of a hill above the Bosporus, looking out on a view of the city and the lights of oncoming traffic that streamed furiously across the bridge from Asia. The bar, sparkling with Art Deco brightwork, reflected the headlights so they were twice seen and devastating. Not that the customers noticed. They were scattered about the citrus-colored divans, lounging and drinking at citrus-colored tables, as if they were at the beach.

"What'll you have?"

"Pepper Parmak," said Levent, showing his identification. "I'm told she's usually here."

"Upstairs in the office," said the bartender.

Levent walked across the dance floor to the stairs that led to the glass-enclosed module hovering above the club as if from the belly of a dirigible. His call to Vice had produced a response from the detective on duty, telling Levent what business the prostitute named Pepper had retired to. "Semi-retired," said the detective. "But now she's got a license to steal and it's legal. She owns the place, it's said, but I wouldn't bet she has the deed just yet."

If Levent had not heard that a prostitute became suddenly respectable, he would have put off the visit for another time. But a woman who serviced an important clientele and came to own more than her body was intriguing. These things did not happen easily, and seldom completely.

She had come to rest on this cliff-like eerie. The room—and it seemed like more than one—made up the entire second story, hanging over the discothèque and the city like a cockpit angled to heaven. Levent had reached the landing and a bright red door when it opened before he knocked. A man, dressed in what passed for fashion these days, almost barked.

"I pay you people to stay away."

So the bartender had warned the second floor that a cop was on the way. Levent did not mind if it gave her the chance to contemplate the sins that everyone, especially a whore, had in abundance.

"I'm not here to shake you down unless you keep on with that tone. I'm Inspector Levent of Homicide, and I'll speak to Pepper Parmak unless she's changed her name with her occupation."

The man looked at Levent as if measuring him for a fight. "I guess you can have your way if you're polite."

"Always."

He stepped back when Levent entered the room, which was circular at the front and so dimly lit for the rest that he did not know what shape it was. The woman came out of the darkness in a shape that could not be missed. Pepper's dress was long, gossamer, and strung with bright beads, following the line of her body as if molesting it. That seemed proper. The things that made her a woman were what made so few women her competitors.

"An inspector," she said. "I've never had the pleasure."

"It should be that," said Levent.

She shook hands like a man and smiled like a businesswoman. Cold, yes. Pepper was all about sales. A closer.

"What can I help you with? I hope it's nothing concerning the club."

"Not exactly," he said. "I'm investigating the murder of Ayla Acheson. Perhaps you heard about it."

"I knew I'd seen you before," she said. "On television, but somehow you look different. Yes, it's the nose."

Levent did not know what to make of the critique. He should have had a new suit and a makeup man when he moved before the cameras. But nothing could be done about the nose that was small.

"Your name came up in connection with a man I have some interest in," he said. "A former client."

She didn't like that, though Levent had used the most deli-
cate word. "I've known many men through business," she said.
"Most of them are gentlemen."

"I'm thinking more along the lines of a continuing relationship," said Levent. "A partnership. The man's name is Ahmet
Gunduz."

She looked at Levent as if trying to gauge how much he knew.
Deciding she could not know, she turned to the man in the pale
lime sweater and spoke like the boss for the first time.

"Leave us, Ismet."

He did it reluctantly, staring at Levent as if he would prolong
his aura as a bodyguard. Pepper waited until the door closed
behind him before moving to a couch that gave a total view onto
her nighttime fief.

"Policemen know how to make themselves unwanted," she
said. "Let's get this over with."

Levent sat on the chair that faced her, taking his time as if he
expected refreshments. When it was clear hospitality would not
be offered, he spoke.

"You've done well for yourself," he said. "It must have taken
serious money to make this place what it is."

She sprawled back on the couch, opening her arms wide on
the back and displaying the full curve of her body. "That's because you don't know how much I owe in loans to the banks,
Inspector."

"I could find out," he said. "But that would mean more time
away from both our businesses. It isn't necessary to intrude on
yours more than you'd like. Ahmet Gunduz is the subject."

"What do want to know?" she asked. "What he always says—
without exception—when a woman sucks his cock?"

"Does that happen a lot?"

"When he puts his money down," she said. "It's my opinion
it would happen to every man who could afford it."

"I defer to your expertise," said Levent. "I might be surprised
if you told me it was something he couldn't get at home."

"What he gets at home is the money to have his wants supplied in other places," she said. "The money's hers, you know, and she guards it like the Agas used to guard the Sultans. Ahmet has a Mercedes and a Porsche, but if he wants to put gasoline in them, he has to ask nicely."

Very deliberately, Levent looked around her penthouse and the activity that had grown on the feral grounds of the discothèque below. "Then how do we account for all this?"

"I don't have to."

"Yes, you do. If I don't have your cooperation, I'll find fifty violations of the health laws and close this place tonight."

She considered her ground as she looked over it again, blinking as the lights from the dance floor cruised the room in steady rhythmic flashes. "What I have to do, Inspector, is find a way to explain that causes me the least grief. I don't think you know what you're dealing with here. I'm a brick in the wall. It shouldn't surprise you to know you are, too. Take out one of those bricks, and the whole building falls around our ears."

"That's why you must be honest," said Levent. "Nothing you say will go beyond this room."

"So it will be a *secret*," she said sarcastically. "In *Istanbul.* There hasn't been a single one kept in this city for the last two thousand years. Julius Caesar was gay, you know, and he came out of the closet here."

"I'm more interested in knowing what's in the closet," said Levent. "If Ahmet Gunduz buys gasoline with his wife's credit card, how did he find the money to open this place for you?"

"It isn't all his," she said. "I'm not like most women in the business. I know how to put part of every transaction aside."

But she had admitted enough to cause the first brick to wobble. "I believe you, Pepper. Up to a point."

"He has friends," she said in a slightly different tone. "Men with good business sense. Some of them are bankers."

"Not good enough," said Levent. "This place is expensive to furnish and takes even more to run. Bankers don't go all the way into a high-risk business for a friend. Where did *Ahmet* find the money?"

"It's a truly remarkable story," she said, floating her voice into a dimension that was less present and hard. "I really wouldn't have believed it of him. You have to understand the man has no business sense—and little of any kind. Give him five hundred dollars, and he'll find his way to the first store that sells solid gold lighters for his cigarettes. His Cartiers. Never was a fouler cigarette ever made, but there's the name on the packet, you see. It's the same name that appears on his new lighter, so now you have a complete set. It's very basic behavior, and it doesn't lend itself to making anything but an impression on fools like him."

"You're sure that's what he is?"

"Totally," she said with no room for doubt. "When I first met Ahmet, I thought, yes, this could be the one who opens the door to the future. Play him well and you might have the money for your apartment. A new apartment. He would have done it, too, if he had anything of his own. And after the second date, too. But I soon found out who rules that roost. Ahmet didn't even have money to pay for a hotel room unless the same night manager was on duty. They were friends from their college days in Germany when they ran their sports cars in rallies. This manager gives him a discount by the hour—and sometimes by the minute if I'm any judge. He allows Ahmet to run up the bills—but only to a point. Then a little piece of paper with the exact total finds its way to Ahmet's wife. You might think that's a problem, but it isn't. For a couple of hours or minutes, she gets the chance to tell him exactly what she thinks of him and his sorry cock. In the end, she pays. She always does. Where else can she find a husband who would put up with the foul things she does?"

"I take it you know all about those things, too?"

"He gossips like a woman," she said with her hand on her breast, as if touching a wound. "He's a typical Turk of the upper class. Every time she fucks some truck driver, Ahmet knows about it soon enough. She doesn't bother to hide it either. If you want to know all the details, you should talk to her chauffeur. That's real pornography he's looking at in his rear-view mirror. I have to say I'm an amateur compared to the mighty Tara Gunduz."

Levent thought she was claiming territory for her new status as the owner of a fashionable business. But it was not professional jealousy that brought out the tirade. Bringing out more should be profitable.

"Have you ever heard the name of Tara Gunduz mentioned in connection with Ayla Acheson?"

"I don't know if they were lovers," she said. "But, of course, Ahmet accused her of going to bed with women, too."

"They were friends, I've heard."

"From what I know, that's true," she said. "But *he* was the greater friend in that way."

"Ahmet and Ayla? A couple?"

"They were lovers, he told me." Pepper shrugged as if she did not know how the movement traveled through her body—glittering and complete. "I don't know if the connection was serious. It sounded like talk. Men's talk. Ahmet, for all his hotel bills, does not know much about pleasing women. He's passive in bed, paying for someone else to work him up, and of course there's that sorry cock. His wife is right about that, and a few other things, too."

"So you doubt the connection with Miss Acheson."

"Not really," she said. "Only that she was his love."

Levent did want to hamper the flow by doubting Pepper's judgment. He was sure it was correct in every way concerning the flesh. And what else was there for men who could afford to shop?

"Go on, Pepper. I'm interested."

"They were in business together," she said. "I don't know how it came about, but I know she was responsible for getting him out from under his wife's hand."

"He said so?"

"Indirectly," she said. "That made me suspect there was more to it. When I asked him the first time about becoming a partner in this business, he said he'd have to dip into the money market to find the funds. He implied that he'd have to talk to her."

Ahmet Gunduz had been confirmed at the meeting in the Marmara Hotel. He was there with Delir Rasfar, who had been to the money market in the bazaar with the victim. That could not be a coincidence.

"When did Ahmet come into his own?" asked Levent. "I mean, to the extent he agreed to finance this place?"

"I asked him for the money about six months ago," she said. "I can't recall when I knew his finances had changed. Several months before that. He was waving money around—cash. I'd never seen him do that before."

"Could it have been as much as a year ago?"

"That's possible," she said. "We didn't have a set date every week or even every month. There were periods when Ahmet found other women. Sometimes even women he talked into bed. He could do that, because he's more a talker than anything else. But usually it would just be in and out. Most of the women who fell madly in love with him were paid to do it."

Allow a couple of months for the effects of the meeting to sift through Gunduz's accounts. Another month for whirlwind spending at every luxury shop in the city. What was left seemed good for timing.

"Is Ahmet still solvent?"

"As much as he can be with his habits," she said. "Whatever he's wandered into, it's profitable. And easy to manage. I guarantee you he's not capable of making money any other way."

"Does he have an office?"

"He does now," she said. "It's in Harbiye near one of the airlines. I don't remember which, but you can be sure it saves him from going too often to the hotels. That seems backward for logic, but he can afford to pay for the room these days." She hiked her thumb into the past. "I talked to one of my friends from those days—about two weeks ago—and she told me Ahmet took her to the penthouse of the Marmara the last time she was called to worship. And he paid her better than she deserved."

"How much?"

"Two hundred euro."

"I'm impressed," said Levent. "It sounds as if Acheson provided the means to drop a great deal of cash into his hands."

"Without another explanation, I agree."

Levent could not think of one yet, and was not sure he had to. "But I'm puzzled about the services such an inept man could provide to a busy woman."

"Connections." Pepper smiled as if she envied that much about Gunduz. "That's the one thing Ahmet has. The people he knows are the richest and most important in this city. Even the politicians know him because of his wife and her family. He could call on any of them at any time, though not to borrow money."

"He doesn't seem to need that now."

"No," she said. "Not today. But tomorrow is a different story. Give him time, and he'll piss it all away."

"It's a good thing you negotiated your loan before that happens."

"Isn't it?"

CHAPTER 14

Home and Heritage

As he glided upward on the elevator, Levent wondered what Erol had found in his follow-up at the Marmara. Nothing much, or he would have called. And not much should be required. Levent was confident he would find out why that meeting had been held in the Small Conference Room, and he was certain it would fit with AylaTur and its ascent to grace.

Many things seemed to revolve around her reversal of fortune. Samuel Wilding could clear up much about it if he chose, but nothing said he would and most things said he would not. That left Emre Oz to report and the Family Gunduz to explore. It seemed a sacrilege to call them a family, but it would be unwise to call them less. No one drew up in battle formation like the rich.

"I'm glad you realize what you're dealing with," said his wife as she placed the white beans on the table. "Your Chief doesn't have a chance with those people. You—don't even think it."

"Actually, I'm thinking the husband may be easy."

"You won't be able to pressure him into talking," she said. "If you threaten to tell his wife about his love affairs, he'll laugh and tell you she knows. She pays for all of them, it's said."

"She did at one time," said Levent. "I'm not sure he needs her help these days. Ahmet Gunduz has become an economic power in his own right."

"You heard that, too?"

"From a good source. A prostitute who knows him well."

Emine drew a coy and very deceptive look into her eyes that began but did not end with her eyebrows. Dangerous. Dangerous for Levent.

"You questioned her?"

"I thought it might be too much for Erol. He's excitable when it comes to attractive women."

"But not you."

"Only the one closest to me," said Levent, thinking he had done that well. "What is it you heard from your source?"

"They say Ahmet Gunduz has to be in trouble. A man with a head like his doesn't go into the business of putting up two of the largest buildings in Istanbul. He's already renting space to some important corporations. The people behind him are using his name and reputation."

"Reputation?"

"His wife's name and reputation."

"Who are the people behind the project?"

"The development company is called Skyline, but no one knows who they are," she said. "That's unusual even for Mafia. All these *maganda* like to brag about how important they are, especially if a project is as big as their ego. But if they're a party to this one, their mouths are sealed."

"Have you heard anything about Moldavians in the mix?"

"Cousin Sema says it's probably Russian Mafia. Is that close enough?"

"I'd like to know what part of the ground Sema has her ear to," said Levent. "She's so ignorant she probably doesn't even know some Moldavians speak a Turkish dialect."

"It's called Gaguaz. And yes, she knows. Sema sees Moldavians in every bad thing. You know, she actually hired a Moldavian *au pair* to keep her house and watch the children before you brought in those two murder cases."

Levent was glad to hear his work had some effect, even if it made its mark on a woman as consistently malevolent as Cousin Sema. There were others out there, and surely they were better off.

"How does Ayla Acheson fit in?"

"She tells me Ahmet Gunduz and Ayla Acheson were partners of a sort," said Emine. "It's even rumored they were lovers. That should be something to pursue if you feel you have to. His wife's jealousy might come into play if the woman was as impressive as herself."

"Is Tara Gunduz really so impressive?"

"It's said her family had a surname before surnames were used. That's how old they are. And how important."

Under the Ottoman Empire, no one had a surname, a condition that changed with the Republic. But a lie of that sort was something only a great family could put about. Levent knew they owned textile factories and villages in the south where the cotton was grown. And, of course, a bank to handle their transactions, and chains of stores to sell the products, and all the steps between.

"I suppose they have good foreign connections."

"Of course," said Emine, who was definitely talking down. "They have factories in Europe now. About ten years ago, they expanded into electronics when everyone in this country thought the computer was a fad. Before that they gave us washing machines that laundered everything but our money."

"I'm afraid they have those, too, now."

She looked closely at Levent, her blue eyes turning the colder, paler shade he had learned to heed. "Is there something you're not telling me?"

"A lot," he said. "But nothing very relevant."

"All right," said his wife. "Keep it to yourself. You're probably not interested in what Acheson said to her psychiatrist. This just happens to be the same psychiatrist that Guldem Sefer uses."

"This psychiatrist talks about his patients?"

"*Her* patients," said Emine. "And yes, dear, this is Turkey."

"I absolutely am interested."

She sat down at the table for the first time since he entered the dining room, and as if she were sitting on nails. She folded her hands and spoke in a hush, although no one else was in the house.

"Guldem Sefer, who has this directly from the source, says there was a good reason Ayla Acheson was so interested in rape victims and domestic violence. She had been raped herself."

Although Levent did not know if that was possible in this case, he would never speak to the subject. "When did it happen?"

"When she was younger," said Emine. "It took place in her own house, and it was her stepfather who did it."

"My God," he said. "She didn't stay on in that house, did she?"

"Not for long," said Emine. "She was in her teens at the time. She left and went to live with her uncle."

"Samuel Wilding?"

"I think that's the name," said Emine. "Yes, I recall now. He looked after her from that point, or at least until she was sent off to school. In England, before she came to Turkey."

So that was how she had gotten here, running from her home to her heritage. She was looking for something, a better place perhaps. Levent felt suddenly saddened by the mean death she had found.

That was bad for a homicide detective.

What was it like for the uncle?

CHAPTER 15

The Purse

Levent sat in a hard plastic chair beside Meryem's desk, feeling he should have slept better. The Chief's answer to profiling was a woman of forty years with a degree in criminology at an American university, and the most remarkably sloppy appearance Levent had ever seen in a college graduate. She did not seem to have washed her face this morning. She certainly had not combed her hair. And her voice, yes, that was the problem. It was somnambulant. Happily, she seemed to have arrived at a place where she could stop.

"You're telling me he's a sick man," said Levent. "But is he a psychopath in your opinion?"

"I'm not much on definitions," said Meryem, pushing her hair from her eyes as if that would help the perspective. "Psychopath. Sociopath. This man's obviously been traumatized. He made reference to his terrible past twice during your chat."

"I'll feel sorry for him after I get him in jail," said Levent. "Not until then."

"You shouldn't," she said. "The violence of the crime tells us he has nothing like a conscience, at least not when he's involved in his work. He's proud of what he's done. Nor would any sane man advertise himself to the police. It's true that a normal person might find himself under a compulsion to confess, but the thrust of this conversation is different. He even went so far as to give you a clue."

"Yes, I noticed. The sky."

"Have you looked there?"

"I looked last night and saw nothing but stars," said Levent. "To this point, I've come across a building rental company called Skyline, and the logo of the victim's tour company—three cranes in flight. If I find anything else, I won't turn my eyes above my head."

"I'd keep looking if I were you," she said with something keen in her voice for the first time. "He didn't make the suggestion idly. He meant you to have something to go on. He doesn't think you're smart enough to find it, however."

"It's good that he's overconfident. It's the most encouraging thing I've heard. He could make a mistake."

"I'm sure he's made several already, and I'm sure you'll find them," she said with great condescension. "You say he didn't bother to disable the alarm in the house. He went straight up and confronted her."

"Confronted is one word," said Levent. "But all that proves is he's a better killer than a burglar. A careful man would have found a way to bypass the system rather than beating the clock."

"I'm sure you're right, but you might have been more careful with him." Her deep brown eyes were critical of Levent's performance. "You should have encouraged him to keep talking, even when you felt he was being difficult. I have the feeling you would have uncovered a deep hatred of women in this man."

"Why do you think that?"

"He wants you to investigate the *victim's* life," said Meryem. "As if she was at fault for her murder. He's hoping you'll find something to justify what he's done. To prove him righteous."

"He wants us to think he's done a good deed."

"Something like that," she said. "This man wants to personalize the killing. That includes his demand that you give him your name."

"You don't think he'll send mysterious letters to me?"

"He said he wouldn't." Meryem scratched the side of her head through her hair. The sound was audible. "These people often can be trusted to tell the truth as they see it. It's a warped version of the truth, however."

"I wish I'd been able to keep him going," said Levent. "If I hadn't been typing in a foreign language, it would have been easier."

"He seems fluent in English," she said. "That should help narrow your search. Have you checked the foreign missions in

Istanbul? And foreign companies with offices here? I realize there're quite a few these days."

"Just what I need," said Levent. "A killer who isn't Turkish. The Chief would be pleased."

"I don't think this man is a native Turkish speaker," she said. "The fact that he chose the handle Karanlik proves nothing. That's dictionary work, not fluency."

"But it speaks to a degree of preparation," said Levent. "He made up the handle before he decided to act."

"He must have lived in an English-speaking country for more than a few months. His knowledge of the language is colloquial."

"Do you think it's American English that he used? Or the British kind?"

"I couldn't tell," she said. "I'd guess British."

"We have some indication of a Dutch connection," said Levent. "They all speak English nowadays. Usually, British English."

"Everything here indicates this man is above normal intelligence," said Meryem, slapping the paper in her hand. "I don't envy you, Inspector. If he's as smart as he seems to be, he was on the first plane out of the country."

"Unless he's a true psychopath with more work to do."

"Yes," she said. "There's that."

* * *

"So she straightened everything out for us."

"In a roundabout way," said Levent. "She pointed out that the killer wants us to examine the victim's life. That means she deserved what she got for the way she lived. And he knew the way she lived."

"He could have talked to neighbors and found that out," said Akbay with his feet up on the desk again. "We did."

"He didn't talk to them, though," said Levent. "Everything this man does or says is an excuse to justify his blood lust. And his hatred of women. You and Meryem agree there."

"That's a terrible thing to say, boss. Leave me out of her fantasies."

Levent was glad to get back to potential facts. "What did you have from Interpol on Diler Rasfar?"

"Nothing on the name," he said. "The description might bring something if they look hard enough. I'm trying to remember the last time we got anything useful from Interpol." Akbay shrugged and reached for a slim package on the desk. "This came while you were solving the case with Meryem. By courier."

Levent took the package from Akbay. No return address. He opened it and saw a computer-generated list of dates and flight schedules. Excellent. Emre Oz had followed through on Levent's request like a good man about graft.

The list covered ten dates that did not fall within specific intervals. The nearest came two months apart and the most distant almost seven. No pattern.

The incoming flights were the usual commercial carriers. The origination points did not conform to a pattern either, though they clustered around the states that bordered the Black Sea. Kiev in the Ukraine appeared three times, Tiblisi in Georgia three times, and Baku in Azerbaijan twice. There was also Amman, Jordan, and Baghdad, Iraq, one flight each. So it was a selection of the states nearest to Turkey with an emphasis on the northern.

Levent was happy the schedules aligned with what he had learned from the maid and the victim's partner, Duran. Acheson's visitors seemed to have carried contraband from Russian states and Arab neighbors. Levent was a bit surprised to see a flight coming from Iraq. The Americans went in and out of that country from their air base in Adana in southern Turkey, but this traffic was civilian. Of course, any number of Turkish firms did business in Iraq when the Americans let them share the danger. And the profit, such as it was.

Levent was looking for something to account for the large sums of money that could be generated from these origination points. He saw some possibilities. The Azerbaijanis and Iraqis had oil wealth. The Ukrainians and Georgians dealt in the arms trade in large quantities. Beyond that—

Levent was still trying to find links in the list when the desk phone rang. Akbay answered it with a grunt, speaking in mono-syllables before he sat suddenly upright in the chair. As suddenly, he got to his feet.

"Stay right there and don't move," he said. "Keep your eyes on the car. We're on the way."

Slamming down the phone, Akbay said, "They spotted a blue Volvo parked on the street at Kabatash. This one, they think, is different from the rest."

Levent followed his detective out the door. In one coat pocket, he put the pages from Oz, and in the other, the printout of the license plates and registrations Akbay had left behind on the desk. They moved downstairs and across the parking lot quickly, with Akbay getting behind the wheel of his battered BMW. That always made Levent nervous.

Erol was a lunatic driver with a certified excuse that made his madness legal. He wheeled the BMW furiously through tight traffic until they came onto the seaside road, where they moved freely until traffic again thickened and came to a halt. Akbay went to the siren at that point.

Levent could not watch as cars—all but the taxis—scurried out of the way. Akbay bulled through one intersection after the next, screaming incoherently over the siren, as if it mattered. Finally, he lost patience and drove up the median on the new railway tracks. No trains in sight for the moment. God would protect them because they were cops.

As a distraction, Levent retrieved the print out of the plates and registrations he had taken from the office. It was a good thing the department had bought a new printer to replace the ghost scrawl they had tried to read for so many years.

But nothing struck him until he came to a name midway in the list. Asiye Kaya. Yesterday, when they spoke to Atilla, he said his partner in the February orgy had been a tour guide called

Mehmet Kaya. That was a match—perhaps a wife—though the surname was common.

Levent settled for coincidence. Akbay was just leaving the part of the road where the construction ended. As he cleared the BMW from the mess, he shut down the siren to come into Kabatash quietly.

The seafront here was always crowded because of the ferry across the Bosporus. A long block of apartment buildings stood tall on an abutment on the inland side of the road, allowing a view for some of the residents. As Akbay turned onto the road in front, Levent saw the police car parked at the middle of the block. Two uniforms with no plain clothes in sight.

Akbay pulled up a hundred meters short of the car. If the killer had driven that Volvo, and he was anywhere in the area, he had plenty of time to clear away. One of the patrolmen, a man named Turcan that Levent knew, came up to their car as if he had done something right.

"There's no one around who recognizes the vehicle," he said through the window. "We talked to some of the kapijis along the street. They say they don't know the car and never saw it before."

"Good work," said Levent. "Now get your squad car out of sight."

"Yes, sir."

"And don't run."

"No, sir."

If the kapijis in the area did not know the car, that meant something. They superintended the buildings and knew all the tenants and vehicles. Sometimes they made extra money washing the tenants' cars, which made for powerful memories.

"This could be a young man staying overnight with his girl," said Akbay. "We're seeing a lot of it on this case."

"I don't think so," said Levent. "And he'd have to be a new boyfriend to escape notice on the street."

Akbay had no trouble accepting coincidence, the detective's best friend, as fact. "I'll go to the store at the end of the street and ask if they know how long the car's been parked here."

"I'm going to cruise by the Volvo," said Levent. "Keep an eye on the street in the meantime."

Akbay headed off as Levent moved without hurrying toward the old blue car parked between a Mercedes and a Renault. Nothing was exactly new in the neighborhood, but it was a stable one with a few businesses on the lower floors of the buildings. The ferry pumped traffic into the area, but not many people moved on foot at this height up the hill and at this distance from the Bosporus. And the ones who did would almost all be local.

Levent thought as he walked at a normal pace that the killer might be up there at any window, watching. It was good he had given that bastard his name the night before last. Levent wished he had upgraded his cep and paid a few more liras for a camera. He could have sent his photograph winging over ICQ.

This is what I look like, you piece of shit. If you pass me in the street, I'll know you know me. I'll see it in your eyes, and that will be the end of the interactive game you made for yourself.

Levent passed no one in the street. He came within ten paces of the Volvo before he read the dirty license plate. Istanbul, then 543. The rest?

Pulling the printout from his pocket, Levent looked over the list he had folded into the palm of his hand. The rest of the numbers were correct. The car was registered to Asiye Kaya, who lived in Jerrahpasha—a long way from Kabatash. Levent knew the district. That's where the morgue was.

He kept walking, slowing as he approached the front of the Volvo. He saw nothing remarkable about it except a dent and scratch on the driver's side fender. Nothing on top the dashboard. Nothing on the front seat and certainly no keys in the ignition. Nothing on the back seat.

Levent had walked twenty paces past the car when Akbay came out of the shop at the corner, moving faster than he had left. He began to speak when he was still several meters off.

"We've got nothing unless he camped for the week," he said. "The car was here all day yesterday. No one knows exactly when it came, but they think it was probably dropped the night before."

That was when Levent had been talking to the Chief, receiving instructions on his assignment. The decision about what to do next had ramifications. If Levent called for more uniforms to canvass these apartments and patrol the streets, anyone watching the car would see the activity. If he was the killer, he would run.

"Make the call," he said. "Get as many men as you can here. We may not find him, but someone could have seen something."

"They're apt to tell us he took the first ferry to the Other Side," said Akbay. "It shouldn't be a coincidence he parked here."

Or he could want the police to think he had. Ataturk, the main airport, was on this side of the Bosporus. There was a newer one on the Other Side, but not many flights went out from it.

"Do you have the jiggler in the car?"

"In the trunk."

Levent passed leisurely back up the street, trying to time his break-in with the arrival of police units on the street. As he moved, he checked the address for Asiye Kaya while he dialed the number for AylaTur on his cep.

"Let me speak to Atilla."

It was more than a few seconds before the young man's voice came to his ear. Levent wondered if he had that weird contraption strapped to his head. The one that made him invisible.

"Yes."

"Inspector Levent here. I'd like to know the whereabouts of your friend Mehmet Kaya."

"He should be in the air and on the way home now, Inspector. I talked to him at the hotel just before he left for the airport in Adana. The plane will be landing soon at Ataturk."

"Are you sure he was in Adana when you spoke to him?"

"Absolutely," he said. "I talked to the bus driver at the same time. They were getting the tour on board the bus."

"How long was Kaya in the East?"

"The last five days," said Atilla. "He couldn't have anything to do with Miss Acheson's murder."

It seemed unlikely. Levent was sure Kaya would have a busload of witnesses to swear to the same thing. Of course, Atilla would tell him to get his witnesses in order. Nothing was at Kabatash except the blue Volvo.

"Where does Kaya live?"

"In Jerrahpasha, sir. The Konya Building."

"Is his wife named Asiye Kaya?"

"That's his mother, sir. She's at the house all the time from all I know. An invalid for the past three years."

Worse and worse. While the son squired a group of tourists eight hundred kilometers from the city, the mother lay bedridden in her apartment. If someone had known the circumstances and the schedules, it would have been easy to take the car. Borrowing or stealing, it came to the same.

"Does Kaya drive a blue Volvo?"

"When he drives, yes," said Atilla. "He sometimes takes the train to work, but not often, because the line doesn't run close to his house. And he'd rather not ride that coffin on rails."

"Thank you, Atilla. Be sure and tell Kaya I still want to talk to him when he gets in."

"I already told him that, sir."

This was a friend who shared everything. Levent tried to remember which end Atilla had occupied in the photographs of the orgy, but somehow the image eluded him. Was that the function of a merciful God?

Levent had reached the BMW. He went into the front seat to pop the trunk and walked to the back to find the policeman's next best friend. It was an amazing tool with ten try-out keys that opened almost any car made in the past ten years. There was even a gas cap pick that made credit cards obsolete.

He had taken a dozen steps back up the street toward the Volvo when the first police units began to arrive, running as silently as Turks and their transportation ever did. Bodies, and plenty of them. That was what the force had. Brains? Not for the record. Even using the concept was an exaggeration. Homicide was the single exception, and even there the crop was all-too-thin.

Luckily—and luck had no part in it—Akbay was the exception. He came up in the street when Levent was nearly to the Volvo.

"Where do you want them?"

"Put two men in the street that goes up the hill," said Levent. "Two more posted on each end here. The rest canvass door-to-door. I don't think we have to worry about our man. He's long gone if he has any sense. But get the uniforms to question all the occupants, and the businesses, too. Concentrate on the front apartments that have a clear view of the street. Some of them can't see much beyond the trees, but try them all. Have them break in the damned door if they think anything's wrong. Tell them exactly what to do, Erol. *Exactly*."

"I'll do that exactly," he said. "But there might be hell to pay with their idea of something wrong."

"That's why you'll be their first call."

As Akbay left to brief the patrolmen, Levent took his time with the Volvo. He started with the first key, and by the fifth the door snapped open. The spring-tempered key did not even need a tension tool.

He examined the glove compartment, but found nothing. Insurance papers and registration for Asiye Kaya, a small flashlight, some tissues. Under the passenger's seat were two small coins and a piece of half-eaten candy. In the back seat, he saw nothing but cigarette butts overflowing the ashtray.

Levent did not disturb anything, though he wore surgical gloves. He would have forensics put their minds to this car, and he hoped it would do some good. Going back into the front seat again, he pushed the button to open the trunk.

He did not expect to find anything there. If the killer had left the car in this spot, he was too clever to leave his trash behind. Only when the trunk swung open did Levent realize he was wrong. Lying atop the worn plastic mat, like a jester at a funeral, was a purse.

It was green leather, nearly the same shade as a twenty-lira bill. And yes, it had golden clasps.

CHAPTER 16

Nur

"He's playing with us," said Akbay, as he pushed the UP button on the three-passenger elevator. "There isn't one damned thing in that purse except a bloody tissue. He left it to tell us it was him—and us who are the fools. And he broke his word. He said he wouldn't be in touch again, and now he is in a truly shitty way. How can we trust a freak like that?"

"He's not perfect," said Levent. "Someone saw him."

"You're not going to like what saw him," said Akbay as the elevator stopped at the third floor. "One of these days I'm going to find a witness with full sight. This one's ninety-three, and she sits by the window every day because it's the only place she doesn't have to use her cane."

Akbay was nearly right, but the old woman named Nur answered the door without assistance, wielding the acrylic pistol-grip cane with an unsteady grace. She might have been in her mid-eighties, if calendars ran slowly. Her hair was ghostly white with pale pink highlights that meant she had not been to the coiffeur lately. When she asked if they would like coffee or tea, Levent demurred because he could not imagine the process or the results. She was insulted by their refusal, giving in finally with hoarse sounds of protest as she turned and circumnavigated back to her chair by the window.

"I'm sorry, but we can't stay long, Nur Hanim. This is a crucial phase of our investigation, and we're very glad you can help."

"I saw him," she said as she lowered herself into the chair, gripping the cane with whitening fingers. "From this seat. I always see the strangers. Last year we had a thief climb up the drainpipe and break into the Aydin's apartment through the window. Since then, I hardly take a break from the watch."

"We're certainly glad you didn't," said Levent. "Can you describe the man who left the blue car in the street?"

"I already described him," she said impatiently. "To those damned barbarians who were here before."

"I apologize for the behavior of the patrolmen, Nur Hanim. They're accustomed to dealing with the lowest elements in the city. Well-bred citizens confuse them."

"You're better," she said grudgingly. "You don't sound like you left your village yesterday."

"No, ma'am. I was brought up in the city. An *Istanbullu*. My family lived at Findikli not far from here."

"What's the name again?"

"Levent. My father was also Onur Levent."

"I missed that one," she said, munching her words. "If he looked like you, maybe I regret it."

"So you have an eye for antiques," said Akbay. "Then you should find it easy to tell us what you saw out this window."

"I was watching the ships, as I always do," she said, glancing after one fast ferry that left a white wake. "It was in the late afternoon when it's hardest to see, so I have to say I don't think I'd recognize his face if I saw it again. I saw the car first. He parked it as if he knew how to drive—in one pass. It was probably what claimed my attention. At least at first. Later, it was because he sat there for a while."

"In the car."

"For a couple of minutes," she said. "I don't know what he was doing. I couldn't see that."

Levent wondered how she could see clearly at her age until he noticed the binoculars on the window sill. They were more like opera glasses, but they gave a real boost in magnification. He decided to say nothing about them, since she had not. She probably watched her neighbors, too, like many people in the city. The really nosey ones had telescopes to watch the Asian Side as well.

"Was he carrying anything when he got out of the car?"

"A green bag," she said. "I thought it was a grocery bag at first, but it didn't hang like one."

"Do you think it could have been a purse?"

"Nothing would surprise me about men these days," she said. "I watch all the soap operas—the ones at night, too. Istanbul Masali, that's the best of the lot. But even on that program they act like fairies."

"You don't like Valley of the Wolves?" asked Akbay, beginning to get into the rhythm of her reminiscence, as if he sensed her mind was more subtle than any beat cop knew.

"I don't care for Mafia," she said. "Who the hell do they think they are—running the city like this?"

"Did he look like one?" asked Levent. "Mafia, that is."

"If you mean that he came from the Southeast by vegetable truck, no," she said with a smile. "When he made up his mind to get out the car, he did it in good order. He locked it and looked it over for a second. As if he was saying farewell. A thug wouldn't do that, I imagine."

"Did he have his back turned to you?" asked Levent.

"As he stood at the car," she said. "When he moved around to the back, he turned his profile my way. What I remember is that he had a short nose. It wasn't longer than his chin."

"His complexion?"

"Fair," she said. "Like an Istanbullu of the better sort."

"Or a foreigner?"

"Maybe," she said. "He had good shoulders. On the tall side, though not so much that it made him stand out. I measured his height by the roof of the car. He carried over it with more than a head to spare."

"Close to two meters then?"

"Yes," she said. "Not less in any case."

"The color of his hair?"

"Black," she said. "Or dark brown."

"Any distinguishing marks? Say, like a scar on his face?"

"I couldn't see well enough for that," she said. "Even with the glasses my eyes are not made so fine these days."

Akbay smiled. He had seen the opera glasses on the window sill, too. "What did he do after he the locked the car?"

"He went around to the trunk," she said. "He lifted it up and put something into it. It must have been the green bag, since he didn't have it when he closed the trunk. At least not that I could see."

"What happened next?"

"He left."

"Did you see where he went?"

"I have a problem there," she said. "I began to look at a tourist vessel that came by at the same time. It was a sailboat, three-masted, though they don't use the sails for anything but display. I'm trying to remember. It isn't easy at my age. Things come and go, and mostly they go."

"You wouldn't be able to recall if he went down to the ferry?" asked Akbay. "I mean, if he wandered that way."

Nur said nothing. Her eyes, which were still a keen brown, narrowed as she took them back to that late afternoon.

"Perhaps if you used the glasses you might remember," said Levent. "Did you use them while you watched the sailboat?"

Now that she had an excuse, Nur reached for the glasses, which had a short stem for her hand. They were mother-of-pearl and might have been bought long ago for the Opera House at Taksim Square. Or for football matches. She looked through the lens thoughtfully, swinging her gaze from the street to the Bosporus. And back again, as if she had located something.

"I would remember if he went down to the ferry," she said. "No, I watched that toy sailboat for a while, then looked again to the street." She pointed. "Yes, I saw him go that way."

"To the left."

She nodded slowly. "I said you were better than the others, and it seems I was right. It's the view through the glasses that improved my memory. I recall now he wore a jacket. A blue jacket, nearly the color of his car. To myself I thought he must be a hardy soul, for it was a chilly day."

"He went to the left," said Levent. "Then it wasn't likely he took the ferry. It's easier to go that way to the right. So either he went north, or he turned and entered the street up the hill."

"Or he passed into one of the buildings out of sight," said Akbay. "We still can't eliminate that possibility."

"I didn't see him go into a building," she said quickly. "No. I would remember. As I said, I watch for prowlers. I'm trying to recall the jacket—that would tell me if I saw it again when I looked back to the street."

Akbay moved his balance from leg to leg, as if the tension made him nervous. And the moment was tense for Homicide.

"I do," she said finally, as if finding the smallest button in her sewing basket. "I remember. He got in a taxi at the end of the street."

Akbay was not the only nervous detective in the room. Levent wondered if she had really seen a taxi, or if she imagined it to please them. In spite of her objections, this visit must be the highlight of her week. Her year?

"But he didn't go to the taxi stand at the ferry?"

"No. He found one at the end of the street."

"A yellow taxi?" asked Levent.

"Sure," she said. "It was yellow like all of them, but there might have been something odd about it."

"What?" asked Akbay.

"The color," she said. "My eyes have lost something on their way to heaven, but my color sense is as good as ever. The taxi wasn't the usual bright shade of yellow. It was pale yellow."

That was good. Thousands of taxis cruised the city, as many as fifty thousand, but ones that came in odd shades were far fewer. There were red taxis from Silivri and others that were nearly orange. Levent had seen pale yellow ones on the streets, though he had no idea where they originated. Akbay, by his look, did not know either—yet.

"Did the taxi have advertisements on the side or the back?" asked Akbay. "You know, for liquor or a television program or the like?"

"I don't think so," she said. "If it did, I don't remember."

"But are you sure of the color?"

Nur drew her glasses to her eye again, searching the street at the end, but finally she shook her head. "I could be wrong. I can't tell you if it was old or new. Pale yellow, that's all."

If she was right, that was a start at tracking their man—and they knew he was their man. It would be hard with a hundred different taxi companies and thousands of drivers, but if they had some luck—

If Akbay had some luck, that is. There were advantages to being an Inspector of Homicide.

CHAPTER 17

Kaya

They were leaving Nur's apartment, carrying all the information two detectives could bear, when Levent took a call from Atilla at AylaTur.

"Mehmet Kaya just arrived, Inspector."

"I don't imagine he drove."

"No, sir. He came by taxi from the airport. I told him to get here as soon as possible. Do you want to talk to him?"

"In the flesh," said Levent. "Tell him to stay where he is. If he moves, every cop in the city will be after him."

Atilla hesitated for his friend. "I don't think he'll go anywhere."

"You make sure of that."

Levent commandeered one of the blue-and-whites that were still in the street, telling the patrolman to make time. A man whose Volvo had been stolen was the man who could have lent it. And if Kaya had lent it? Then they knew the murderer.

That was Levent's last thought. He called ahead to the station in Sultanahmet and told them to get some men to AylaTur's office immediately. They were to take Kaya into custody and hold him.

With rush hour two hours off, Levent arrived in twenty minutes. The station at Sultanahmet was better than most, in case tourists found their way to it, but the holding cell where they had put Kaya was like any in the city. He stood in the cell like a horse that had never been to the barn, pacing the cramped area as Levent appeared in the corridor. He looked up at his visitor as if a man in a suit was the mark of civilization. When the jailor put up the lock, he stepped back against the wall.

Kaya was even more handsome than his friend Atilla, taller and leaner with a body that looked gymnasium-strong. His profile could have been chiseled from any workable stone—a dimpled chin and well-bridged nose with a forehead that seemed unaccountably intelligent. His hair rose from his milk-white skin like a black coxcomb—and thickly. If Levent recalled, it was that way over the parts of his body he displayed only to his lovers.

"Sit down. You make me nervous."

Kaya sat on the edge of the bunk warily. He was still dressed in safari clothes—corduroy pants, a cotton shirt, and a canvas vest with pockets everywhere. That was what tourists expected when they went to the badlands of the East. One wrong turn and they ended up in Iraq.

"I'm Inspector Levent, and you're the man whose car was used by the murderer of your employer. Tell me how that happened. Do it convincingly, and you might not spend the rest of life in places like this."

"My *car?*"

"Your mother's car," said Levent. "The Volvo with the dent in the front fender. I suppose you put it there on a drunken night."

Kaya did not seem confused. He seemed to expire. As if he had become used to this place, he sat back on the bunk and slumped hard against the wall.

"You can't think I had anything to do with this." He bumped his head against the wall again, deliberately this time. "A *murder*. I didn't even know about Miss Acheson until yesterday."

"You had something to do with the killing," said Levent. "I don't know the full story yet, but I will soon."

Kaya accepted the threat as he accepted his innocence—totally. "I can explain this. I left the car here when I went out to the East. My mother never uses it, and I park it behind the office while I'm gone. I've done that several times. They have two spots in back of the building, but they can fit three in a pinch. And they usually do. So I leave my key in case they have to move the car."

"Where do you leave the keys?"

"In the office."

"Exactly where?"

"In Miss Acheson's office," said Kaya. "There's a hook on the wall by the storage cabinet. I have to leave it, you know, with such a small parking lot."

"How many other people park in the back?"

"No one's allowed to except Miss Acheson and Mister Duran," he said. "It's a wonder they let me do it."

"Not a wonder," said Levent. "A reward for after hours' work."

He blushed to the roots of his hair and halfway down his neck. All his emotions seemed lodged in his blood. Levent almost believed what Kaya said, but it was better not to now.

'I shouldn't have had you taken to this cell," said Levent. "Your mother's home would have been much better. You could tell her all the things you do in your time away from her."

Levent took a step closer to Kaya. He removed the victim's cep from his pocket and snapped it on, thumbing slowly through the photographs. Kaya's eyes followed the slideshow as if he saw doom in those images. His eyes could not grow wider without permanent damage.

"I'm going to have these done up on paper and hung all over Jerrahpasha," said Levent, flashing the camera again. "They'll make you a hero to some. The others, well, you'll have to learn to live with their scorn."

"What do you want?" he asked, lowering his head. "Please."

Levent was always amazed by the way a son who lived at home with his mother regarded his embarrassment as a greater crime than murder. It had happened before, or Levent would not have believed it.

"I want you to tell me how your car came into the hands of a murderer," he said. "To whom did you give it?"

"I didn't give it to anyone," he said. "I never have and I never would."

"Then explain how it moved itself."

"I can't," he said, almost sobbing. "How can I know? But it wouldn't be impossible for someone to get the keys from the office."

"Could a stranger do it?"

"I don't think so," he said, shaking his head and maintaining the movement. "Clients don't usually enter the boss's office. And a man would have to pass by everyone to get there. Someone would notice."

"Then we should look for someone on the inside," said Levent. "A co-worker."

"Yes," he said slowly. "That should be correct."

"If you left the car, and it had to be moved while you were gone, who would be the one to do it?"

"Anyone," he said.

"Yes, but who would normally do it?"

"The job would fall to the least senior person," he said. "The newest."

"And that would be—"

"Atilla," he said.

* * *

It was three long blocks on foot from the station house to the offices of AylaTur, but the trip was as arduous as any Levent ever made. He did not call ahead to have the staff wait on his arrival. He took Kaya and three patrolmen to be sure the confrontation was complete and that no one absconded.

When they arrived at the office, all the staff waited at their desks, but not on their phones. Everyone was present but the least senior man, Atilla Kocaman. It seemed he had gone outside for a smoke after his friend, Mehmet Kaya, had been picked up by the police. He had not returned, but they were sure he would.

Levent blamed himself.

CHAPTER 18

The Graveyard Look

Atilla was not stupid. He would be found, though not in the usual places, like his girlfriend's apartment in Atakoy, which he had been careful to mention to Levent. He would avoid his immediate family, normal contacts through his job, or obvious locations where his co-workers could direct the police.

Levent spent some time with Mehmet Kaya, trying to find a pattern in what had happened. Most of what Levent discovered was a lack of planning and a talent for improvisation. The evening Atilla and Mehmet found themselves in the same bed was an example.

Atilla had been unemployed at the time, but working hard for his lack of bread. He hustled the streets, stationing himself around the square in front of the Blue Mosque, trying to hire his services as a guide and luring tourists to merchant shops in the area. As a guide, he was rejected more often than not, but the merchants kicked back a portion of the profit that he occasionally drove to their doors. That small share hardly paid his expenses in the end. There had to be a better way of making a living.

There was, by and bye. One of the numbers Atilla stored in his cep belonged to AylaTur. Occasionally, a random tourist could be persuaded to sample the nine-tenths of the country outside the city of Istanbul. When that happened, Atilla directed them to the offices just down the way. Would they perhaps like to see the wonderful fairy chimneys of Cappadocia? Or would the Kurdish lands to East appeal to a Euro tourist who kept a place in his heart for terrorists?

That happened often enough to bring Atilla to the attention of the powers that be. One day, after he had brought in a family of seven Italians who left St. Sofia in disgust at the bad lighting, Atilla was introduced to the woman who owned AylaTur. It was

Kaya who did the deed. He vouched for the young man who had nothing to his name but a stolen Icelandic sweater and his gall.

The last quality was nearly all that was needed in the business. Harassing strangers and their money was the chief requirement for salesmen to tourist venues. Atilla auditioned one day in the office, impressing everyone with his quick tongue and lack of scruples. If more had been required, there were his not quite wholesome good looks.

The particular winter day was so bitterly cold that Atilla would have had to steal a second sweater to survive on the streets if not for the intervention of Mister Duran. He called Ayla's attention to Atilla, and worried her into thinking twice about letting such a fine prospect go. Balls like that could only be found on the finest animals. Why waste such talent?

She was not one to do so without a reason. As the brains of the business, and its heart, Ayla followed hers without pause. When the chance meeting adjourned to the bar of a nearby historic hotel to discuss the future of tourism, Ayla, Atilla and Mehmet were joined by three of her friends. All these women were past the sensible age for marriage, but clearly none were above marrying again. Kaya knew they were spoken for by their husbands—if those men had been interested in speaking to their wives.

They did not often, it seemed. That became obvious early on. Kaya spent half the evening—for it was that by then—guessing which of the women was flirting, and which were more seriously inclined. In the end, he left the decision to the lottery of who turned in her wine or raki glasses last.

The clear winners were Ayla Acheson and her friend, Tara. The latter had an odd name, which she said arose on the night of her birth as her father watched an old movie about the American South. But much of Tara's conversation from the first turned upon the subject of circumcision. Why was such a great to-do made about a simple matter of hygiene? Why were such huge parties thrown to celebrate what was merely a loss of skin on the most sensitive part of a man's body? It was as if that solemn rite of passage was just a curiosity.

It became that when Tara followed Kaya to the men's room and asked if she might look at his manhood in a more private place. Curiosity? Yes, but that was not all. In her car, the largest model Jaguar, she caressed his cock until it was hard in her hand, whereupon she began to move her fingers faster and faster as she breathed hot in his ear. She brought her hand into a fist and him to consummation as Kaya lurched in the rich leather upholstery.

He was amazed that she had done it with such skill and pre-meditation, even to the fact that she kept a tissue at hand to rescue the come that had blown from the sanctified part of his body like a geyser.

What was a geyser? She explained that, too.

When Kaya returned to the table in the bar, he could see this would be the end of the evening, but not of the relationships formed. Miss Acheson told them she would host a party the following week for a group of guests, and the presence of both young men would be welcome. In fact, she said they must put in an appearance no matter what their prior engagements might be.

What engagements? For what parties? Kaya had a tour scheduled to Konya and the historical mosques at that place, but he could not refuse an invitation from his employer. Atilla, Ayla's man, did not lodge the weakest protest. Afterward, he wanted to know everything that had happened when Kaya left for the men's room, and exactly what he must do to cement the most promising lines of his future.

Atilla was far from bashful. He came from a family of five children in which he was the only son. His father worked as a guard in a plastics factory and his mother as a domestic servant. How she managed to raise a family of five was a question with a short answer. She delegated the job to her daughters. From an early age, Atilla had learned to please women. The details of his education were a family secret.

The two young men augmented their education through a course of home study on the Internet. The things that could be learned there, the downloads with wonderfully graphic pictures, elevated their pursuit to on-the-job training. Even the vocabulary was new and exciting.

They soon turned their learning to good account. The things they practiced were the same as men have dreamed of from the darkness of the caves onward, though every one of them seemed fantastically new. The party came and went. Other, more private auditions, were held, usually at Ayla's apartment in the city. Atilla's claim that his relationship with Ayla barely survived being hired was a grotesque but understandable lie. He came to her when called and performed to specifications. He also knew that he stood in a line.

It became clear in time that Atilla did not like the place he was assigned. He tried to advance his position by every means. His zeal included making up to Mister Duran, who was as gay as a summer in Bodrum. The fact that Ayla let her partner tease her lover was a confirmation of Atilla's place in her life and her firm. He was something to be played with when she liked.

Kaya knew of his friend's dismay because Atilla had come to him with his lament. He wanted Kaya to use his influence with Tara to reestablish Atilla's relationship with Ayla, but that could not be. Tara had let Kaya know after the third meeting that he could not continue as her steady lover. Her husband, she said, was insanely jealous, but his wrath would likely take the form of revenge against Kaya. And for that she could not be responsible.

Kaya did not believe a word of it, but he knew his options did not exist. A woman who flogged the highest government officials for backward behavior was not one to be contradicted. Besides, she said in parting, she was sure one of her friends would be interested in an attractive young man like him. And she said she would circulate his number.

Kaya waited bitterly for his phone to ring, thinking of all he had lost, especially the way she sucked him until he cried out and used her fingers to take him back from the edge, and then went to him with her mouth again until he came within or without her like a seismic event.

To take that away was like making a whole new world vanish, because that's what it was. Just when Kaya was certain the phone would never ring, Tara proved as good as her word. The friend she thoughtfully provided as her substitute was not as beautiful or accomplished in love, but every bit as eager. Indeed, they were still dating, as she called it.

Kaya told Atilla more than once he could do nothing to advance his friend's career or his love life. And he was glad he had refused. When he thought about it, Kaya suspected Atilla's purpose from the start was blackmail.

It had been Atilla's idea to photograph their group session. The women agreed and participated with an enthusiasm born of raki, but in the end Ayla kept a forceful hold on Kaya's cep, the one he had bought on the gray market. She replaced his property, of course. She replaced everything she wanted to control, including employees who presumed too much.

Restive at his demotion, Atilla grew resentful. A whore and a closet queer, he called the management. The only thing they did properly was seduce the staff. It was cheaper than paying them well.

Kaya was glad the last two weeks kept him out of the city on tours most of the time. He was afraid Atilla had decided to work his way to the top by way of the bottom, though he said nothing that indicated violence.

Kaya had not suspected him of being involved in Miss Acheson's death when he heard of the event while visiting a Syriac monastery on the last leg of his Eastern tour. The only thing Atilla said that stayed in his memory was the suggestion he made the day before yesterday. He told Kaya he might want to remain in the East to meet another tour that would be landing at Adana the next day. Good money, he said. Lady alumni from Bosporus University.

Since tour guides depended heavily on tips, Kaya was tempted. If his mother had not been in such poor condition, depending for her food and almost every need from the neighbors in the building, he would have done it. And he had to admit that rich women were on his mind.

Atilla may have tried to prolong Kaya's stay in the East, think-ing it best to delay the discovery of the missing Volvo. It was not the finest automobile in the city, but it was reliable and not bad for gas. Atilla had no car of his own, though with steady pay these days, he was looking. He could have had one already if he had been willing to drop down in class.

He was not. Atilla had had a taste of the good life. If only Ayla had furnished a replacement lover, as Tara had, his temper might have eased. But Ayla was too possessive. She kept a hook into Atilla that lasted long past its time. In between his trips from the city, Kaya learned that Ayla and Atilla were still inti-mate, at least for one night. The event took place about two weeks ago, just after she opened her country home.

Atilla had not said anything of the meeting except that it happened. If his attitude was a guide, nothing good came of it. Atilla said Ayla was just another bitch, but smarter than most. She would have her comeuppance one of these days.

A threat?

Kaya didn't see it that way. He thought it was the talk of a relationship gone sour. Or of dreams gone the same way. Atilla built his castles big, knowing that if he failed at AylaTur his next stop was a return to the life of the streets with a slightly better wardrobe and memories like bitter orange. He would do any-thing to avoid that. And it seemed, at last, that he had.

* * *

"So Atilla knew the layout of Acheson's country house."

"I'm sure he got a good look," said Kaya. "Good enough. He has a keen eye for detail. One of those who know the make and year of a car that moves past them at a hundred K. Spend enough time working on the streets in Sultanahmet and you can tell a man's life by his T-shirt. Or a woman by her shoes."

"He never spoke to you of another man or woman he had taken up with?" asked Levent as they sat in the office crowded with policemen taking statements, noise he had learned to shut out years ago. "Try to remember. Even if the words were casual or not meant to be heard."

"No one I can think of," said Kaya. "But I don't imagine he would tell me if he planned to kill someone."

"He has a partner." Levent did not want to give information to Kaya that could find its way to Atilla, but the description of the man who had left the Volvo did not seem to match. "It could be someone he met through work. Was he close to any others in the firm? Or outside it?"

"Atilla has some contacts who wouldn't blink at breaking the law," said Kaya. "All that time on the street—"

"Who comes to mind?"

Kaya cupped his hand before his mouth, as if that was how he thought. And yes, it was the most familiar pose of a tour guide, speaking into a microphone at the front of the bus as it soared through the countryside.

"Most of the merchants around here are rogues," he said without taking his hand from his mouth. "Atilla knew them all. But it takes something more to put an end to a life. At least that's what I think."

"The murder was slow and very brutal," said Levent. "It wasn't done in a minute. More like an hour. We're looking for someone who had the leisure to enjoy that kind of work."

"I don't know anyone who fits the description. If I met any through Atilla, I can't recall them." Kaya removed his hand from his mouth as if his train of thought had come to a moving halt. "But there was a man I saw when I was with Atilla in Sirkeci one day. I can't say what he was. He might be a plumber or a killer. All I know is that he bothered me."

"Mafia?"

"Something makes me doubt that, though he could have been. I don't know. It might have been just the look in his eye."

"That's a start," said Levent. "How did you meet him?"

"I didn't have time to get to know him," said Kaya. "I was with Atilla when he went out after work about two weeks ago. He wanted to buy a new cep to replace the one he lost at Ayla's apartment. She'd given him one that belonged to the firm, but he wanted his own. We went to Sirkeci, because Atilla had just met the owner of a cep shop when he arranged a tour for his wife. He was looking for a special price, of course. As we came into the street, I saw this man leaving the shop. I'm not sure if it was the same shop, but I think so."

"What did he look like?"

"Not a common sort," said Kaya. "Brown hair, brown eyes. A bit taller than normal—about two meters. He wasn't badly dressed and he wasn't badly favored. But that's not what I'm trying to say."

"What struck you about him?"

"It started with his name," said Kaya. "It was Can. I *thought* that was his name, and I *thought* he was Turkish. The way they exchanged greetings—the kisses and a handshake—made me think so. I can't be sure, because they met for just a moment, but it isn't my recollection that he spoke perfect Turkish. Later, when I remembered him—and I did remember—I thought he wasn't Turkish. I thought his name might be the same name, but in English."

"John."

"Yes."

The pronunciation of the names was identical. The Turkish c was the English j. In Turkish, the name meant life, and in English, God only knew. It was a fairly common name, however, and more common in English.

"So we have a man with a name that's different but the same in two languages. And you thought he could do serious harm."

"Yes," said Kaya. "I'm sorry I didn't ask Atilla who he was, but it was as if I wanted to forget him. I mean, he looked at me for just a second, but it was the longest second I ever passed with a man. He had that look—a graveyard look—if you know what I mean."

"Maybe I do."

CHAPTER 19

Husnu

Akbay called to say he had found the taxi company that painted their cars pale yellow. They operated out of Nishantashi not very far from where the man had been picked up, but of course roamed the city, going where their fares took them. The important thing was where the man had been dropped. And that would not be known until they found the right taxi driver. Akbay and the management were more than halfway through the list without a nod yet.

Levent left Kaya in police custody with instructions to treat him like a guest for the night. It did not seem as if Kaya was involved in the plot, but there was no trusting two marginal people like those. If nothing else, Kaya's sympathies might resurface and get the better of him.

With Kaya out of the way but available, Levent dropped down to Sirkeci. He wanted to see if the owner of the cep shop could supply more information about a man with graveyard eyes.

It was a short hop down the hill to Sirkeci, where people came from all over the city to bargain in the stores that lined the crowded streets and passages. Levent found the cep shop with ceilings three meters high and communications goods piled all the way on the vertical. The proprietor, Husnu Hilal, was a pioneer in Sirkeci, a small, shrunken, and totally bald man with glasses piled atop his head. He kept a long pole with a hook on the end when he went aloft for his stock. It looked so much like a weapon that Levent was glad when Hilal stacked it aside to address the question.

"Can," he said.

"Yes, John. He's about two meters tall with brown eyes and brown hair. His eyes are the things that people don't seem to forget."

"I'm having trouble with the description," he said, coming from behind the long counter where there was not a single open space. "I'd be better off if I wore my glasses, but they're bifocals, and I can't see my feet for walking when I have them on."

"My information says he might not be a Turk," said Levent. "He speaks the language less than well."

"That would be almost everyone these days," he said, looking off Levent's left shoulder. "I wonder what they teach in the schools."

"I think you know," said Levent with the impatience that a busy day brought. "I'm sure you can tell me something about John. If you get many tourists in this shop, it's because they're lost and looking for the train."

Hilal scratched his head—the most vigorous gesture he had shown. "Let's be honest and say I have a small problem with your people, Inspector. Last week one of your men came by and said I was selling stolen goods. Now, I never did that in my life, God knows."

"Write his name there." Levent pointed to the small pad on the countertop. "I'll have a word with him."

Hilal, who was accustomed to bargaining and winning, turned to the counter and the notepad and pen by the phone. Strangely, for a man who made his living in the wireless world, it was not a cep. He wrote the name, ripped off the sheet and handed it to Levent.

"Can," he said again. "I believe I know the man, though he never spoke his name. If that makes him a foreigner, so be it. He used the language well enough, but a bit slowly, as if he had something in his mouth and couldn't clear it away. I thought he had false teeth to tell the truth."

"Did he look like he did?"

"No," he said after a pause. "They were his, I'm pretty sure. Made ones would be more perfect. Not that his were terribly bad."

"How many times has he come to the shop?"

"Twice," he said. "Each time for a new phone."

"A better model?"

"He said he misplaced his." Hilal shrugged as if that was common. "It's practically the only thing he said."

"What plan does he subscribe to?"

"Avea," he said. "It's the best."

"He'd have to leave his name and address when he signed up for it."

"True," said Hilal. "If he did it here. But he didn't."

"He made arrangements elsewhere?"

"A lot of them do," he said. "Especially if they have a cep already. What can I say—they get used to what they have? Their bank or credit card gives them free phone points for the things they buy. They won't give up that extra three or four seconds they don't have to pay for. Even if they're paying for it right up the ass."

The stranger could have come to Sirkeci for price, but if he was who he seemed, he was probably being careful. Scattering his cep purchases was one way to make them hard to trace.

"Do you think this man lives around here?"

"I never saw him on the street except when he passed through," said Hilal. "And the first time he was in, he asked for change. He was probably going to take the train out toward the airport. Or the new line into the city center. He could go either way from here now."

So he did not take taxis every time. If he knew his way around the city well enough to use public transportation, he might know much more.

"Did he ask for anything but change before he left?"

"Not this time, but, yes, the other," said Hilal as if his thought was important. "That first time he came in he wanted to know if he could do something to make his phone operate in another country. You know, switch the chips. Make them compatible with another system."

"What did you tell him?"

"I said sure. It's just a matter of putting in a new SIM card. But he'd have to go to the country where he wanted to have it done. We don't sell phone plans from Argentina here."

"But it wasn't Argentina he wanted," said Levent. "Which country was it?"

"We were obviously talking about some place in Europe," he said slowly. "Not America and not Asia. I'd say it could have been England. I might be wrong, but it was some place over the water."

CHAPTER 20

Sibel

England. Possibly Holland. Their man was a traveler. He spoke Turkish reasonably well, which made him very uncommon if he was a foreigner. He had a knowledge of surgery, if Derya Silme was right. He had made the acquaintance of Atilla on the streets or otherwise. Was he a tourist who decided to stay on? A foreigner working for one of the multinationals? There were other possibilities, but all made a biography that was unusual.

John or Can would be easy to track in time, but every hour that passed allowed him to distance himself from the crime. Levent did not know why the man would stay when doing so placed him at increasing risk. If he was still in the country, there would be a strong reason.

Levent had already called Passport Control to alert them to any man who left the country matching that first name and description. He did not expect results, but if he got a call, it might be worth the trip to check it out. In the meantime, he checked with Forensics to see if they had anything on the car.

Although the Volvo had been wiped down thoroughly, they found some prints, and plenty of hair samples. They would be able to start eliminating suspects when they received the hair and fingerprint samples from AylaTur. Levent had remembered to send them over—Atilla's from the desk where he worked and Kaya's from his body. Where in traffic hell were they?

Tavshan had no answer. Nor did he supply much useful information on the results of the tests at Acheson's house. The tumblers of the lock on the front door were scarred by the kind of pick machine that was easy to come by. The bloody fingerprint found on the printer in the same room had brought no result except to confirm by the diameter that it had probably been left by a man—one with fairly large hands.

"Miami CSI would give you more noise," he said. "They probably could tell you he used surgical gloves that were made in mainland China. Not Taiwan, mind you."

"And that's all you have?"

"Not quite," he said. "I found a ghosted footprint in the room where she was cut up. I matched the pattern to one Converse shoe. Converse has a presence in any number of countries, including Turkey. If you really want to know, they're a fad among students and the rich. My cousin wore a pair to her wedding last month. White gown with black high-topped sneakers. Everyone thought it was insane except the people who thought it was cool."

"Cool?"

"There's no Turkish for that," he said. "In my opinion, there's no Turkish for this killer either. I'd start looking in Australia."

That was the problem, and Levent now had another. Rush hour had begun and would continue for the next three hours. He wanted to work around it, but had trouble mapping his next move. He had not heard from Samuel Wilding, and his calls to Tara Gunduz's house were not returned.

Levent wanted to call Wilding to remind him of his pledge, but decided against it. The man would come in his own time or not at all. Should he drive to the Gunduz house on the Bosporus and knock on the door? What was the chance a woman like her would be at home at any hour?

The only people who wanted to be in touch with Levent were peripheral figures. Sibel Burgaz was one who appeared on Emine's list of feminist contacts. When Levent had called her earlier, she said she would be in her office in Gumushsuyu until six, so he diverted the driver to the five-story building that stood across the street from the German Consulate.

Her office was in her home, which she shared with the cause. The two front rooms were filled with communications equipment, including two computers and a multi-function printer. A female assistant attended the links to the outside world and seemed busy. A feminist, perhaps, but stylish. Turkish.

Sibel Burgaz had been a beauty in her day, and the memories were still there for reference. Her eyes were remarkably bright, as outward-looking as they were inner-fed. Her long dark hair, daubed with red highlights, fell across her large and growing breasts like any wind-tossed thing. Her blouse billowed loosely and her trousers, too, making her presentation into a professional state-ment. She told Levent to sit on a bucket chair and got down to business without preliminaries.

"I told you before I have no idea who would want to kill Ayla," she said. "I've thought about it, but still come up with nothing. No one who knew her could possibly have done it."

"She was well liked, I've heard. Particularly in the women's movement."

"*Revered*," said Sibel, fingering the reading glasses that hung by a golden chain from her neck to rest on her breasts. "Every-one who knew her knew what she did for us. This place is an example. It was financed by Ayla. Still, I wouldn't know what to do tomorrow if she hadn't set up a trust to continue supporting the office. She understood that this was a struggle that would go on for a long time, and she provided for it, too."

Levent knew the money had gone somewhere, and this did not seem like the worst place. It was certainly one of the places. "Have you ever known her to go around covered?"

"*What?*"

"You know, headscarf, long coat, etcetera. I talked to a man who said he saw her like that one day."

Sibel reared hard in her seat. "Tell me this man's name, and I'll tell you why he lied. Ayla would never do anything like that. You're talking about sacrilege. One day when we were in her car, I saw her try to run down two women in the street simply because they were in *tessetur*. Ayla took her calling seriously. And it *was* a calling."

Levent could not reconcile Sibel's words with those of Acheson's partner. Duran said money had caused the sacrilege, but he had his own transgressions to hide. One way to remove suspicion from himself was to throw it on someone who could not protest. Duran was one man who bore a closer look.

"It does seem like going covered would be out of character for her."

"Like killing a baby," said Sibel, wringing a neck in her hands. "Beating back the barbarians from the gates was the most important thing in Ayla's life. Barbarians in high places were her special thing. This organization is dedicated to doing exactly that through the *law*."

"But I thought the women's organizations had gotten what they wanted in the last revision of parliament," said Levent. "At least I hear that from the home front. Many reforms were passed."

"Most of what we wanted," she said. "Not all. It's like carving laws on stone tablets. Those Neanderthals in Parliament still see honor killings in the same light as traffic violations rather than what they are—the slaughter of women. Virginity testing is another vestige of the past that means a lot to weak minds. And the treatment of rape and marital abuse victims by the police is a scandal that never ends."

"I couldn't agree more," said Levent.

She smiled as if she had found an ally among her enemies. "You do?"

"The laws are in place, but behavior has to change," said Levent. "Women must have the protection of the law. Otherwise, they might carry guns. Like Ayla Acheson."

Sibel nodded, drawing the stem of her glasses to her mouth. "Yes, she did buy a gun. I knew about that."

"But she didn't use it when she had the chance," said Levent. "It wasn't at her apartment or her house. No matter where I look, I can't find it."

"You won't," she said with authority. "She bought it two or three months ago, but decided to do without it. I was with her one night a couple of weeks ago when she threw it in the Marmara Sea. We were out on the water with one of her cousins, and Ayla had been drinking. A rash decision, it seems, but to tell the truth she was worried about your people."

"The police?"

"Ayla was at the demonstration in Kadikoy on Women's Day, but she wasn't beaten like a lot of people were. When the riot started, a policeman chased her down a side street with blood on his mind, but she changed his mind when she turned the pistol on him."

A dangerous thing to do. A cop with his blood up might not stop. And he might draw his weapon. "And that's why she threw the pistol away?"

"I told her it wasn't necessary," said Sibel. "It would take an ambitious cop to track her down from the Other Side. I haven't met one of those until today."

Levent accepted the compliment, if that's what it was. "But I'm puzzled about why she needed a weapon. She bought it some time ago. Most people don't think as far ahead as a demonstration that might get out of hand."

"A woman wouldn't have one unless she felt threatened," said Sibel. "Threatened in a personal way, that is. And Ayla did feel that she was."

Progress. A little more and Levent might have what he wanted. "By whom was she threatened?"

"I don't know," she said. "I got the impression it was someone from her past. She said when she spoke of it that there was nothing like thwarted love. Or perhaps she said perverted love. Whatever it was sounded unsavory."

"That's all she said to you?"

"It seemed like enough," said Sibel. "She was not one to be easily frightened, but those moments do arrive. Whatever you think, it's not easy being a woman alone here. That's one reason almost every woman marries, even to a man not of her choosing. Adjustments are made later by those who can manage."

Especially by the rich. The woman who was most on Levent's mind was one of the chief proponents of adjustment in marriage. A guru.

"Do you know Tara Gunduz?"

"Of course. If you'd come here at this time yesterday, you would have found her in the office."

"I've been trying to get in touch with her to talk about this case, but her phone doesn't respond."

"You should try her private number," said Sibel with a smile. "It's the one she doesn't share with her husband."

CHAPTER 21

Tara

As the driver jammed the car through traffic, Levent gave Tara Gunduz a chance to redeem herself. He was surprised when she answered her cep immediately, as if she wore it around her neck like the traders in the Bazaar.

"I wondered where the police were on this case," she said after Levent introduced himself. "I expected to hear from you before today."

Levent did not take her words seriously. He understood that criticism of city government was her means of entertainment. Nor did he say he would have contacted her earlier if he had the ammunition. When he asked where they could meet, she gave the address of an art gallery in Beyoglu. It was the opening night of the exhibition, and there would soon be a crowd, so he should hurry.

Luckily, the blue-and-white was not far from the turn up to the Old Town. Beyoglu sat on a hill across the Golden Horn from Sultanahmet, a sprawling knit of narrow streets and alleys with a wide promenade that ran most of its length. At one end stood Taksim Square, where Tara's husband kept his harem. The art gallery was more along the slope of the hill toward the tunnel.

If Levent had to worry about parking, the trip would have taken an hour; but he arrived at the top of the hill in five minutes, telling the driver to drop him on Istiklal, where only police cars and the antique trolley were allowed to pass.

Levent always thought of the Old Town as the heart of the city, the place where its citizens heard the beat best. Crowded, always crowded. The young men and their younger girls, the tourists, the scavengers who preyed on tourists, the shops, restaurants and bars that filled every commercial slot. Two blocks along the street through dense foot traffic, with the trolley bell tinkling and music booming from the CD shops, Levent found

the Lighthouse Gallery on the second floor of a lavender building with white escutcheons.

The sign said the exhibition would open in fifteen minutes,
but people had already spilled out the double door of the gallery
into the hallway. On opening night, the hors d'oeuvres and liquor
flowed freely, attracting every artist in the city, as well as his mistress. Others were gathered about, dressed as if for the opera,
and these were the patrons of the arts.

Tara Gunduz was one of them, and not the least. Having her
appear at an opening was the mark of greatness for an artist.
Talent did not matter, nor did draftsmanship or a sense of color
greater than the average mule. Levent knew her at once from her
pictures, which did her justice. Though well over forty, she had
been into the shop for steady repair. Blonde from the best bottles,
her cheeks botoxed like balloons, her nose chosen specially for
the occasion, she stood several paces behind the painter, who
stood at the door. It was clear she allowed him the task of greeting
the guests, while leaving no doubt who was the personage of
importance.

Levent shook hands with the painter—a short hairy man with a
long ponytail—for politeness. He advanced to the next station along
the line, trying to calculate how much Tara Gunduz cost to maintain.

His pay for the year in a day, he decided. Her dress was of a
scarlet and gold silk that could never have come from worms.
Her coat was sheared mink, scalloped in patterns that echoed
the gross abstractions on the walls. These were the paintings,
ranged in no special order, and they were horrific. By comparison,
Tara was attractive. She was very attractive.

"Police Inspector Levent."

She smiled with the lips that were the fashion, bee-stung and
everted. "I should tell you that I called your cousin Sema for a
report," she said. "I wanted to know you to the bone."

"Then you do."

Her laugh said yes, but not completely, and not yet. "Sema
tells me you're the only brilliant man in your office. I hope it's
not a lack of competition that earns you the name."

"It could be," said Levent. "We all try, but the prize for the best detective usually goes to the man with the greatest stamina."

She laughed, closing the mink over her breasts, which rose. They continued to rise against all the rules of gravity. "I've found that quality to be the most lacking in our city. The Bosporus can't be cleansed in a day, or prejudices changed. To say nothing of less important things."

"Unfortunately, I've come to talk about other things," said Levent, as he handed her the cep with the photographs of her friends at play.

"Do you want me to call someone for you?" she asked. "Or should we talk from across the room? It's done, you know."

"The second might be best," said Levent, tapping the phone in her hand until it came alive. "You may want to sit down."

She turned her back, surrounding the cep as if she had recognized it from some dim episode in the past. As Levent waited for her reaction, he looked at the first painting in a series that depicted the lights of Istanbul underwater. Interesting. Seen one way, the lights looked to be both below and above the water. Yes, the dimensions had been made to intrude. Levent suddenly knew he had just shaken hands with a genius.

Tara, of course, had known it first. He wondered if she provided inspiration for the man first in line at the door. The way Kaya had described it, her fingers were more important than her new mouth. Her touch, he said. It's unbelievably fine. Or perhaps, simply unbelievable.

Nothing in her face or demeanor as she turned back to Levent indicated she was upset by what she had observed in the phone. "How much do you want?" she asked, as if she were at a fashionable boutique in Teshvikiye. She was not bargaining. She had made a demand.

"Nothing," said Levent. "Certainly not money. And I'll want the pictures back. They're evidence."

"We can talk about that," she said in a very different tone. "These things have no bearing on your case. I guarantee it."

She began to walk slowly toward the rear of the gallery, still with the cep in her hand. Levent followed quickly. He could not let her confiscate the phone as she had the painter. When she turned into the doorway to a room halfway down the hall, he took two quick steps. That damned thing had a delete button.

She probably would have hit it already if she had been familiar with the model. Her thumb was in the correct place as he entered the room. Tara sat down behind the manager's desk. As if caught doing something naughty but not wrong, she tossed the cep on a stack of papers.

"Now you'll tell me your purpose," she said. "No nonsense. I can have you removed from this case with a phone call. With *that* phone."

"'Perhaps," said Levent. "But that tells me you're not interested in helping to find who murdered your friend."

She nodded briefly to acknowledge her grief. "It should tell you something else, Inspector. Most men in your position think about starvation and how it pertains to their survival. They also think about sex, and sometimes as it pertains to the survival of their name. If they think of anything else—a third thing—I've never seen it."

"Some men like to solve problems," said Levent. "Puzzles. It's a subspecies, I believe."

"Very well."

"When you were finished with Mehmet Kaya, you passed him off to one of your friends," said Levent in a voice with a beat. "That was intelligent. Perhaps even prescient. If the victim had done the same with Atilla Kocaman, I think none of this would have happened."

"You're telling me that well-hung donkey is mixed up in Ayla's death?"

"Yes."

"Jealousy," she said with disgust. "Men kill for that, I know. It's a glandular thing. But to think Ayla's murder is simply a matter of her having taken the honey pot away—"

"It was more than that," said Levent. "I'm sure it began with a wounded ego, but Atilla had spent too many years on the street learning its ways to forget them. The street told him that revenge is best when it has a hidden purpose."

"Money," said Tara, as if she cursed its name. "But that doesn't make sense. Ayla would have given it to him if he threatened her. She knows—she knew—it's simply a means to an end."

"Money, yes. But when the amount is large, it changes the equation and produces a catalytic effect. And the amount is very large."

Tara looked closely at Levent and the changing calculus he had drawn. This was the woman who doled out her husband's allowance to incorporate but not exceed a stated sum for his whores. Levent had no doubt she was the brains behind the family firm and all its subsidiaries. She knew everything she needed to know, but did she know everything she should?

"What kind of money are we talking about?"

"Millions of dollars," said Levent. "I've managed to learn about several million that passed through the victim's hands. Probably, there's more I haven't been able to track yet. It's almost certainly the reason she was murdered."

"I don't believe it," she said forcefully. "Ayla did well in her business, but nothing like that came out of it."

"That's what I think, too," said Levent. "It would help me if you could suggest where it did come from."

"If I knew," she said, "I'd be there in the morning. So would every commercial being in this city."

"I've heard that one man has been there already," said Levent, putting a burr in his voice. "He's someone you know well. As I'm sure you understand, money must find a safe home if it's not completely legal. In other words, dirty cash has to be laundered. In a country with no mortgage system to speak of, that presents a problem, but it's one that can be solved with ingenuity. The money is put into property. Now, a man could travel this huge city buying up all the available apartments units, and some do. No one traces the purchases and no one really cares to. But that's a tedious way of going at the problem. It would be better—far better—to buy up space in an office building. Whole floors, perhaps."

She seemed to know where he was going, but said, "Go on."

"It would be best if this office building was a tremendous undertaking. A new and grand enterprise. Two towers rising high in the sky."

She nodded. "And that's how you come round to me?"

"Yes."

"No," she said. "I have no need to put money in any amount through the laundry here or elsewhere. We *make* washing machines. We make them in Turkey and Romania and sell them everywhere across borders. We move in and out of currencies in the legal money market and generally do well by the exchange. Now the question becomes: How stupid do you think I am?"

Levent said nothing. His eyes moved slowly onto the cep with its digital camera as it sat on the desk.

"All right," she said, looking away. "But that doesn't prove anything except indiscretion. The things you're describing take planning and execution. A criminal enterprise. I can assure you I've never been involved in anything like that. I can't believe Ayla was either."

"Ayla and Ahmet," he said. "Ahmet being your husband."

She laughed, and without stopping, laughed again. Her voice was still merry when she spoke. "Inspector, one of us here *is* stupid."

"I don't think so," said Levent. "But anyone can be fooled."

"And you think it's me?"

"If it isn't, I'm going to arrest you."

She held his eyes long enough to see if anything in them was serious. In the end, she saw more of that than she liked. "Inspector, I'll tell you flatly that my husband isn't capable of serious deception. He has a need to confess his sins, and he does in almost every case without prompting."

Levent believed that, as well as he knew that she had needs, too. "Do Ahmet's confessions result in you giving him money?"

She didn't like the question because of what it implied. "Usually," she said. "Yes, I usually give Ahmet money when he beats his breast. I've been known to give more money when he weeps."

"And what do you think would happen if he found someone else to give him money?"

"I don't know anyone who's *that* stupid," she said. "Even his friends don't like throwing money away."

"You didn't answer the question."

"The answer is yes," she said. "If Ahmet found someone who was foolish enough to give him money, that is."

"Your husband not only has money," said Levent. "He's become a partner in at least one business I know of."

"What business?"

"A nightclub called Mine or Yours."

She scoffed. "I know about that and have for some time. One of his whores came into some money. He goes to her now and then. If she's busy, he stands by the bar hoping to collect the overflow in women."

"Probably. But he gave her the money to open the place."

"That's absurd."

"She's not," said Levent. "Not at all. And she told me about the arrangement herself. Some small amount of duress may have been involved, but I'm sure she was speaking the truth."

Levent could not tell if Tara was thinking of her husband or her pride. She licked her surgically altered lips. "Duress," she said. "You're better at it than you seem."

"Information is duress in some cases," he said. "It's what we *don't* know about the people we love."

She weakened. "Yes."

"What do you think when he goes off to work every day?" asked Levent. "This man who never did."

"He got the job through a friend," she said. "I simply didn't imagine it was anything that couldn't be done by an Angora cat."

"When can I talk to your husband?"

"After I do," she said.

CHAPTER 22

The Heavens

Ahmet Gunduz could not be found that evening. It was impossible to find him when he did not want to be found, and that condition was unfortunately common. His phone at work did not respond because that criminal enterprise had ended for the day. His friends had no idea where he might be because they were his friends. His cep rarely answered when his wife's name announced itself in the display, unless he needed money on the spot and the spot was tight. And that, Tara was forced to admit, had not happened in some time.

She promised a meeting the next morning sometime before lunch, and if not, as soon as possible afterward. Levent believed her because he had to. Depending on what she found out, he would see a contrite husband or one that was missing from everyone's directory for the balance of the century. Gaining leverage over the rich was a minute-to-minute event that stood constant revision.

Levent left the gallery where the crowd had diminished in relation to the food and beverages. When he reached the patrol car in the street, he checked his cep for the calls that had come in while he was with Tara. Three showed, and only the last seemed important. It was sure to give some direction.

"Mister Wilding. This is Inspector Levent."

"Twenty minutes if you can make it," he said. "The Heavens."

Levent thought he could make it and nearly did, arriving less than five minutes late at the complex of tall apartment buildings half a kilometer from the Bosporus. In the tallest of the buildings, he took the elevator to the penthouse floor, where a club called Soho and a restaurant called The Heavens occupied the space and commanded splendid views of the city.

Wilding, who sat at the best table by the window, rose when Levent approached. "Let's order now," he said. "We can thrash out our business when that's done."

This Englishman so familiar with the lesser parts of the world would pay in this expensive place. He would determine the agenda. That was obviously his idea.

Levent conformed to the thinking that would move the best bottle of wine in the house to their table. He did not fail to note as they ordered that this was another of those places where he should look to the sky. The best parts of it swarmed around them in odd multiples of stars to city lights. A competition?

"A striking place," said Wilding. "A bit too New York, but the food is good. At least, that's what I remember when I was here with Ayla."

"No bad memories, I hope."

"It's impossible to have them about her," he said. "But not, of course, about what happened to her."

"It must be terrible for the family," said Levent. "Are you here to represent her parents, too?"

"Her father's dead and her mother's very ill," said Wilding. "Terminally ill. It's the end of something, and very sad for us all."

"And her stepfather?"

Levent knew he had tumbled onto something. Wilding's eyes grazed his for an instant, but it was that fraction of time when all bad things are conceived. The civilized man in him smiled.

"You must have heard something."

"Rumors," said Levent.

"They're probably true," he said. "Say Louis Tekel to me and you've spoken the name of the devil. What Ayla's mother saw in him I can't say. But she was lonely after her first husband died, and he appeared like an unwrapped gift. A countryman in exile, like her. Handsome, of course."

"The name sounds Turkish."

"It is," he said. "If I thought we bred men like that in England, I'd change citizenship. But of course we *do* have them. Everyone does."

"He abused her, is that true?"

"For six months, as I hear," said Wilding as if he had heard very late. "When I found out what was going on, I offered to take Ayla out of that situation. If you must know, I insisted. I wouldn't say I did the best for her. It was the only thing I could think of. The school I sent her to was for children with special needs. And she was certainly that by then. I wasn't sure she would recover, but she did, nicely. And went on to college without missing a step."

"Do you hear from the stepfather?"

"Never," he said. "And I made sure Ayla didn't. I like to think I was successful in that."

"So he left her alone afterward?"

"I'd know if it was otherwise."

"You were close to your niece?"

"Of course not," he said very quickly. "I don't know if any man was close to her after . . . that."

Levent had to agree. The woman he had come to know never let any man close to her unless they were furnishing a service. She hired them and fired them, as if it was that simple.

"I'd like to know where I could get in touch with Louis Tekel."

"Why?"

"I have a suspect," said Levent. "I can't give you the details, but his background makes him relevant. He may be a foreigner who speaks Turkish."

Wilding was smart enough not to press the issue too quickly, and he was glad of any focus that kept Levent from asking the more loaded questions that lay behind their meeting. Wilding moved his pale complexion just this side of fascination, and opened his thin lips in a smile.

"You want to know more about Louis?"

"If it's not too much trouble," said Levent. "Gathering information is a more than a hobby. It cuts several ways."

"I believe I know you well enough not to doubt you." Wilding hunched forward across the tight convivial table. "Louis came to us on the run from one of your coups, if I remember correctly. I don't know how he managed to stay in England past his visa, but he became legal when he found a citizen to marry. She wasn't the usual desperate sort, but had a little money of her own. A flat of her own with a walk-in wine cellar that was always building. Louis stayed with his English wife until it was convenient to leave her. That was about the time my brother died, and that's when he made overtures to my sister-in-law, Nil. Interesting word, overture. A beginning that states all the themes but not to the point of boredom. Louis was all about that. He had a real talent for making sure the facts never intruded on his life."

"So he was divorced from his first wife?"

"Bitterly."

"Children?"

"Two," he said. "From all I've heard, the father made the divorce bitter for them as well. He didn't pay much attention to either of them after he found a better object for his affections."

"Their names?"

"Amelia for the daughter, and I believe for the son, John."

Levent reminded himself that John was a common name. But it had appeared in context. "Are you sure of the names?"

"I could check on that, but yes, I'm reasonably certain. Why?"

"It's nothing," said Levent. "Any foreign connection to your niece could be important."

"You're not saying enough, Inspector."

"I'm sorry, Mister Wilding."

"It's Samuel."

"Of course."

At that moment, conveniently, Levent made way for the appetizers that came to the table in several stages. They were not Turkish except as they were made in Istanbul by cooks who followed New York fashion. But they were dressed nicely by the wine, which was as good as Levent had expected from his host. Everything he had gotten at this meeting so far was choice.

"Not bad for an interruption," said Wilding, as he sipped the red burgundy. "But you were saying—"

"I meant to ask what happened to Louis' children once he pursued the bitter divorce with their mother."

"They grew up," he said. "You'd think they might suffer without a father, but in this case I doubt that was true. Anything that might go wrong was already embedded in the genes."

"Do you know anything about their lives?"

"Not a lot," he said, as if he might be holding back. "The girl tried to make a career in modeling if I recall. The boy went into the military several years back, but that's the last I know of him."

"I'd like to hear more, if you can find out."

"I could, perhaps."

"Anything on the children's background should be helpful," said Levent. "Especially anything that might have occurred lately."

"You mean trouble?"

"I mean information," said Levent. "I've told you I'm obsessed with it. I'd very much like to know, for instance, what you can tell me now about your niece's bank accounts."

"These questions are a one-way street so far, Inspector."

"It won't stay that way much longer, Samuel. I'm close to him now."

Wilding chewed on the guarantee with his Chicken Cholesterol Divan. To this point, he had given rather than lent information at no cost to himself. He did not want to cross to more dangerous territory.

"If I had an option in this case, believe me I'd pursue it." He put down his utensils as if surrendering weapons. "I *was* able to check the accounts here in Turkey. And they *did* come to more than I imagined. Not the figures you had in mind, but on the high side. So I went further along. I got in touch with Ayla's man in Antalya. I know him—Metin. Well enough, in any case, to make demands on his time. That's the advantage in being a partner in the business."

Metin was one of the victim's overnight guests at her country house, according to the maid. So was a *Mister* Samuel. They might have met and enjoyed each other's company on the same summer weekend.

"Yes, Metin. The name's come up."

"Well, it should have if competence means anything." Wilding looked over his plate as if it held the answer in boneless breasts. "Metin directed me to Luna Bank in Dubai. Ayla usually made out her accounts with me as the adjunct party of record. So it was relatively easy to obtain a count. And I'll admit I was surprised by the figure they gave. It was two million five. In dollars."

So most of the money the victim had exchanged found its way to the safe haven that she, and probably Wilding, had devised. He had probably called Metin to be on the safe side of surprise. And there was certainly more money elsewhere.

"Is that all you have for me, Samuel?"

"I'm afraid so. If another account is hidden away—even from Metin—it should show itself in time. I'll let you know, you can be sure."

And he might, once the money was safely transferred to London. Or a more obscure destination on the real-time globe. Levent could do nothing about that. An arrest would not stop it.

"Did you manage to find out how all this money got into the accounts? I mean, were you able to trace the origin of your niece's wealth?"

"I asked," he said. "Metin was no help there. He claimed all Ayla's management decisions were strictly hers."

"Not yours either?"

"In this case, not at all," he said, putting regret like a pulse in his words. "I'm afraid I let Ayla do what she wanted. I suppose I was afraid to pile damage on damage. She wanted to make her way, and I wanted it for her. I should have paid more attention to the business, that's true."

This was the exact point where fact deviated from self-interest. Levent knew he would not find the answer to his question from this source. If he wanted more information about John Tekel, he must agree not to disagree.

"The beef carpaccio is excellent."

"Yes," said Wilding, more relieved than concerned. "They really do have a good kitchen."

CHAPTER 23

Tarabya

Levent had reached his car when Akbay called. "We have our taxi driver and his destination," he said. "It's Tarabya back from the water."

"I'm on the way from Beyoglu."

"We're not far from Second Bridge up the hill," he said. "I'll use the time to look around until you arrive."

"Be careful. He's smart and he may be skittish."

"I'd like to see that."

Levent told his driver to hit the road hard again. It was a half hour to Tarabya, and since it was on the inland side, they made for the highway. Traffic had eased, but there was no clear run in Istanbul before midnight.

The chances the killer had camped for any length of time in Tarabya were not great, but Levent's anticipation had grown enormously. Talking to Wilding of his niece's life brought her closer, surrounding her with a living population. He could not forget the image of her in her office chair, bloody and one-eyed, but other images, quieter and as powerful, had begun to push it aside. One was particularly strong. His name was John. Or perhaps even Can.

When they reached the six-lane highway, Levent went to his cep. He ignored the calls that had come in and punched up Peter Nocking, Her Majesty's man about intelligence, at the number that was said to connect to his wireless.

They had known each other since the day Nocking called for help in rescuing a citizen of the commonwealth who found himself in trouble due to his drug habit. Levent, who was always ready to help addicts of good family, had cleared the man from any part in the death of the woman who appeared one night, and died, in his flat. It had not been easy, but finally it was just.

Clearing the crime created a debt that had gone uncollected until now.

Nocking answered the phone lazily, as he did everything but drink. He was not one to admit what he did for his pay, or that he did it in more than passing. His voice sounded like two men vying for the same tongue.

"Yes, I'm well," he said. "Very well, thank you. How are things in the criminal department?"

"Busier than usual, Peter. We're up against a deadline. And one of the suspects has a connection to your homeland."

"Not another doper?"

"Nothing so easy," said Levent. "But this man has been in military service, so you should have something on record."

"Got a pencil, yes, sir. Blaze away."

"His name is John Tekel. He grew up in London of English and Turkish parents and should be in his late thirties. I'm sorry I don't have a date for his service, but that may give you a rough idea."

"All we need, you know. Computers."

"You'll get back to me as soon as you can."

"In the morning, Onur, as soon as I've checked all sources. It's a race to see which of us greets the sun with a happier face."

Levent believed Nocking would return the information, but only after chewing it over thoroughly. That was understood. How much he chose to keep to himself was a question. Levent hoped it would not be too much.

He checked the calls that had come while at dinner—one from his wife and his Chief. Levent returned the first, righting himself at home. He passed on the second, thinking more time might bring something worthwhile to report. Even standing in the shadow of the killer should bring them closer to the end.

The complex of apartments where the taxi had taken Nur's blue jacket sat near the top of the hill at some distance from the Bosporus. The *site*, as these things were called, comprised three nine-story buildings in sunset colors that had been built in the last decade. That meant a lot of units to check, and a lot of time spent, but Akbay had begun the job. He had just come out of the second building at a quick walk as Levent got out of the car.

"The kapiji doesn't remember seeing anyone enter the buildings when our man was dropped off," he said, turning and leading Levent back into the building. "But he knows all the tenants, and he gave me his opinion on everything they've done in the last two years. That's as long as he's been here and a bit longer than the tenant in 604. She's a woman alone. If you believe him, another prostitute. But this one's different. More of a professional. Moldavian."

"A passport Moldavian or a real one?"

Akbay hit the elevator button. The door stuttered twice before it opened like a tomb. "The kapiji doesn't know what he doesn't know. She's real enough for him. They certainly become more real when there are more of them. I wish they'd find an economy and stop borrowing ours."

"They haven't come close to that yet," said Levent, watching the floors pass in silence. "I've heard somewhere around ten percent of their young women are sold out of the country—usually into prostitution. Maybe as many as half a million."

"I had some Moldavian wine a couple of weeks ago," said Akbay. "They're on their way to developing an effective poison and having people pay for it if I'm any judge. We shouldn't be surprised if importing whores is next. It's bound to be safer for the client."

Levent was willing to follow Akbay's instincts, especially when they had nothing else to go on. When the elevator stopped at the sixth floor, Akbay already had his lock picks out.

"The kapiji doesn't have the keys to the apartments, probably because no one with sense would trust him. So we may have to go in quietly."

Although it was time for citizens to be in bed, no one answered the doorbell. Akbay had to go to the picks, where he found some trouble with the lock, a Kale Kilit that still had a factory glow. He backed out and tried twice more before the tumblers finally aligned and the door snapped open.

The lights were on in the main room, illuminating nothing but the furniture. It looked heavy and Russian, though it probably had been bought locally at stores catering to bad taste.

Levent stepped across the room from carpet to carpet until he reached the kitchen. Nothing there. He moved to the beginning of the hall. The doors were closed for the entire length, as if something private was happening in each. Akbay had already moved down the hall, opening the first door and looking his way in carefully.

A bedroom, no occupants. Levent moved to the next door down the hall, the bathroom. He pushed and the door opened partially, but the bottom struck something. He pushed again, harder, and the object, which was heavy, moved hardly at all. Dead weight.

With a smell.

Levent flipped on the light switch, looking obliquely into the mirror over the sink. He saw two feet sideways and parallel with the floor. A woman's feet in slippers. He put his shoulder to the door and bulled it open wider.

"We're late," said Akbay.

Levent took a long step that brought him to the other side of the room beyond the body. She was almost prone on the floor, her head wedged against the long vanity. Her hands were tied behind her back with plastic cord, the fingers wide apart and rigid. She had been dead for a while. It was not hard to see that her throat had been cut, or where it had been done. A scum of dried blood rimmed the porcelain sink. The killer had not changed his method.

"It should be easier when they're Moldavian," said Akbay, sidling through the door into the narrow room.

"It was hard," said Levent. "Look."

A small amount of blood smeared the front of the vanity and the floor below, so she might have tried to crawl to the door. Or dropped when the killing was done. She had not gone far.

"We can add neatness to the things that make him what he is," said Akbay. "He doesn't want this bright red stuff dripping through the floor into the dinner of the family downstairs. So he made sure it went down the drain." Akbay nudged open the shower stall with the tip of his pen. "It might have been better to do the job in the shower, but it's small."

"No sign of torture."

"Let's say he didn't want much from her. Only one thing."

Her silence. There was one way to guarantee it. Kill when in doubt. It wasn't safe to have a cup of coffee with this man. And perhaps that was all she had done.

Levent was glad her eyes were closed. She looked as if she had been attractive. Her hair was a medium blonde that did not have darker roots. Her nose was wide and flared at the base, reaching for the angle of her cheekbones. Something Oriental there. Something still Slavic in her color, too—white with bruised highlights, but as mellow as a rose. If she had been selling herself, there would be buyers.

Akbay was already on the phone to the technicians, and for a change their presence would be welcome. Forensics should have a good chance with this one. A bathroom with a drain-well in the floor and ceramic tiles where minute things became visible would generate possibilities. The killer had probably manhandled her into the room, not being gentle about it. Killing was almost always an act of desperation, but this man went about it like work.

Without knowing it, Levent had his phone in his hand in his pocket. Yes, he had to call the Chief. It might be time to change inspectors again.

This one was always late.

* * *

Levent was puzzled when he learned that the killer did not seem to have slept at the apartment of Maya Pongash. The sheets on the bed in the spare room were laundry stiff and the sofa small. Unless he slept with her—or slept in an apartment with her body growing cold in the bathroom—he had simply made a stop.

He might have done that. It depended on when he had killed her. He might have done it as he was going out the door.

Pardon me, but your life is required.

The medical officer, not Derya Silme but another called Kibar, did not want to pin down a time of death. A day, he thought. Possibly more, but not a lot. So the killer might have settled down for a while. He might even have slept with the victim if she was the woman the kapiji thought.

Levent was not sure. In her hall closet, he failed to find the slippers most Turkish houses kept for guests of any length. That might be expected of a foreigner, but this young woman also kept three coats—men's coats in different sizes—hanging in the closet.

Turkish-made. Small. Medium. Large.

Levent could think of no obvious explanation for it unless she had been running a private hotel. That might account for the traffic in men that the kapiji had seen going in and out.

A hotel and haberdashery. As he passed through the apartment, Levent found a number of shirts and pants in the closet in the spare bedroom that were also of different sizes and locally made. Several belts in different sizes, which seemed more telling. Everything but extra underwear.

The bed was also more than expected of a place used for the occasional guest. It was queen sized and large enough to sleep two people. If they were Russian, three adults and a child.

Until he knew better, Levent called the apartment a safe house. Was it kept for illegal immigrants—countrymen needing a place to stay—while they became acclimated to the city? They could have come down from the north on one of AylaTur's Black Cruises, landing on the coast or shuffled through customs quietly. That would account for some of the money in Acheson's pyramid, though not all.

But this was part of an organization. Loose, but probably effective. Unless a foreigner had passive income, staying in the country for any length of time under the radar was not easy.

Learning the language was harder. Levent found in a dresser drawer a Turkish-Russian dictionary, a Turkish-Russian grammar, and some audiotapes. They might have been the victim's, but notes had been made in the margins in two sets of handwriting. Perhaps more. Even if the immigrants spoke Gaugaz, they still had to pass plausibly on the streets.

If these things added up to a safe place for Moldavians in Istanbul, the killer had come knowing what kind of place his victim kept. He could lie low—for a while if need be—and for less if he wanted.

He had wanted less and more. Levent found a steel blue laptop computer on a bookcase shelf in the main room. It was slotted upright like a book and had the size and weight of an abridged dictionary. After finding the power supply in a desk drawer, Levent plugged it in and checked for ICQ on the desktop. Not to be seen, but in the program files he located an ICQ directory. Empty. Someone had deleted the program.

For Levent, that was as good as a signature. He did not think the killer stopped at the apartment only for that reason. Going online to talk to the police might have been an afterthought. A chance to taunt.

The killer had moved on, and he might have gotten all he wanted. Levent wanted to know exactly what those things were, but had no idea until Akbay appeared with the building's kapiji. Stopping at the door of the apartment, Akbay left the man in the hallway like a dog.

"He's got something to say, and he wants to speak to the Chief."

"The *Chief?*"

"You'll do," said Akbay. "What can I say—he left his village three years ago. He'd keep a cow in the back yard if he could."

Akbay, who had grown up in Istanbul, disdained immigrants. He led Levent to the ill-shaven, elongated man who stood upright in the hall, moving from side to side like someone waiting his chance at the toilet.

"This is Chief Inspector Levent," said Akbay with a flourish. "He's in charge of everything here, including me and you. Now tell him what you found."

"Alp Otgar," he said, extending his hand.

Levent took the calloused hand without enthusiasm. Alp had that village look, both callow and corrupt, that took some time to erase. His skin looked dusty, and would remain like that until he had been here five years and learned to wash more than once a day. His eyes were sharp and clouded, reflecting an alternating current of alienation that would last even longer.

"I'm Inspector Onur Levent. I understand you have important information to add to our investigation."

"I imagine it's important, Chief, or I wouldn't bother you at this late hour. For the same reason I didn't notice it at first because of the dark, and then your people came with all your cars and commotion. I finally remembered to check, but I didn't see it anywhere. I looked around, too, since they don't always park in the place where they're assigned."

"We're speaking of a car," said Levent, translating from Turkish to Turkish. "The victim's car?"

"Of course," he said.

"You say it's missing?"

"It ain't anywhere in the lot," he said, correcting Levent with a frown. "That's what we can say at this point."

Levent did not ask from which television program Alp had absorbed his dialogue. He would know about the car. The hard part was treating him with the respect he was sure he deserved.

"Thank you for your help, sir. Mister Otgar. Where did we say your village was? Black Seacoast?"

"Why, yes." Alp seemed stunned, as if he had eradicated with great care every trace of his past. He looked in the palm of his hand as if Levent had read his future there. "How do you know?"

"It's my job."

Tonight, it seemed like more. As Levent drew information from Alp like a village dance between two old men, he wearied of the day. The car belonging to Maya Pongash was a late model Opel Astra, electric blue in color, license plate 34-BU-7374. It was a hatchback in which she kept a small mattress snug against the rear window (for the customers she took in from the road), a gozboncu hanging from the rear view mirror (which only a heathen would put any faith in), a ten liter plastic water bottle, the usage of which did not bear a second thought, and a lot of maps in the slash pocket on the driver's side that told what she was better at than anything else.

"Whore's gear all," said Alp, riding his obsession hard. "I mean, if you want to know where you're going in this city, it ain't like there's a shortage of people to ask. She could have come to me for what she needed, but that would mean looking me in the eye. And she wouldn't do that. None of them can these days. They're all too busy selling themselves, tempting men and giving them the back of their hand when it's done. I say it's good she's gone. The man that did it is a saint—if he ain't a garbage collector. My money says he's both."

That was the trouble with money and men who were tempted. Levent had no clear indication that John Tekel was one of them, but he could not help thinking along those lines. Too much money was involved. Too much organization. Another swinish killing, but not nearly enough torture.

The pattern of the psychopath had been broken almost from the start and now seemed complete. What was left was a man with motivation that should become clear. And a car that could be traced. Levent rubbed the small blue talisman that his wife had attached to his key ring. Not a gozboncu, it was a tiny prayer slipped inside a cylinder of silver filigree.

Get lucky soon. It's time.

Part Three:

The Ninth Crusade

CHAPTER 24

Two Englishmen

Levent did not really awaken. He came from the place he had been to the place he visited. Home. His bed with the duvet in startling floral colors. He was the only one in bed, so it must be late.

Like a clock that ran in step with his consciousness, Emine came into the room with a mug of coffee and the telephone. She placed the coffee on the nightstand and the phone in his hand.

"It's an Englishman," she said. "But not Prince Charles."

He wanted to ask how she knew, but was simply glad it was not the Chief. Their conversation last night had been their most dismal, filled with recriminations and shouted threats. Levent never shouted.

He took a sip of coffee—more than a sip—before he spoke into the phone, wondering which of his Englishmen had called. Two were involved in this case, and both could return significant information if they chose. As it happened, the voice belonged to Peter Nocking, the intelligence arm of Her Majesty in Istanbul.

"If I knew you were in bed, I'd have sent a carrier pigeon," he said. "The fax machine is broken again."

The fax machine was always broken when it came to written communications from Nocking or his colleagues in Ankara. Levent knew that from the scattered times he had asked for information.

"I was up late, Peter."

"More dead bodies from the tourist department?"

So he knew of the first murder at least. Levent expected that Nocking would do his own rambling as well as the research requested, especially when they were so much the same. How much was the question.

"No," said Levent. "It was an unrelated matter. I wish the two were better related. It would save time."

"I see," he said, meaning he did not quite. "I've always thought of this as a safe city, but then I don't see the things you do. Tell the truth, I don't have the stomach for blood."

"No one does," said Levent. "Except psychopaths. Do you have anything for me in that way, Peter?"

"The dossier of one John Tekel," he said. "As requested, but perhaps not as psychopathic as you'd like."

"Whatever you have is appreciated."

Nocking knew he had to oblige, though he would keep fishing for information as he fed out the chum. "This Tekel is interesting. According to his service record, he was born in London on June 22, 1973. His father was an immigrant who married locally and turned to importing Turkish tobacco. It comes from your State Monopoly, which, as you know, is also named Tekel. So our people thought his name was a laugher, and he might be working for your intelligence. But it wasn't true, and the only thing it did was get him into our files. His name really does seem to be Tekel, and he made a little money at his business. Had two children, Amelia and John."

"Are they British citizens?"

"That's correct. They could be dual citizens of Britain and Turkey, but if they are we have no record of it."

"Staying with the record is good enough, Peter. I'll check passport controls from this end."

"I'm sure you will," he said. "Better than ours, in fact."

Nocking probably could have summarized his information in one paragraph, but because he was intelligence, it was standard procedure to shake the tree to see what fell.

"Now, Peter, what about John Tekel, the son?"

"Grew up in London under the usual conditions," he said breezily. "Or so I suppose. It all depends on what's thought normal."

"Normal," said Levent, "is normal. Even in England."

"Yes, well, after he came into the service, that assumption was called into some doubt."

"How so?"

"John Tekel was given an assignment some people thought was important," said Nocking, as if that happened as a matter of routine. "And in the end, he fucked up badly."

"What important assignment?"

"He was with one of the advance units that went into Iraq. Everyone thought that was important at the time."

"What unit?"

"Can you believe that's still classified?"

"All right," said Levent, who was beginning to know how far he could go. "Tell me if he's still a member of that service or any other."

"No."

"No what, Peter?"

"He was dismissed from service."

"For what reason?"

"That's classified, too," said Nocking, as if he could say more. "But I can put forward some items for you to chew on. I'm using what has never been called my best judgment in telling you about it. If one of our citizens wasn't the victim in this case, you can believe I absolutely would not."

"Ayla Acheson," said Levent.

"There. You said it."

Levent did not know if Nocking understood the relationship between Acheson and Tekel. It all had to do with asking the right questions.

"Peter, it might help my investigation a great deal to know why Tekel was turned out of service."

"There was an incident," he said without much follow through. "It's something everyone would rather forget. Heat of battle, so on."

"Heat of what battle?"

"An action near Basra," he said. "Nothing significant. It seems that Tekel and another man were found too near the bodies of three dead people. Iraqis. One male, two female. The women's throats had been cut. Tekel and his friend claimed the man killed the women before they could stop him. No one understands why he'd do it. They were his sisters."

"No witnesses," said Levent.

"Correct," said Nocking. "But Tekel's friend wavered just enough to create suspicion in the minds of the investigators. Frankly, he must have created a lot of suspicion to get the military moving on it."

"Enough to cashier those two?"

"Some pressure was applied," said Nocking lightly. "They were given the choice of leaving the service without penalty. That isn't much of a penalty unless you think of yourself as a career man."

"What sort of career did Tekel follow?" asked Levent. "I mean, what was his specialty in the service?"

"A simple lieutenant," said Nocking blandly. "Nothing too complicated. He wasn't even supposed to be where they found him, if the truth was known. His was a medical unit."

Levent tried not to let satisfaction slip into his tone, although it was the single and purest emotion he felt. "Did Tekel have medical training?"

"Yes. Some. Don't know the details."

"Ayla Acheson's spinal cord was severed by a man who had surgical knowledge," said Levent. "At least our people think so."

"Lord."

"Please tell me John Tekel was not a surgeon."

"Best of my knowledge, no." Nocking paused like a gong. "But things can be learned in the field. One of the better laboratories for that sort of thing traditionally. I'm sure if he put his mind to it—"

His mind. That was the issue. "How long was he in the service?"

"Three years."

"Dismissed when?"

"Two months after the invasion."

"So he's been free for the last two and half years. A medical man without a practice, a citizen with a country he'd rather forget."

"Forced to agree."

"You should lock these people up," said Levent. "He's a maniac who's causing havoc all over this city."

"And a damned fine city it is."

That was the diplomat in him talking. Levent did know where he would find the sensible man, or the spy, but he was sure one or the other resided behind Nocking's blue eyes. It was time to spook him.

"Peter, I want you to think of this. A man murders two women in Iraq, and two more later in Istanbul. He seems to have done that, and the second body was just found in Tarabya. Now, you could think of these numbers as one through four. But what if the numbers are six through eight? Or higher?"

"Yes, I follow. These people go by the bushel. The peck. We don't know where he might have begun."

"We do roughly," said Levent. "You should have Scotland Yard run for similar murders in London. And where his family vacationed. And where he went to school, and where he was stationed in the service before going to Iraq."

"You really are serious," he said. "You think we'll find he was a busy fellow at home, too?"

"I'll find him if he's here, Peter. You find him if he comes up on your patch. It would be comforting to think he'll come to the same end in either country."

"Comforting, yes. Something about this must be."

* * *

The satisfaction Levent felt as he spoke to Nocking was replaced by nagging regret as he hung up. The information he had received did not matter unless it could be turned to finding the killer.

But Levent was as sure of his man as he could be. The decisive factor was how Tekel had killed in the past, which was the same as the present. The repetition rarely varied in people whose minds were frozen by the first blood they had drawn. Levent never understood why, but he accepted the fact because it was so often true. The method of murder was like a path through the wilderness where any deviation meant a complete loss of way.

The wilderness.

Didn't Karanlik use that word in their cyber conversation? Levent still did not understand why he had called and spoken to a man he knew was the police. Nor did he understand Tekel's motivation in slaughtering his half sister in such a brutal way, though that should be clear in time.

Before Levent signed off with Nocking, he asked what contacts Tekel might pursue in the city. The answer brought dismay. Istanbul was Levent's city, and the Tekel genealogy was not something Her Majesty's servants or Her computers kept. Try the phone book.

Levent tried headquarters. He was surprised when Akbay answered from the desk. Had he slept at all? Last night, and the night before, he said he would go home to bed, but Levent had learned not to believe him. When Tekel was put down, Akbay would put himself down to rest.

Levent hesitated to pass on the new information from Nocking, thinking Akbay did not need to personalize the killer more than he had. But he did it in as few words as possible. Akbay took the facts in without asking questions until the end.

"When we know what the victim and Tekel were doing together, we'll find him."

"Nothing on the car yet?"

"He's not on the road with a two-year-old bright blue Astra," said Akbay. "We might get lucky if he crosses ones of the bridges. They've got the plate number posted at the booths on both sides."

"That's a thought," said Levent.

"That's all it is," said Akbay in a murmur that spoke to his lack of sleep. "I'm puzzled about why he stays around, but he's probably looking for something. It could be the last batch of money. You should put the uncle to the wall, and ask him if the cash showed up in any of the accounts. I just called Fatma, the maid, and she said Mister Samuel and Mister Metin came to the house on the same weekend last year. They got along just fine, she said."

"I'll see what I can do with Wilding, but I'm not optimistic," said Levent. "He's one man who doesn't want to enjoy our hospitality to a fault."

"But it would be nice to invite him to stay."

"That's what I do, Erol. I sleep, and then I go at them again."

* * *

Levent called Wilding, but received no answer at his hotel or mobile numbers. He left messages, and then wandered through another cup of coffee, giving Wilding a chance to return the call. Levent did not like holding important conversations on the road, traffic being what it was, but he finally got in his car.

He drove into the city by the ridge road that overlooked the highest hilltops. In early spring, Istanbul came alive with flowering Judas trees. The purple-pink blossoms—the true color of Byzantium—appeared as if they had been hiding, climbing the hills on both sides of the Bosporus like psychedelic snow. It was the best sight on land that could be had in the booming city of so many millions, the death of winter symbolized in the blaze of a tree that had no function but beauty.

A lull in the onslaught of late morning traffic was something to be appreciated, and Levent did as he came most of the way into the city center without a serious backup. When he found himself bumper-to-bumper, he was already on city streets. It was then he got the call from Wilding.

"Yes, Inspector. I'm sorry not to get back quickly, but there are things to be done with my niece's affairs. I'm clear to talk now."

"Why don't we get together," said Levent, wanting another chance to confront Wilding at a mean distance. "Where are you?"

"Coming in from TEM," he said. "I can meet you at The Last Chance in Etiler in twenty minutes."

"See you there."

Levent tried not to make anything of Wilding's current location, but those two gigantic towers were just off TEM, the outer ring highway. He could have been visiting his niece's house in the same general direction, but Levent had heard nothing from the men who were guarding the place. And they would have called if a foreigner had come to visit.

Levent noted that the apartment in Tarabya was within convenient parameters off the highway. Could the killer have stayed there before *and* after his first strike? Convenience meant a lot in Istanbul, where a blip in traffic could disrupt any schedule. Tekel was as careful a planner as he was a ruthless killer. It would be good to hear the report from Forensics about the place in Tarabya, though on first call it was clear they had found nothing. A man who stayed at one location for a while should have left something of himself behind.

When Levent arrived at the chic cafe on the main boulevard, he called headquarters and asked for an experienced man to be put on task to follow Wilding. The meeting would make the uncle easy to pick up and traffic would provide a cloak for surveillance. Levent did not expect Wilding to leave the country at a run, but it should be interesting to know where he went and the people he met. Anything else would be a bonus.

The waiter at the cafe wanted to put Levent in a corner on the way to the kitchen—the only place the police belonged in this part of the city—but changed his mind and discovered a table at the front window where reservations had suddenly been canceled. Levent then put his two-way radio away and lowered the volume. He had settled in and ordered coffee, his fourth of the morning, when Wilding clambered through the door the worst for traffic wear.

"These people should *not* be allowed to drive," he said, as they greeted each other again. "They might as well be on a horse. No lanes, no signals, no courtesy, nothing but general direction and a wave of the hand at that."

"There's an old expression that tells what a Turk needs," said Levent. "Horse, woman, weapon. Make the horse a car, and you'll find the numbers still work."

"I'd have said that if I wasn't a visitor to your city. It's too civilized a place to put up with this shit."

Wilding sat in a civilized chair and ordered a cappuccino along with two chocolate soufflés from the waitress. Levent wondered how the man kept his figure gorging on things like that, but passed off the mystery to his heritage. The English ate more sweets than Turks.

After the waitress had gone to fetch the order she said would take twenty minutes, Levent selectively outlined the progress of the investigation, as he had promised Wilding. It was difficult skirting the facts that might alert him to John Tekel's identity, but Levent put enough flesh on the bones so the victim's uncle could discern a tightening and more violent circle. In seven minutes and thirty-nine seconds, Levent was able to sit back and relax expectantly. The uncle seemed nearly satisfied, and he knew it was his turn to inform.

"I spoke to my sister-in-law to see if I could find the things you wanted," he said. "It wasn't a happy occasion and I hope never to repeat it."

"How is her illness?"

"She was operated on for a cancerous tumor five months ago," he said. "That bought some time, but the results won't differ. The cancer has already returned. She gets smaller every day. She was never a big woman, but seeing the flesh melt in such a terrible way—"

"I'm sorry to hear that."

"Losing her daughter hasn't helped," he said. "I told her the killer would be caught soon, and I described your efforts. I thought that might mean something to her. The problem is it's just talk when they're like that. You're reporting from another world. They don't quite live in it any longer."

"Still, the conversation must have been trying for her."

"Don't you listen?" said Wilding abruptly. "She can't *afford* to care. It's her daughter we were talking about, and it's as if I was describing a traffic accident in South America."

Levent thought Wilding told the truth as he had felt it. His emotional rhythm vouched for that. But it might also be a desire to throw the focus from the things that would touch him in his money.

"Yes," said Levent. "I've seen that happen. I don't suppose she was helpful in other ways."

"That's where you're wrong," he said, as if contradicting Levent was a thing he had come to like. "She knew a lot about Louis' children. More than I thought. I haven't been so upset at hearing simple words in a long time. It seemed clear that Louis and his world were more important to her than any other. I could tell they'd been in contact. They split up years ago, but she'd been talking to him—lately. He wouldn't care about her condition, not for a second. He must think there's money to be had."

"As you described him, I agree."

"Damned if there'll be any for him," said Wilding angrily. "That man is a plague. He walks and talks, and as it happens, he's passed the disease onto his children."

"His natural children, you mean?"

"If anything's natural about Louis," he said, pushing his words as if he could not stop them. "I doubt that. They say an octopus has brains, real intelligence, and can solve problems if its self-interest is great enough. Open a can of beans on the sea floor, suck up the food, so on. That's Louis. An inch is better than a mile. He starts slowly, charming his way in, and he's extremely patient. It's a virtue, they like to say. Of course, they've never seen a truly evil man or they'd change their minds. I did, and it was a shock to learn my sister-in-law really hadn't. I think she's still in love with that man in spite of all the harm he's done."

"I'm sure he must have come at her very slowly," said Levent. "All the time in the world."

"Yes, yes," he said. "Probably sent her flowers every day. I didn't see him at the hospital when she had surgery—that's too close for comfort—but I'm sure he called often and worked his way back into her heart like any predator. After he and Nil broke up, the bastard went back to his first wife. Moved into her house, if you can believe that. As if he'd just been round the block for a decade. Of course, he moved out again when he found another woman to charm. It was just too bad his children—his natural children—had the benefit of his stay. It didn't last long, but by the time he left the house a second time, he'd sewn chaos in their lives a second time. Both children were under psychiatric care for a while."

By Levent's count, that meant most of the people in the family had been driven to seek professional help. On the evidence, Louis Tekel's presence was a catalyst to mental aberration—a psychological plague. And there was the genetic component, too. The blood.

"Do you know what disorders the children suffered from?"

"They were serious," said Wilding grimly. "The girl tried to kill herself, and that alerted everyone. A call for help and all the things they go on about in that profession. It's not a profession, you know, but a damned screwy way of communication. It took eight months on the couch to find out the real problem was the way the girl and her brother were having at it."

Levent was not sure he understood all the varieties of that verb in English. "You mean, having . . . sex?"

"It's the way they went about it," he said with a grimace. "Undercover, so to speak. They weren't calling it incest or much of anything, because they invited their friends to enjoy the frolics, too. Thursdays at my father's pied-a-terre in Chelsea, that sort of thing. No one knew who and what was being found when the lights went out."

"Did Louis have a hand in that?"

"I don't know, but something about his presence causes what they used to call a lust for forbidden things." Wilding paused as if he had considered the coincidence at length. "He wouldn't have directed the orgies. His wants are more private. Hands on, and more a quick mouth than hands. I don't have any reason to suspect his involvement except for one strange thing."

Levent waited several seconds to hear the reason until the silence began to build. He was about to prompt Wilding, when the man spoke with muted force. "Ayla was involved," he said.

"With what?"

'The group," he said. "And the boy. John. I'd sent her away to school, and she was doing well there. Louis was out of the house by then, but he was still in London and close enough to his children to give off infection. When Ayla returned home from school for visits, something happened between her, the boy—and his friends. Ayla and John had of course known each other before that. Had for some years, but not in a special way and certainly nothing to worry about. This time was different. I gathered from Nil that the results were distressing."

"Distressing for whom?"

"Everyone concerned," he said. "Ayla had apparently taken part in one of their group meetings. But when the lights went out, she wanted out of the fun, thinking it wasn't really. There was a lot of bad feeling that day—or night—and the upshot was that Ayla let their secret out. She told her mother what was going on. And Nil eventually told it to John's mother."

"So Ayla spoiled the parties."

"They ended abruptly, yes" said Wilding. "The children went into therapy. I'd like to think it did some good, but there appears to be little evidence of that. The boy—John—ran away from home and found some trouble on the road fast enough. The girl went into a tailspin that began with drugs and ended when she eloped with one of the other party boys. From all indications, she went off the boy but not the drugs. I told you she was a model. I suppose I meant it based on my information. But model is sometimes a synonym for prostitute."

Levent was not thinking of definitions. Sibel said the victim had bought her pistol months ago when she felt threatened by something from her past. Thwarted love. Perverted love. Something unsavory. These events qualified.

"So John lost his love," said Levent. "A perfect love."

"That's a strange way of putting it."

"Perhaps." Levent hardly noticed that he shrugged. "It seems to me the loss must have been greater for being so illicit."

Wilding stared across the table of brushed metal and pressed bamboo. "I'm sorry if I said negative things about your second profession. You're obviously a talented psychologist."

"What I am doesn't matter," said Levent. "What happened must have been serious for John."

"I'd think very," he said.

"The trouble you said he found while he was on the road. Do you know what the problem was?"

"I don't have all the details," he said as if he didn't want them. "Apparently, after John ran off, he found a girl to share his bed. They lived together for several months, but were never on the same page emotionally. It seems she didn't quite share his mood swings. They seem to be extreme at times, and not always amusing. The police were called in one day, and when they arrived to find this one-room mattress, they also found the girl beaten up."

"Badly?"

"I don't know if you'd call something like that good," he said. "And I can't tell you if he learned to abuse women from his father or if things like that are hereditary. All I can say is it was fortunate for the family that the girl was no one. That still matters in every part of the world. Some money changed hands, I believe, for plastic surgery or the like. That's all I know."

Levent would have liked to know if the plastic surgery began with cuts on her neck—call it practice—but he did not want to point Wilding too far in the direction of revenge. He seemed close to it already. He had sat back in his chair as if preparing to sit out a siege. Clearly, he knew more than he was telling, and that included his opinion of the Istanbul police.

"Do you have any idea of John's whereabouts now?"

"I'm not sure anyone does," said Wilding. "Nil seemed to think he went to work for a private security service after he left the military. There are far too many to count these days. The Americans need an endless supply for their obligations in Afghanistan and Iraq. The British can use help, too. In any case, Nil thought John was far away and gone."

"Can you describe him physically?"

"The last time I saw him—" Wilding tossed himself into the past as if it were a place to jump from. "John is just above two meters in height. Average weight for his size with a good build. Fair complexion. Brown hair from his mother and pale eyes from his father."

"Pale?"

"Call them more gray than blue," he said. "A strange effect. I once saw a holographic postage stamp. Austrian, I think. It seemed to follow you around the room until you put it in the box. Something like that."

Although Levent did not think there was anything like that, he said nothing as the waitress returned with Wilding's order. It had been challenging for the kitchen to fill, but the results were worth the wait. The cappuccino was hot and frothing, the twin soufflés hot and steaming.

Wilding did not wait for the soufflé to cool. He addressed both like a man starving for calories—or a distraction. Levent waited until the Englishman had done his best work before coming to the question that Akbay wanted him to press.

"Tell me, Samuel, did you get a good look at your niece's bank accounts? I'm particularly interested in the Dubai account?"

"Good enough," he said.

"Do you remember if there were any recent large deposits?"

"I don't recall. Good enough does *not* mean I memorized the transactions."

"Then perhaps you could call the bank and find the answer," said Levent. "It's important, or I wouldn't ask."

He put his fork aside and looked at the raspberry swirls on his plate that spelled out the name of the cafe. As if he realized there could be sense in decoration, Wilding bobbed his head.

"You're asking about the last conversion Ayla made. The one you *think* she made."

"It's not my opinion," said Levent. "The man who handled the transaction was positive about every aspect of the conversion. He guaranteed a heavy count, and I told you how much it was. Eight hundred thousand dollars approximately. You really should have noticed, and I'm disappointed that you haven't."

Wilding shook his head as if he could shake the question. "I don't recall seeing anything like that as a recent deposit."

"Failing to recall isn't good enough, Samuel. You must do better. Please, call the bank."

"That's unnecessary," he said in a growl. "I'm *sure* the money was not there. Nothing had been deposited to Luna in the last three weeks."

The money. Something in the way Wilding phrased the words was revealing, as if currency had gone beyond itself. He did not want to admit the money was missing. Why? Because he wanted it back?

But how would he get it back? Had he written off the eight hundred thousand, or was he lying about everything that had to do with it? The last, unfortunately, had always been the best guess.

"Thank you, Samuel. You've been a great help."

CHAPTER 25

The Towers

The killer now had a name that could be traced. Levent called Akbay and told him to put Tekel's name through Passport Control and every less official place he could think of. Those were not as many as they had been. Few places asked for the identification of a man who spoke Turkish, and the ones that did could be put off with plastic cards in the name he had in his pocket.

Tekel had shown he would go far to avoid the usual places a visitor might be found. Levent gathered from Wilding that it would not be a surprise if Tekel had entered the country under a false name. Or had more than one identity in his pocket for the trip to his father's homeland. Levent wanted to know the surnames of his relatives, but Wilding said he could not supply them. Perhaps that was true.

Tekel might be wary of presenting himself to people he could not kill and abandon, but the killing definitely included relatives. The death of Ayla Acheson now fell into the most common category of murder. The domestic. This family quarrel had an unwholesome twist, but if Tekel had murdered his estranged half sister, a lot of things fell into place. From the beginning, the killer had known too much about his victim. Levent had wondered how Karanlik appeared on Acheson's ICQ, but that could be explained. She was Tekel's enemy, true, but only in the version given by Wilding. She might have been less. At one time, much less.

Levent knew that he followed an equation written by a man who was heavily involved in his niece's affairs, including her money. Wilding had every reason to have Tekel accept the blame. The story he laid down was perfect in outline.

Perhaps Wilding's movements would provide an answer. Levent had not yet received a report from the man who was following him, but would soon. At some point, Wilding's actions might require attention.

Levent parked on the street in Harbiye where a spot magically opened up. Emine said it was a sign of heavenly intervention when that happened in Istanbul. Levent hoped Ahmet Gunduz would open up as easily. He was said by his wife to await Levent's questions eagerly. Tara also made it clear she would not be present as a censor.

The office of Skyline Real Estate was newly renovated, and even more modern than new, with desks the shape of painter's palettes and startling counterbalanced bookcases. The oldest thing in the place was the secretary with gray hair who was the advertisement for Gunduz's good behavior at work. Levent wondered whom he was trying to misdirect. Certainly not his wife. His partners?

Those men were nowhere in sight as Levent entered the huge, megalomaniac office where only Gunduz sat. He did not get up to greet the police. He put his hands flat on his desk as if to rise, then slowly sank down for the insult. Things like that worked with the people he knew.

"Call me Ahmet, Inspector. Have a seat if you will."

Levent sat down in a plush spring-loaded chair before the desk.

Gunduz smiled as if he had won the first skirmish in a battle. "It's always good to meet the man who's responsible for your divorce even if he didn't take off his pants."

"She won't divorce you, Ahmet. Love conquers all unless the embarrassment is extreme. I know you won't allow that to continue."

He swiveled wide his Versace chair. Ahmet was a good-looking man, which counted. His fleshy mouth and heavy eyelids spoke of a clear sensuality and his dark brown eyes of a man in motion from his neck down. His ornaments were fine—Italian shoes and a Swiss watch with a pink band that matched the stripes of his shirt. His hair had thinned with the years, but it was cut short, baring the scalp that was deeply tanned. Their winter house was in Miami, and they occasionally occupied it together.

"I have my instructions," he said, steepling his fingers to prepare. "Ask any questions you like, Inspector."

Levent looked at the replica of the two towers that stood on a table near the window. Even in miniature they were impressive—black, phallic, and translucent. Istanbul architecture was always calculated to impress as it rose toward the heavens. Except for some hunchbacked slums scattered about the city, the entire population should have altitude sickness.

"Last year you attended a meeting in the Small Conference Room of the Marmara Hotel," said Levent abruptly. "I'd like to know the parties involved, what was discussed, and the decisions that were taken."

Gunduz was surprised by a question so exact. Plainly, he had been expecting room to maneuver as great as his office. "It was a strategy meeting," he said to end the pause. "We were setting out the scope of the corporation. You understand these things have to be done and roles settled beforehand."

"Then begin by telling me who's on the board of your corporation."

"I'm sure you'd recognize some of the names," he said. "They're among the best-known in the country. Tamer Bosh of Electric Textiles, Nihat Ferlanli of the Bodrum Group. Several others of the same prominence."

"I'd like a list."

"My secretary will provide it," he said with a nod toward the door. "The ones who serve on the board, that is. Two of the men at the meeting did not join us. They will remain nameless."

"Those two didn't like the odor?"

"There was no odor," he said with a flash of anger. "No one was under any compulsion, and some had better things to do."

"Who were the Mafia at the meeting?"

"There were none," he said in the same voice. "I don't know what you think was going on, but the men in that conference room would no more associate with Mafia than they would take their mistresses to their daughter's weddings."

"What about Diler Rasfar? How did he fit into the summit meeting?"

The first pertinent question brought hot color to Gunduz's cheeks, pushing through his tan. He turned to face his inquisitor directly, collapsing his fingers and drumming on the arm of his chair.

"He was a coordinator," said Gunduz as if that answered the question. "And not a great deal more."

"What did he coordinate?"

"The meeting," he said. "Of course."

"So he was a key figure. The organizer."

"I don't know what you're getting at," said Gunduz with frustration that showed how naive—or slow—he was. "Rasfar was a facilitator. He understood his position. The men at the meeting were such that he would never have been able to know them without my assistance."

"I understand that you put a good face on money laundering," said Levent. "But I want to know who Rasfar is and where he can be found."

Gunduz must have known that it would come to this question, but clearly he had not been able to invent a story to hold his basket of lies. For the first time, he sputtered. "I'll tell you what I can about him. Diler Rasfar was born an Iranian. He might have remained a citizen if the country had a sensible government, but we know that's not true. He carries a Moldavian passport, though I don't know how committed he is to spending time in his new homeland. He can usually be found in Chisinau and London these days."

"Where in those two cities?"

"I have numbers for him," said Gunduz. He buzzed the phone line of his secretary, asking her to look up the phone numbers and bring them in.

Levent did not wait for her appearance. "How did you meet Rasfar?"

"Through a friend," he said.

"Ayla Acheson?"

"Perhaps."

"Perhaps isn't your word for the day, Mister Gunduz. Your wife will tell you as much. You're in a great deal of trouble, and she knows it. Tell me about your relationship with Miss Acheson, and how you came to know Rasfar."

He went down the road to the past again like a map of Antarctica, as if nothing could be seen for lack of definition. The compass Levent had provided was clearly not one he liked. "Ayla and I became good friends about a year ago," he said. "We knew each other before, but not on the same basis. I'd rather not go into the details."

"Gentlemen don't talk about their lovers," said Levent with a smile. "But I can't believe your affair lasted long."

The implied insult made the color rise in him again. The man's problems with women were at the heart of his life. Unfortunately, they were not opportunities, though he saw them that way.

"No," he said. "The relationship didn't last. It was far too dangerous a connection to maintain for long. Tara and Ayla got to be friends—actually through me—and that made things impossible."

"But not impossible in a business sense."

"She came to me with a proposition," he said. "This was after we had gone our separate ways. There was nothing wrong in it that I could see. Ayla had access to considerable funds from outside the country and she wished to put them to work here."

"Put them to bed," said Levent. "Hide the traces."

"All right," he said as if he really was a businessman. "No one thinks money like that comes as clean as spring water, but who gives a damn in this country—even if he can afford to? Tamer Bosh, for instance, is not only the head of Elektrik Textiles but also a representative to Parliament for the current government."

"Yes," said Levent, who knew exactly where the stone wall began. "And these connections were what you brought to the table of the conference room."

"Others could have, I suppose."

He meant there were no others like him. It was true there were not many whose wives who ran a fair portion of the country. And he had seen the means to get out from under her hand in Ayla Acheson.

Just then his secretary, who was surely his resident brains, entered the room with a slip of paper that she handed to Gunduz across the wide desk. He received it and nodded to her like a servant. After waiting for her to clear the room, Gunduz passed the paper to Levent.

There were three phone numbers, complete with country codes, but Levent could not tell if any were cellular. He doubted it for the first London number because the note said Tri Cities, as if it was an entity.

"Tri Cities is what? A company in England?"

"Yes." Gunduz shrugged lazily. "They're in transportation, but I'm afraid I don't know as much about them as I should. Delir can be reached at their offices if he's in the country, but you're better off with the cellular number. It's the last."

"You're not very curious about the people you do business with," said Levent. "I would be. Your wife will be. My next call is to her."

Gunduz ran his fingers around the gozboncu embedded in the glass on his desktop. His defense against the Evil Eye was chic, an elliptical blue bead embellished with yellow horns.

"I can't prevent you from calling Tara," he said, circling his fingers. "All I can say is that Rasfar is a first-class manager. He was at the meeting to guarantee that a portion of the buildings would be financed from banks in Dubai. He provided those guarantees well enough to ease the minds of the partners."

"That wasn't his only function," said Levent. "You're providing a massive shelter for illegal money in those two towers. Rasfar, with the cooperation of Acheson, was bringing it into the country until the last day of her life."

Gunduz did not react to the statement. Perhaps the others did not trust him with a close knowledge of their transactions. That was a problem.

"What can I say, Inspector? People have the need to protect themselves."

"To protect their money."

"Exactly."

"And who protected Ayla Acheson?"

"A woman alone," he said, shaking his carefully barbered head. "I spoke to her about that same thing on several occasions. Granted, she never found the right man. But she should have had family around her."

So much for the instinct of Ahmet Gunduz. That mechanism was so faulty that Levent held no hope of finding a lead to the killer. But he would try.

"Did you ever hear Acheson mention the name of John Tekel?"

Gunduz laughed. "The only Tekel I know comes from a bottle."

"This is not your day for jokes either," said Levent. "I want you to think about what I asked. John Tekel is Acheson's brother through marriage. He lives in England, but is in this city now. And he's closely linked to her murder."

"I am thinking, Inspector. On Tekel, I have a definite no. But on a half brother, yes, I believe there's something."

Levent watched Gunduz as the messages from his body seemed to reach his brain without interference. "They were *not* on the best terms," he said finally. "I recall Ayla mentioned him—perhaps not by name—a couple of months ago. They'd been in touch for the first time in a while. He'd asked her if there was any possibility of returning here to work. He must have been out of a job, or planning a career move. She said she wasn't comfortable with the request, although she thought he could make his way here. Multi-lingual, I understand. And well-traveled."

The time line had begun to fall into place. Sibel said the victim had bought her weapon about three months ago. That was probably when Karanlik appeared in cyber-night like a ghost, or a hologram.

"Do you know if Acheson followed through on her relative's request?"

"I'm having trouble with that," said Gunduz. "Perhaps she didn't say. Or if she did, she referred him to someone else. Yes, that was probably it."

Tekel had gone through Atilla for the Volvo, but Levent did not think Atilla was the chief liaison man. That task would fall to someone more in command of himself and the business.

"In your opinion, to what person did Miss Acheson direct that job?"

"I don't know," he said. "People don't tell me as much as they should, and I will do something to correct that in the future. But if you're asking who *would* Ayla refer him to, that has an answer. Anything she did *not* want to deal with herself—jobs of small importance—she usually passed off to her partner."

"Faruk Duran?"

"Correct. Faruk wasn't worth much, she always said, but he could be counted on to shepherd old ladies and dogs. He's a bit scattered, yet easygoing when all's said and done. There's a story about him when he was starting his career as a tour guide. He was out in the East, talking to his group, telling them a certain mountain was, say, three thousand meters above sea level. One lady raised her hand and asked 'Yes, but which sea?' And Faruk, God bless his heart, didn't have the answer."

"I've been told that Duran's interest runs toward young men," said Levent.

"His interest runs in a direct line," said Gunduz archly. "The younger the better. If the half brother is handsome, I think he might be seeing a lot of Faruk. Perhaps more than he'd like."

"But you don't know if they have seen each other?"

"Ayla never told me," he said with a regret that wandered. "She was closed-mouthed in some ways. But I think Faruk has another boyfriend these days. I saw him on the street with his latest catch a couple of days ago."

"Who is he?"

"I don't recall the name," said Gunduz. "But I've seen him before. Good-looking boy. I believe he works in the office."

That would be Atilla. Damn it, but Levent should have known those two were on better terms than he thought. Now that he had confirmation, he did not plan to make the mistake again.

"Do you know where Duran lives?"

"It's not far from here," said Gunduz. "Just down the hill in Cihangir."

"I'll have his address from your secretary," said Levent, as he rose from the desk and walked quickly out the door.

CHAPTER 26

Cihangir

While Levent was still inside the building, he called Akbay and gave him the address of Duran's apartment. Another call to AylaTur told him that the surviving partner had not come to work in the morning, nor had he shown at the office at any time, though he had called in the morning to say he would be late.

Duran was very late at two-fifteen in the afternoon. Levent felt he was running against the clock. A madman roamed the city, while the people he had used to facilitate his crime ran free. And they would be smart if they did run.

Levent thought of Atilla and Duran as a unit now. They might not be found together, but they had been in touch. For a man like Atilla, money was the same as resources, and Duran had those. Duran needed a knowledge of the street to make his way clear. Atilla had that.

As he moved down the back street to Cihangir, Levent called a number he had not used in a while. Jason Ender was a member of the American State Department whose connections were wider than his job indicated. If he was in the U.S., he would be getting out of bed now, but Ender spent less time at home than any man Levent knew. They had worked a case together two years ago in Istanbul that resulted in a spectacular conclusion. Knowing Levent as he thought he did, Ender expected a repetition.

"What have you gotten into this time?"

"Not the usual," said Levent. "A woman was murdered, and the killer talks to us like your serial crazies do."

"What does he say?"

"He told me to look to the sky. I found so much there I was confused, but today I came across reference that sounds promising. Can you tell me anything about a transportation company called Tri-Cities? They may be Moldavian or English."

"Trip Cs," said Ender, lending unexpected depth to an abbreviation. "I can give you one reference. They're a private carrier operating out of England. Maybe Gatwick. The name is Tri-Cities Expeditors, but no one calls them that. After last week, they'll be called a whole lot worse."

"Why?"

"They're running a lot of cargo in and out of Iraq for us," he said. "It's high risk stuff. Until last week, everyone was wondering why they wanted the work. We learned the reason when one of their planes went off the runway in Baghdad. Some cargo was thrown around and broken open. What they found strewn around was about three million dollars. Probably more if you checked the pockets of the ground crews."

Levent liked what he heard. He had always been puzzled about the source of the money, thinking it was a chain of smuggled goods. If money was simply being moved, everything became clearer. It was money that would not like to be traced by account number. And at last, Levent had found what he should when he looked to the skies.

"Where does this money come from?"

"That's obscure now," said Ender. "They'll probably find out in time. When we first went into Iraq, the troops found tons of green. There's been a huge spike in the price of oil since. That means billions in oil revenue. From what I hear, the new government is more corrupt than Hussein at his worst. Many millions are already missing."

"And the money's hot."

"As hell."

"The British are in Basra," said Levent. "They were from the beginning."

"Our allies," said Ender. "The Coalition of the Just."

"We call them Crusaders. The Ninth Crusade, by our count."

Ender laughed, but not loud. "The Crusaders went home with their tails between their legs. All except those who managed to fill their pockets with loot."

"Again, it seems. But I'm puzzled about why the money wasn't shipped directly from Basra."

"They don't have an airport," he said. "There is one, but it never was much of a show and it was badly damaged in the invasion. The British haven't been able to get it back in operation."

"Three years later?"

"Is that criticism I hear?"

"It's disbelief," said Levent. "But I've come across some loose money here, and it seems to predate the invasion."

"So did Hussein," said Ender. "He had plenty of money managers when he was managing more than a jail cell. No one knows how much cash he trucked from the country to foreign banks. Probably billions."

"I'd like to know more about Tri-Cities," said Levent.

"I'll ask around," he said. "I can't promise anything, but it seems like nothing is what you have plenty of."

Not quite. Not any longer. Levent had a trail that led from Baghdad to Istanbul. One of the flights in Oz's list had come directly from Iraq. They must have been in a particular hurry that day.

* * *

Levent double-parked on the street two blocks from Duran's apartment on the wide boulevard that was the only open space in Cihangir. The rest of the streets were as narrow as any in the city, the roadways like walkways and the pavement a thin berm. Cihangir was one of the older sections of Istanbul, inhabited since Byzantine times or long before.

The street leading toward the water was so steep that Levent had trouble keeping his balance as he descended. He lost face when he turned sideways, digging his feet like skis into the slope, as two people passed going up the hill. Their sex was indeterminate, their hair chopped more than cut, and their clothing bizarre even for Cihangir, which was the Bohemia of Istanbul and the bedroom of its gay life.

All the houses on the street were old, but many had been restored. Duran's four-story building had the patina of the past overlaid with the modern—a weathered gray plaster with satellite dishes hanging at every angle. It sat at the verge of the cliff like an eerie with strange blisters.

Duran rented the top two floors. Everyone bought in this city, even the poor, but this man was used to running against the herd. Being gay in Istanbul was no ticket to the top. The wise man took his pleasures as privately as possible. And that was expensive.

For the money, something should have been done about the stench of cat piss that swarmed out of the alleys in superheated waves. Duran's building was no exception, with the smell of mildew and the ages overlaying the piss. A rubble of ruins from ancient times lay chock a bloc in places against the hill that overlooked the Bosporus, adding to the look of chic decay.

As Levent drew up to the courtyard of the building, he marked all possible escape routes. There seemed to be only one that led in the direction of the Golden Horn. Good.

He had rung for the kapiji to let him into the building when Akbay called saying he had arrived with three more men.

"Just wanted to check with you, boss," he said. "I took a call that claims a police inspector was raped on the street."

"Get down this hill now—and not in the car. Your brakes aren't good enough."

The kapiji came up the stairs from the basement as Levent shut down his cep. This man looked flighty, sporting a piratical mustache and a leather vest over his bare chest. He was either dirty or had just woken up, and did not complete the job until Levent showed his ID.

"Do you have the key to the two floor apartment at the top?"

"I used to," he said. "But that cunt changed the lock."

"I don't see outside stairs or fire escapes. Is there any way up there except by the inside?"

"If you can fly."

Leaving the kapiji at the door to let Akbay into the building, Levent began to climb the stairs to the double floor apartment, ignoring the old two-passenger elevator that would make a lot of noise going up. The marble steps were steep and worn like coins, growing less traveled until at the fourth floor they were nearly new. And there they stopped. The stairs leading to the fifth floor were inside the apartment and inaccessible to outsiders.

Duran could not be surprised by anyone, including the police. The door to Apartment Eight was an impressive slab of reinforced steel. One lock had been fixed to the handle and the other, separately, near eye level. Both looked new. Not unpickable, but trouble. It would take a full-scale effort to breach the apartment, though perhaps that was unnecessary.

When Levent heard Akbay and two other sets of shoes coming up the staircase, he rang the doorbell. And waited. Duran might have left for parts unknown, or he could be up on the top floor and making his way down.

He was not. Levent saw an eye flutter at the peephole. It did not linger and did not respond in any way. Levent knew something was wrong when he remembered that Duran's eyes were blue. Although it was hard to say for sure, the eye behind the peephole seemed to be darker. Probably brown.

Still, the door did not open. Although he was certain Duran was not on the other side inches away, Levent called out.

"Faruk! This is Inspector Levent! I want you to open the door now!"

The multiple shoes clambered up the stairs, gathering momentum. Akbay came onto the fourth floor first, followed by two men, both detectives, Kar from Burglary and Kemer from Homicide. At Levent's hand signal, they flattened against the wall on each side of the door.

"Faruk! You have to talk to me now! All your options are exhausted! The game is over!"

Still no response. The eye had disappeared, too. Not a graveyard eye, but one that was on the way.

"We'll break in if we have to!" said Levent. "It's your choice!"

"Don't try it!" said a voice that was not Duran's. "I have a gun! I'll use it to scatter his brains!"

The voice was muffled by the door, but Levent thought he recognized it. Akbay knew he did.

"It's our friend Atilla," he said. "The stud became a pussy after all."

It seemed so. Akbay had been right about Atilla from the beginning, going at him that first day not like a police detective but like a police dog. Akbay's instincts were usually good, and he trusted them all the way.

Was Levent losing something? If he had gone through the offices of AylaTur with a pickaxe that first day, the investigation would have found a quicker end. And the killer might already be theirs.

Now, not even Duran was. Atilla's threat had surely been directed at his boss. That was dicey. Losing either man was a loss, but it seemed as if the loss of Duran was more serious.

"Atilla, we have to talk!" said Levent. "I'm going to ring your cep! You'll answer because you don't want to die today!"

While Levent searched for Atilla's number in his directory, the door to the other duplex apartment on the floor opened. A woman appeared with hair that had last been seen on the dead. With a mouth wider than the breadth of her eyes, she spoke in a low nasal voice.

"Do you want to stop that racket?"

Akbay moved quickly across the hall to her. He had his pistol in his hand where she could see it, and he put it in front of his lips to hush her. "Easy now, ma'am. Just tell me if there's a way onto this fellow's terrace from your terrace."

She shook her head no, staring at the pistol, but spoke in contradiction. "I'm not a ma'am, and I suppose you could go over the wall. You'll need the skill of a monkey and the ass for it, too."

"That's a fair description of a Homicide detective," said Akbay as he turned back to Levent. "Give me five minutes! I'll get in there."

Levent waited until Akbay pushed through the door before he pressed the button for Atilla. It rang seven times, the seconds thickening like mud, before a familiar voice answered.

"I don't want to talk to you."

"Talk to me or talk to God," said Levent. "There's no other way, Atilla."

"Do you want to bet on that?"

"We're not betting here. What we have to do is get you out of there alive. And your employer, too. Let's remember all things are possible. I know you haven't killed anyone. I know you want to get on with your life."

"Just like that," he said. "A free ticket."

"I can't promise that, Atilla. If you help us, I'm willing to help you. That's the best I can offer."

"I'm not going to jail," he said in a voice that almost broke. "And that's what you have on your mind."

They all said that, but Levent had seen several men who meant it. He could not decide if Atilla was one. He knew the streets, which was almost the same as knowing prison. He could survive there if he survived today.

"You have information I want, Atilla. That means bargaining room. If you help us find John Tekel, I'll do my best to see you don't serve longer than you have to. You can believe that if you know anything about me."

"I don't," he said. "And I don't want to. A man who believes a cop is a damned fool and twice damned."

Levent was about to answer when he heard Atilla's voice rise to a shout that flew through the door. "Shut up!" he said. "Shut up you filthy faggot and don't say another word."

He was talking to Duran, who must have been trying to talk him down, too. That was not a good idea. Whatever had gone on between them ended when Atilla put a gun to Duran's head. And it had probably been nothing good.

"Give me something," said Levent. "Anything I can use. That's a beginning."

"Fuck you!" said Atilla, shouting into the phone. "This is the end of all of it. You're going to be the one who kills this sorry bastard I've got three feet from your face. And then what do you have?"

What Levent had to work with was Akbay's monkey skills. He had no idea if they existed, but of the ass he was sure. All Levent needed was more time to let those two things coordinate.

"It would be a start if you take that gun away from Duran's head," said Levent. "Is that what you want to do—kill an innocent man?"

"*Innocent?*" Atilla's voice rose hysterically to laughter. "This bag of shit is the reason we're here today."

"If what you say is true, there's no reason for you to kill him. We'll take care of Duran. We'll see that everything's put right and all the lies put aside. Now tell me why you think he's responsible for this trouble?"

"Because he ain't a man and he ain't a woman and he doesn't have the nerve of either," said Atilla in a tumble. "If you want to know how Ayla ended up choking on her own blood, you have to know who sold her like a harem girl out of the palace. He did it and gladly—did it for a low-life promise—thinking he could manage the business without getting out of bed too early in the morning. That's a joke, Levent. A stinking joke. The only thing he can do right is what he's doing now—and that's pissing himself!" Atilla whooped, loud, into the phone. "God, if it isn't running on the floor!"

Levent heard the glee and hatred in Atilla's voice, knowing they were the same. This was going to end soon, and for the worst unless Akbay got in that apartment.

"I'm sure it makes you feel good to see him like that," said Levent. "But it won't help anything now."

"It's helping me," he said. "You should see the color. Pure gold. It was her favorite. She put it everywhere to remind her of what's important. I'm sure she meant something else—something she could put in the bank—but in the end it all comes down to waste. You can't know that, can you, until you see it making puddles on the floor?"

"Atilla, listen, I'm going to tell you exactly what to do," said Levent with deliberate calm. "I want you to—"

His words were taken from him by three pistol shots that merged within a one count. The shots broke so close together that they might have come from the same weapon. It was hard to tell through the baffle of the door. Nine millimeter, probably. The police carried them. Everyone carried them.

And then Levent heard the sobbing.

CHAPTER 27

The Princess

Atilla had been hit twice, once low on the thigh and a second time in the chest. He was beyond questions, breathing in heavy gulps that only brought him pain. Levent wrapped the leg in strips of clean bed sheet, but nothing could be done about the chest wound until the ambulance arrived.

Atilla had gotten off one shot. He had not turned it on Duran, who stood inches from him. Instead, he brought his weapon onto Akbay, who stood at the base of the stairs that led down from the top floor. Atilla's shot went wild, like the man who squeezed it off, ripping a long gash in the banister. Akbay's answers under difficult conditions found the mark.

The weeping came from Duran, who had hoarded his emotions like a man under siege. Akbay made sure he did not return to a secure place. Duran was allowed to move to the nearest chair, but not far from where Atilla had fallen. Every time Duran closed his eyes, Akbay smacked him on the back of the head.

"Keep your eyes open and watch this man die," said Akbay. "I shot him, but I didn't kill him. That was your doing."

Duran said no, and what he said no to was unclear. He spoke the word repeatedly, as if he could say nothing else. But he could. And would.

"You might think you'll catch a break when the medics arrive, but I'll make sure you goddamned don't," said Akbay, smacking him on the head again. "If he's not dead by that time, I'll hoist you into the back of the ambulance, and you'll hold his hand all the way to the hospital. You'll watch him going to God, and you'll be right there every step of the way. Don't close your eyes! Look at him, you stinking son-of-a-bitch! Look at what you've done!"

"Please," said Duran. "I never thought anything like this could happen. Not in my home. In my . . . life."

They usually said that even when they did not piss their pants. Duran sat on the edge of the green velour chair with his leg—the right one—held out straight, as if he could not bear soiled fabric.

"What did you think?" asked Akbay. "That you could murder a woman in her home and not have it come back to you?"

"I didn't kill Ayla!" he said. "I had nothing to do with it. What you're saying is wrong. So wrong!"

"Tell me where John Tekel is and this will quickly be done," said Akbay. "Lie and you'll be as far gone as Atilla."

"I can't tell you that," he said, almost weeping again. "I never had anything to do with him. Only Atilla. That's the truth."

"Don't say that's the truth when you know it isn't!"

"But it is! It *is!*"

Levent did not believe him either. Duran had recognized Tekel's name instantly, but it was clear the process of divination would proceed step by step. And they would be as miserable as his life had become.

"Tell me what you had to do with Atilla," said Levent. "You're speaking for your life, so make it good."

Duran cheated. He turned his pale eyes away from the gore that was once Atilla's chest. He looked at Levent with pleading so rank it was like shock. It was probably that, too, revisited.

"I didn't begin this," he said, "no matter what you might have heard. Atilla came to me. To me *here*. One night, after I parked the car in the lot, I came upstairs and found him waiting in the hall."

"How did he get in the building?"

"I don't know," said Duran anxiously, not wanting to turn his eyes to the blood again. "The kapiji might have let him in."

"So he'd been here before," said Akbay. "A guest for the night."

"Yes."

"How many times?"

"It might have been three." Duran looked at Akbay. "Yes, it was three times, I'm sure."

"And he loved it," said Akbay. "I mean, you. He wanted to get married, settle down, have babies."

Duran looked at Levent again hopelessly. "I know it's great fun being hard on a queer," he said. "I've done it myself."

"*You?*" said Akbay. "You're the rankest queer in Cihangir. You'd take the kapiji to bed and have him beat your ass with his vest."

"I've done worse," said Duran humbly, slipping into the role of pity. "Denying nature is worse than you know. I was married when I was twenty to a young girl who was a guaranteed breeder. And I did my part for three years. The first man I went with was someone I knew. A cousin. When I saw him again, I turned my back and told the first person I saw that I thought the cousin had problems deciding which side of the fence he liked. But it wasn't he that had the problem. It was me. And I thought it was like that with Atilla."

"You knew which street he came from," said Levent. "He was a hustler before he found you."

"I understood that, of course," he said. "But I suppose it meant nothing under the circumstances. I thought if he was good enough for Ayla, he'd be better with me. Much better."

"He was used to being on top," said Akbay. "I don't know about you, but the size of that cock would put my asshole off."

"If you think that's what we do—"

"I don't care what you did in bed with Atilla," said Levent. "I want to know what happened when the lights came on. What did he say that made you betray your partner?"

Levent heard the sound of the elevator as it cranked up to the fourth floor. Duran heard it, too. He pretended not to notice, but the stillness of his head said he hoped for a distraction.

Before the elevator stopped, Levent slammed his hand down on the arm of the velour chair. "Answer my question!"

"It was *money*," he said hopelessly. "In the beginning, money. Atilla said we could have enough of it to last us the rest of our lives. He said Ayla would be getting a shipment of cash soon. And we could have it without raising a hand."

"How were you going to do that?"

Duran did not answer. Detective Kar opened the door, and three medical technicians from the emergency unit came through it carrying several bags and a collapsible stretcher.

"Bullet wounds," said Akbay. "The count is two."

They set to work immediately, one man on the leg and the others on the chest. Levent did not know if that was better or worse for Duran, but it was decidedly worse for the Inspector. After Atilla's shirt had been stripped away, the blood spread on the meat like a secondary blaze. A piece of white bone rose from the vicinity of his ribs. No, it seemed to wander.

Levent took Duran by the arm and lifted him from the chair, knowing he had begun to find a place where he could collect himself. Nothing about him seemed feminine, and now that the crying ceased, he rose from the chair like a man.

"Come with me," said Levent in a calm but not gentle voice.

Akbay stayed behind at Levent's signal as he walked with Duran from the main room of the apartment to an alcove that had been carved at the side from the larger space. It would have been a library if there were books, but it held nothing except two chairs slanted toward the Bosporus.

The view might have been worth the money Duran paid. Kiz Kulesi, the Princess Tower, sat on a small island that seemed to hover just off the water. Legend had it that a Byzantine Emperor built the tower for his daughter to keep her safe from harm. His plan had not worked well in the end, but this was Istanbul, where a good story was always better than facts.

"Please, have a seat."

Duran hitched up his soiled trousers again and sat in the overstuffed chair like a stubborn child who had been subdued. Levent did not take the other chair. He spoke in a low conversational voice, as if he did not want to be overheard. The stupid would call it fatherly, but Duran was not quite that. He had put his shock far enough behind him to put self-preservation first.

"You'll find you have plenty of time to work up a story with your lawyer, Faruk. All that will come later, and it's no concern of mine now. Frankly, I can see you as the victim in this mess.

Atilla was a hard case who looked for the main chance before he looked for anything that might be right. You know that now. I have no trouble believing he came to you with a proposition that must have seemed irresistible. I know he was in contact with John Tekel at least two weeks ago. I'd be willing to swear to that if it helps your case."

Duran nodded yes as his hand rubbed the back of his head. "My case," he said as if it was something he had found in the street. "Yes, I'm sure that would help. But why are you doing this?"

"You have information that will help us track Tekel," said Levent. "It may be buried in your memory, or your subconscious, but it's there. It could be something that requires a bit of interpretation. An educated guess."

Duran began to shake his head until he realized that was an unproductive way to explore his future. "I'm thinking, Inspector. It wasn't until a week ago that I even knew that man existed. Atilla kept him completely to himself."

"Let's say I believe you, Faruk. Atilla was Tekel's contact. That's plausible and should make sense to the court. But how did you find out that a delivery of money was about to enter the country?"

Duran was obviously trying to devise an explanation that pushed his participation to the distant margins. He seemed to find what he wanted after a cursory search. "I discovered that quite by accident," he said. "I took a call from her uncle about a week ago. He said that Ayla should call him back on a matter of importance. It had to do with an accelerated schedule, he said."

"For a delivery of money?"

"I took it to mean that, yes. As you know, I was aware of what Ayla was doing by then. I asked Samuel if there was anything I could do to help. He said no, but I was to tell Ayla that something unfortunate had happened. The matter demanded immediate attention."

"Why didn't he call her cellular?"

"He tried, but couldn't raise her. He hoped she might be in the office. I don't think he meant to say as much as he did, but we knew each other, and I like to think he trusted me."

That was his mistake, but it confirmed what Levent suspected. Wilding was involved in the smuggling scheme with all his consulting skills. It would not be a surprise to find him on the Tri-Cities Board of Directors, along with Rasfar.

"So you had an approximate date for the delivery," said Levent. "You must have tried to pin it down."

"Atilla wanted me to keep close track of Ayla's movements," he said. "That wasn't easy in the best times, but it became more difficult when she began to stay at her summer place. So I wasn't very successful. I told Atilla I simply couldn't keep an eye on her well enough."

"He didn't believe you?"

"He insisted I give him time off to do the job on his own," said Duran, as if his subordinates usually got the better of him. "I know what that sounds like, but I was aware that I wasn't in control of the situation at the time. I wasn't in control of Atilla at all, though I thought I could be. I probably never would have been involved if he hadn't been so willing to meet me after hours. But he did, and I believed him because of the things that passed between us. So when he left the office at odd times, I covered for his absence. Two days before the murder, he took a call from a friend who worked in the money market at the bazaar. And I covered his absence that time, too. Let's say I knew of the arrangement, because spies have to be paid. Atilla borrowed some money from me to reimburse his man."

"It doesn't seem to have worked out well for Atilla. What happened? Was the friend late with the information."

"Apparently."

"So it became necessary to obtain the information from Acheson."

"I hate to keep agreeing with things I never knew, but yes, that seems to be true." Duran looked at his trousers, which were returning to their natural state, as everything did with time. "You have to believe I never knew who was going to retrieve the money. As Atilla described it, no one would suffer. Robbery is robbery, and when the money is illegal, it should be difficult going to the police."

"The only thing you really had to worry about was each other," said Levent. "It seems you should have."

"Yes."

"You should have been worried about John Tekel, too," said Levent. "He's a killer's killer. If he left you alive behind his back, there must have been a good reason."

"Atilla was the reason," said Duran. "He helped the man with information, a car, and God knows what else."

Levent wanted to know exactly what else, but he looked up when an organized commotion began at his back. The medical team had loaded Atilla onto the stretcher and had begun moving him toward the door. Akbay did not follow, but Kar, Kemer, and finally Levent did.

"Still alive?" he asked the man at the foot of the stretcher.

"He shouldn't be."

"But he's young," said Levent. "Strong."

"That's what he's got to get him through."

Levent watched them pass out of the door to the elevator, wondering how they would fit all that bulk into the miniature machine. They would, he knew. They would do everything they could to save a homicidal man. But Atilla wasn't that now.

His lover had watched the departure with interest fused with self-interest. Levent was sure Duran overheard the words, and that he had begun to understand what it could mean for him.

Levent sat down in the second chair turned to the Bosporus. He said nothing as he watched the blue water churn toward the Marmara Sea, swarming beyond the Princess Tower.

"Do you think Atilla will—"

"I don't know," said Levent. "No one can."

"Well, I hope he does, of course."

"I'm sure you do," said Levent. "But your hope will be in exactly the wrong place if he survives. The man who regains consciousness in a hospital room knows he isn't with God. The policeman sitting at the foot of the bed tells him so. Shortly, someone will appear to take his statement."

"But what can he say?"

"That isn't the question to ask," said Levent. "Think of what he'll say that will differ from what you've said. And think how it can be used against you."

Duran put his face stubbornly toward the water and the island tower, as if it held the answer in a princess. Not much time passed before he knew there would be none. He turned back to Levent again with bright lonely eyes.

"So we wait."

"You'll have to wait—and it could be longer than you think," said Levent. "I have a killer to find. Whether Atilla recovers or not, your best chance is to help me do that, and do it quickly."

"I told you I don't know where he is."

"And I asked you to search your mind for—let's call it a clue."

Duran nodded tentatively. "Something that requires inter-pretation," he said. "An educated guess."

"That should be good enough."

After a pause to find the right thing among so many wrong ones, Duran spoke to the point. "Atilla took a call yesterday evening. I could tell it was important, because he left the room after he exchanged greetings. I didn't eavesdrop, but I was curi-ous about something he wanted to keep away from me. You know what it's like when you're with someone new."

"With Atilla, no, I don't. But go on."

"The problem is that he didn't say much, at least not that I overheard. He told the person he was talking to that he didn't know. He said that twice. But he said yes, he would find out if possible."

Levent said, "That's all?"

"Not quite," said Duran, adjusting the total. "When Atilla returned to the room, he was quiet for a while, then we began to talk about the future. The firm. How everything was going to be afterward. Gradually, Atilla began to ask questions about Ayla. It was as if he hardly knew her, and perhaps he didn't want me to know how well he really had. I tried to answer his questions. In retrospect, I can see that two of them may have meant something."

Levent was sure they all did, but he would play by the rules of this game a little longer. "What were those?"

"He wanted to know about Ayla's relatives here," said Duran as if that had puzzled him and still did. "Her mother was Turkish, and of course she left some people in this country. I'm afraid I wasn't as helpful to Atilla as I might have been. In fact, I've known one of Ayla's aunts for years. She's a nice woman, and I didn't want to involve her in anything, well, questionable."

"So you didn't tell him about the aunt," said Levent. "Who did you put out as bait?"

Duran did not like the phrasing. He backed off before he came at the truth less directly. "It wasn't like that at all, Inspector. It was just a quiet conversation. But Atilla persisted, and eventually I gave him the name of another of Ayla's cousin who lives in Florya."

"Who is he?"

"Ibrahim Gurman."

"Tell me what you know about him. Everything."

"He's a man of about forty years and well kept," said Duran. "He wears glasses by Fred, if you know what I mean. Four hundred dollars an eye without the frames. He has an active social life, and he works in banking. For the last couple of years, he's been the manager at a local branch of Luna Bank. It's not far from his home, and he doesn't venture far from it for anything important."

This was the second time Levent had heard of that international bank in connection with the victim's family. It might be the last.

"Does Gurman live alone?"

"Yes."

"Is he like you?"

"Somewhat," said Duran with a knowledgeable smile. "He pretends not to be, and he's known as quite the lady's man by everyone who knows nothing. He has a servant who comes in twice a week to cook. He says he can't bear to get rid of her, because he could never find another to make *imam bayildi* like that. There are people who believe him."

As Levent listened to Duran's lies, wondering what catfight put Gurman first on the list, he took out his cep. Before Duran finished speaking, Levent had connected with Bakirkoy District, and Inspector Baran, a man he knew well.

"I want you to look in on the Luna Bank branch in Yeshilyurt and a branch manager named Ibrahim Gurman. If he's not there, call on his home in Florya. Get back to me at once. This is top priority. Put everything else aside."

Levent snapped the phone shut with Baran's demand for an IOU still in his ears. But he would do what had been asked.

"Now what of the second thing, Faruk?"

"Less interesting," he said. "At least, I thought so then. Atilla wanted to know the name of a hotel where a man could keep himself safe. A place where they wouldn't ask questions. I didn't want to give him the information, because I thought he might use it for his own purposes. But of course I did, after a while."

"The name?"

"I could have given him ten," said Duran. "But I told him to try Pension Chisinau in Laleli. I also gave him the name of the manager there."

CHAPTER 28

Hera PLC

Levent left Duran with Akbay, who was sure he would have more information from the suspect after they got to know each other. "We use the same aftershave lotion," he said. "Who knows what else we share?"

Levent thought Akbay would do well with Duran, but slowly and in small pieces that would allow Tekel to make his way out of the country at his leisure. In the meantime, Levent borrowed a car from Kemer of Homicide and set off down the seaside road in the direction of his two leads. He was halfway along in the southbound lanes, checking the time and knowing the business day had ended, when he received a call from Inspector Baran at the bank.

"I'm here, and I've got the important staff to remain past closing," he said. "I don't think you'll be happy to know that Ibrahim Gurman did *not* report for work today. It's said to be unusual, though not highly unusual."

That was bad news, but Levent was more concerned with the time line. He did not understand this trend of events. If Atilla had talked to Tekel last night, giving him information he was sure to act upon, he should have done it quickly. And if Ayla Acheson kept an account with her cousin at his bank, Gurman should have appeared to access it. But there was another possibility that was worse. Gurman might have been able to get into the account another way.

"I want you to have them check all the accounts that Gurman handles personally," said Levent. "He could be able to get into them without showing his face. We're looking for any large withdrawals that were made today."

"How large?"

"Half a million dollars or more."

Baran's murmur said he was impressed by the scale. "All right, Onur. I'll have them look under the hood and check the tires. Something as big as that should have a smell, too."

"What did you get from Gurman's home in Florya."

"Nothing so far," said Baran. "He doesn't seem to be there. At least he doesn't answer his door."

"Break in the door."

Baran's pause was long, ending in an uncharacteristic sigh. "Maybe I should call the Chief."

"Do what you like, but do it fast, friend."

Baran said he would, and not to worry about getting to the bank. He would stay on, holding the key personnel, until Levent arrived.

Levent was glad he had someone as steady as Baran to hold things down there. Since he was at the turn to Laleli, he took it in rhythm, heading into traffic that was not as it bad as it would be. He told Kar and Kemer, who were following in their car, to continue south to help Baran.

Levent found Pension Chisinau three blocks off the main boulevard in the hotel district that catered to tourists of the second class. Although much of the clientele came from the Russian states and the Balkans, Levent knew enough now not to put too much weight on those locations. He was sure the contraband money had come from Iraq in a line that was anything but straight. Scattering the origin between Baghdad and Istanbul was an inconvenience determined by the need for secrecy.

Tall and pale green, Pension Chisinau looked as if it had been built as a grain silo for one of those hard winters that occasionally came from north. The front of the building and the lobby had been remodeled in the last five years, sealing everything in plastic and smoked glass.

That included the thin man behind the desk, who was not the manager known to Duran. His dark face and darker eyes moved to the rhythm of the calendar. Once a week for a shave, and for a bath, seasonal.

"Do you expect me to remember everyone who comes through the doors?" he asked as if he could do exactly that for the right price. "This place gets a plane load of traffic every day."

"Put the whores aside," said Levent. "I'm looking for a man just over two meters tall or better, with medium brown hair and a fair complexion. He speaks Turkish, but not quite like a native."

"That's half the hotel on an average day," he said. "The other half is the whores. Some of them are Moldavian, if you're interested. Good looking and skillful. You can rent or you can buy."

Levent made a note to return to this hotel sometime and bust this man down to his shoes, which were pale green. "Let's try something else," he said. "The man's eyes. Everyone who's seen them thinks they're looking at frozen food. They'd be a long time dead if they weren't so deep in the freezer."

"Oh, sure," he said. "That one. He came in yesterday evening."

Levent took the guest book on the counter, turning it to read the register. "What name did he use?"

The clerk put his finger less than halfway down the page. "There he is, between Natasha and Natasha."

The name Tekel had chosen for his alias was Volkan Bir. Volcano One. Again, the show-off. The boy who loved his sister was the man who loved himself to the exclusion of everyone else. He seemed to be saying that he was the original eruption—the one that spewed death. And Tekel did say things, especially if he thought the police would come across them.

"Did he check out of the hotel?"

"This morning without a bag," said the clerk. "I can't tell you if he came with one because I wasn't on the desk last night."

"What time did he leave?"

"It wasn't long after I came on duty. About nine or nine-thirty."

Not an early riser for a man who meant to raid a bank. But he hadn't done that, had he? Not in an obvious way.

"Did he have a car?"

"A blue one, but I can't tell you the make," said the clerk. "Bright blue. You see a lot of that color around here—and none of it's natural."

Levent left the hotel knowing he was close. Tekel's lead had shrunk to less than a day, and he had kept the car that he stole from Tarabya. A mistake. If they could pin him down to an area, they might spot the car. And they might be able to narrow the area soon.

Back in traffic and fighting to stay ahead of the rush, Levent heard his phone ring in his coat. He had to answer, but moved into the fast lanes that opened for southbound commuters before taking the call.

"Detective Topuz here, Inspector. I'm the one following this man Wilding. You said you wanted to know if anything out of the ordinary happened."

"Absolutely."

"I could use some help with this tail," he said. "About ten minutes ago, Wilding picked up two men at Taksim who came by taxi from the airport. I don't like their looks. I mean, you'd like them if you were looking for trouble, but nothing else. Big and taking up space. I'm sure you know the kind."

"I'm sure you're right, Hakan. Three sets of eyes will make it easier to spot you, especially if they know what they're doing."

"They know pretty well," said Topuz. "I could see the biggest one scanning for visitors while he put his baggage into Wilding's car. I'd say it's a matter of time before they know I'm here."

"Call headquarters for some men in cars," said Levent. "Tell them this is my case and it has priority."

"Yes, sir."

"Where are you now?"

"We're in traffic coming to the bridge from the Golden Horn," he said. "They must be headed south, though that's just a guess. If they wanted to head another way, they should have gone over the hill."

So they were at Levent's back by twenty minutes. That was almost too close. But if they were heading south, they probably knew something would happen there. That was the direction everyone, including Tekel, seemed to favor.

"Don't let them spot you," said Levent. "Tell headquarters to have someone from Sultanahmet or Bakirkoy relieve you. Switch the look as often as you can."

"I'll try, Inspector."

"And give me five minute progress reports."

"You'll have them."

* * *

Levent arrived at Luna Bank in Yeshilyurt to find Inspector Baran still examining the accounts that had been accessed today. He had found nothing so far that matched the money the victim had exchanged in the money market two days before her death.

Nor had Baran found Ibrahim Gurman. The men he sent to Gurman's home in Florya had made their way into the apartment without demolishing it, but found no trace of the man. For the time being, it seemed that Gurman had disappeared without extracting money from Luna's accounts.

Levent was puzzled by those facts, or the lack of them. Bank activity had closed for the day, though Baran made sure that two of Gurman's assistants did not leave. Levent used the time to ask questions of the assistants that Baran did not have the background to put forward.

Neither of the young women had anything critical to say about their supervisor. Gurman was a model of consideration atypical of any man they had previously worked for. Everything they said confirmed what Faruk Duran had told Levent in less generous terms about Gurman's predilections. Atypical seemed to mean uninterested in women in this sort of code.

Levent was looking for a link to where Gurman might have taken himself all day, and how he spent the time. His questions brought no leading answers from any of the bank personnel. It was not until Levent received a call from the four-man team now following Wilding that he thought to ask the proper question.

They said Wilding's destination did not seem to have changed. He was still driving south, less than five minutes from the bank unless he made a detour.

Where was Wilding headed? Not to a bank that had closed for the day. Apparently not to Gurman's home, though that was still possible. To this area? That seemed more likely. One of Gurman's assistants might be able to point to a destination.

"Do you know any of Mister Gurman's friends in Yeshilyurt?"

Berna Taner, Gurman's first assistant, worked at one of the corner slabs of desk near the back of the long deep room. She was in her thirties, with a banker's pinstriped suit, a woman's bouffant blouse, and a manner that marked her as fiscally responsible but not entirely boring.

"I really don't know of any friends in this area, Inspector. Mister Gurman kept his private life separate from his work. In that way he was a bit strange. Perhaps you'd have better luck asking at his home."

"Are you sure he had no friends here?" asked Levent. "Someone he lunched with perhaps?"

"I'm not aware of them, sir. We always go out to eat at different times so we don't leave the desks unattended."

Conscientious. The virtues of banking were often at odds with the needs of the police. That was understandable but annoying.

"What about relatives?" asked Levent. "Does Gurman have any nearby?"

"Just his cousin," said Taner as if it was of no consequence. "She came in the office from time to time, so I do know her. She has an account here, but I think her visits were more in the way of paying respects to Mister Gurman."

"Her name?"

"Emel Demir. She lives on the seaside road."

"Her address?"

"I don't know the number, but I can tell you where it is."

"Please," said Levent. "And while you're at it, check her account to see if any deposits or withdrawals occurred in the past week."

Levent noted the address while the second assistant searched the Demir account. The computer quickly found that Gurman's cousin was associated with more than one account. The first was in her name, but the second had overdraft links with a company called Hera PLC. That was a plain advertisement for Ayla Acheson.

"Get into that account."

Levent watched as the computer churned, and the screen began to fill with dates and numbers. The account of Hera PLC had been opened three weeks ago with an initial deposit of five hundred dollars. Six days ago—the day after Acheson made her last conversion in the money market—more than seven hundred thousand dollars had been deposited in the account. That was a bit shy of the total, but perhaps the rest had gone to one of her causes.

Today, however, the money had been withdrawn. The Emel Demir-Hera PLC account had seen three separate withdrawals, the first at 12:33, the second at 2:09, and the third, less than forty-five minutes ago. By the end of the day, the account was flat. Even the original five hundred dollars had disappeared.

"Could Mister Gurman have made the withdrawals?"

"It's possible, Inspector." She shook her head slowly like many did when they looked into the past and saw gross possibilities for error. "He has his own computer, and it can link to the system. He shouldn't do something like this, however. It would have been against regulations in the old days, but now that we've become part of a large international bank—"

But he had done it repeatedly. "Has Mister Gurman ever done anything like this before?"

"Not that I'm aware of, sir."

"Why would three transactions be made instead of simply one?"

"I imagine it's so they wouldn't draw notice," said the second assistant. "The computer flags any transactions over five hundred thousand dollars. They're brought up for review at the central office. A safety measure."

A bank officer would know that, and he would know exactly how to circumvent the restrictions. The question of why Gurman did that had only one answer Levent could imagine.

"Where did the money go?"

"Just a moment."

The second assistant traced the destination of the money with a sequence of keystrokes that required two sets of code names and passwords. She found what Levent had asked for with a flourish, bringing up a screen that was a surreptitious map of the banking world.

"It was transferred to another Luna account," she said, pointing to a coded series of numbers at the bottom. "The same account each time. In Amsterdam."

CHAPTER 29

Convergence

Levent, with Baran and three of his men, left the bank in separate cars for the apartment of Gurman's cousin. As they sped along the central shopping street, Levent called for a tactical unit to meet them at the apartment. Several officers were usually stationed at the airport ten minutes away. They should be able to converge quickly.

The building overlooked the Sea of Marmara with the shoreline street and a strip of green land intervening. The basement level was recessed several meters below the street, so the second floor apartment of Emel Demir did not stand high off the ground. It should be possible to gain entrance through the balcony for a man with monkey skills. Levent would have some of those on hand soon, but did not want to wait for their appearance.

After telling Baran's men to cover the street front and back, Levent rang the building's kapiji. No response. Starting with the ground floor and ringing every bell except the second floor apartment, he finally received an answer from the fifth. Yes, the police could be let into the building after the owner came down from the top floor to verify who they were.

Levent waited impatiently before he heard the elevator bump to a stop in the lobby. When the front door opened, he pushed past a woman of fifty years, or sixty without the makeup.

"Get back to your apartment and don't come out until we tell you to. Call all the neighbors and tell them the same. All but Emel Demir."

Levent left her sputtering in outrage and confusion. With Baran, he moved up the staircase that seemed never to have been used. At the landing were two apartments with Demir's on the right.

Not a steel door, but thick wood and recent. Like the building, it was not old or new. Just an expensive place with a view—or an expensive place to die. That might have happened already.

Levent punched in the number he had been given for Demir. He expected no answer and did not have a quick one. As he waited, he thought of the paintings he had seen at the gallery where he met Tara Gunduz. The strange dimensions. And the intrusions of one into the other.

Geniuses and lunatics homed on frequencies that were not available to the rest of us. What they found was chaos, and only the best made sense of it. The others plucked out eyes so they could see.

On the tenth ring, Levent closed the phone. He punched the doorbell, standing well to the side in the hall.

Three rings and nothing. Levent took his pistol from the holster. He was preparing to do something he had never done before—blow the lock on a door—when two people in dark uniforms bounded up the stairs.

Tactical. Levent knew the first officer. Her name was Ferhan, and she was the most beautiful woman on the force. In a trained unit of hard-asses only, she was one of the hardest and the only officer with a shield on her helmet that matched the red patch on her shoulder.

"What's the problem?"

"The door," said Levent. "A killer may be on the other side. Or his victims."

"Stand aside, Inspector. This is what we do."

When her partner turned his back, she went into the pack he carried. Along with a detonator, she took out a length of detcord and a charge of explosive. After shaping the charge to the lock, she strapped on her helmet and stepped back.

"This shouldn't hurt your ears," she said, holding the detonator in her hand and a machine pistol in the other.

Levent turned aside as the explosive suddenly jumped. Before the sequence had ended, Ferhan's partner kicked open the door.

Ladies first. She went in without hesitation, skimming to the left and dropping to the floor, then rolling as her partner dropped and rolled to the right. With no return from the interior of the apartment, they were up quickly, moving down the short hall-way that led to the main room.

Levent and Baran followed close behind. There were no sounds in the place, and no feeling that it was occupied. A weak pulse of light peeped from the front rooms that faced the sea, but nothing could be seen. Not even a shadow.

Especially not that. Levent stopped at the entrance to the main room. He saw nothing to indicate that he had found a slaughterhouse again. The room was large, chairs and couches, a television and a sound system, along with one bookcase set mostly with bric-a-brac.

Ferhan and her partner were already moving into the back of the apartment in murky light. Silently, they began to check out the bedrooms and baths. Most of the doors were open for a quick look and clearance. They encountered no resistance all the way down the long hall.

Levent waited for the signal at the last door before he crossed the main room. On the far side in front of the sideboard was a long dining table that filled most of the space. Only guests were invited here. And there had been one recently.

On the table sat a laptop computer with its hood open and the power supply still plugged into the wall. Turkish-made, the equipment and operating system were current—EXP with a picture of the calcified mountain of Pamukkale as wallpaper. Weird. All white and all innocence.

But the machine did not look like a professional model. If this computer had been used to transfer the bank money to Amsterdam, it should have a special interface and programs. He saw nothing like that on the desktop.

When Levent looked closer, he noticed a small rectangle pinned to the side of the screen. It was a Windows Note with text so small he could not read the words.

Levent expanded the note. Quickly, it became clear who had written the words. Tekel had paused on his bloody path to leave a message behind. A taunt. Another taunt from this digital killer:

Inspector:

By the time you find this, I'll be
having a drink at your expense.
I told you to look to the sky, where
all good things come from, and
you've kept your nose to the ground.
You're a fool for a detective.

I deserve better.

Volkan Bir

So he liked the alias he had left behind at the hotel for his
audience to discover. He liked masks, starting with the appearance of Karanlik. Did the man have a problem with his identity?

No. He knew who he was, and what. He loved what he was
except during those infinite times when he despised himself. That
must be confusing for him, and it was hell for Levent. All he
could really say was that being late with John Tekel was like missing
a commuter flight to Mars.

It was just too bad the communication was one way this time.
Levent had something to say in return.

Greetings, John. I understand how you feel. You think the
game is over, and you have a need to crow.

But know this, prick. When you get where you're going, and
you try to pay for that drink, you'll have to go into your pocket.

Because your account in Amsterdam has been frozen. And
everything you've done will be for nothing.

CHAPTER 30

Patterns

No bodies were found in the apartment. Not even the smallest trace of blood. Tekel had been in this place and gone. That meant he had broken his pattern. He must have taken at least one person—Ibrahim Gurman—and possibly Gurman's cousin if she had been at home. Now his hands were full.

Very full.

Levent wanted to call it another mistake by a desperate man, but Tekel had never been predictable. Unless something broke quickly, Levent had nothing to do but back up and find a thread that would lead him to the next move. Some had been left behind, but all would take time to unravel.

Levent had Baran pull every available man into the area, telling them to look for a sign of the killer or his car. They were still behind Tekel, but the gap had closed to less than an hour.

As he stood on the balcony of Demir's apartment, a call came from the detective following Wilding. Topuz had checked in twice, the last time to say that Wilding's party had stopped at the airport, where they picked up a fourth man. Although Levent was not sure from the description, the addition could be the Iranian, Diler Rasfar.

"We seem to have a destination," said Topuz. "Wilding and his men left the car in the street that leads down to the harbor. They're headed that way with no doubt. I can have him cited for a parking violation or stay close."

"Don't close on him, but don't lose him. I'll meet you at the harbor in five minutes. I want to know exactly what he does."

"I have three men from Bakirkoy for surveillance. It shouldn't be hard."

Levent always worried when they said that. Four men could vanish, especially if two of them had been trained to spot

segurança

surveillance. Why they were headed for the harbor would become clear quickly.

Levent left Baran's men at the apartment to question Demir's neighbors, and to cover if something turned up later. Tekel probably would not backtrack, especially since he had left the note, but this was not the time to guess.

With Baran and the two Tacs, Levent drove his car to the harbor along the shore road. It would have taken five minutes except for the beginning of rush hour. When he grew frustrated, Levent put up the flasher, but did not go to the siren, as he fought traffic in crowded streets.

They were nearly to the harbor, pulling to the curb a block from the water, when Baran's phone rang.

"Yes, that's the one," said the Inspector. "Good work."

"They found the blue Astra," said Baran to Levent. "In an alley three blocks from here." Baran pointed to a large low building in the near distance with two fish restaurants on the bottom floors. "It's behind that place. Do you want to look at it?"

"Not now," said Levent. "Tell them to watch the car, but don't be conspicuous. He could be anywhere in the vicinity. I don't want to scare him off."

Levent knew the alley behind the restaurants. Wide enough to put one car to the wall with room for traffic to pass. Probably Gurman, who would know the area well, had told Tekel to use the alley to park and hide.

As he moved down to the harbor on foot, Baran and the Tacs following, Levent tried to calculate the sequence of events. Tekel had a reason for coming to the harbor area, and nothing said he had to confine his activity to land. He might have gone onto the water. A little lead time was all he needed.

That guess became more likely when Levent received an update from Topuz. "We're at the marina near the end of the harbor. This looks like a decision point. Wilding and his two men just went on board a small cruiser."

"Local?"

"It looks that way. Do you want us to invite them to tea?"

Levent hesitated. If Wilding got on the water, they might not see him again. The Sea of Marmara was open to every body of water in the country, including the Aegean. The last could put them out of the country.

But Levent decided the risk was acceptable. They might be able to run down Wilding's boat even if he made the water. There was a chance—a good chance—Wilding knew where he was going. And that meant he knew where Tekel would go.

"Let them run."

"Sir?"

"Do what I said. We're right behind you."

Levent saw the marina ahead, clustered on the sweep of the harbor. Scanning closer, he saw Topuz at the end of the jetty as he raised his hand to locate. He did not point out Wilding's location, but that was fine. The direction at this time of day was mostly one way—into port.

Quite a few boats were tied up at the marina, rocking on their moorings in a quiet wind, but none had begun to move out yet. Levent picked up the pace along the waterfront, drawing within a hundred meters of Topuz and the two men who had taken staggered positions along the breakwater. They were not easy to spot.

Using Topuz as his marker, Levent saw the boat Wilding and his men had boarded, a fairly new cabin cruiser flying the Turkish flag. It probably worked for fishing hires or day trips to local destinations, and it would have some speed.

As he moved, Levent went to his phone to call the Coast Guard. He anticipated trouble getting them to move at the order of a police inspector, but Levent made it clear he was speaking for the Chief. The man who answered the emergency number immediately switched to his supervisor.

"We don't have a boat in that area," he said. "The nearest one is around Yenikoy. They might be able to make your position in ten to fifteen minutes."

"This is a priority that could become a chase," said Levent. "I'm sure the vessel can be here faster if you tell them that."

"Damn, but I never hear from you people to say hello. I'll do what I can."

"The name is Levent. Inspector Onur Levent. And I pay my debts."

"I'll file that under bullshit. We'll see what it turns into."

A pumpkin, Levent hoped. He would give a lot to see one of those Orange and Whites roaring into the harbor. They were faster than anything else on the water because they had to be.

Any Coast Guard vessel was faster than the cruiser called the Poyraz. Levent saw the name on the stern at the same time as he saw its passengers. Wilding, tall and slim, stood near the wheel with a shorter man who fit the description of Rasfar. They were talking to the captain. He looked like a Turk, which meant he would do what he was paid to do and not ask questions if the price was right.

Levent stopped beside the fish seller who had set up a row of boxes on the pavement. He did not think he could be seen from the boat among the small crowd that gathered to examine the catch. Salmon, young blue fish, sea bass. None were fresh, but the buyers did not seem to notice.

"Go to the end of the jetty," said Levent to the two Tacs. "The Coast Guard vessel will be coming in, and I want you to be the first thing she sees."

They continued walking toward the end of the long jetty. Now Levent saw the other two men aboard the Poyraz as they came round to the stern. Both were as Topuz had described—as tall as Wilding, but thicker through the shoulders. Each man carried his coat bunched tightly in his hands, as if it was important not to leave them behind.

Levent wondered what was in them. He did not think they had gotten into the country with weapons, but Wilding had thought his way this far into the game. A man with resources could find firepower here.

What Levent needed was to squeeze out some time before the Poyraz put to sea. He watched the vessel closely as he punched up Wilding's cellular number. On the first ring, Wilding's head turned to the right and downward, looking to the belt that held his cep. He stared at it for three rings, making no move but weighing a move as if it were the most important thing in life. Quickly then, his hand reached to his belt.

"Wilding here."

"Samuel, it's Onur Levent. Inspector Levent. I'm glad to hear you're still in the country."

"Yes, Inspector," he said, looking back toward the harbor as if he sensed the call came from close by. "I'd say I was enjoying my stay if conditions were different. The sea looks very inviting today from my hotel."

"Yes, it usually looks very good when poyraz blows from the north," said Levent. "It's the southern wind, lodos, that we have problems with."

"I'll take your word," he said. "Is there something you have for me?"

"Yes," said Levent. "I wanted to tell you that we have a line on the killer. We should have him shortly."

"You saw him?"

"It's John Tekel. He's been a suspect since I heard his name from you. When I heard his story, things began to fall into place. We have him headed south toward the airport. If he has a flight out, it's a flight to jail."

Wilding took a step away from the captain at the helm. He made a two hundred and fifty degree turn, looking toward land, but not as if he sensed something wrong. The Tacs were behind his line-of-sight, moving up the jetty.

"That's very good news, Inspector. You'll let me know when you have him in custody."

He had forgotten to show surprise at the identity of the killer. He had not thought of anything but hanging up the phone. "I certainly will keep you informed," said Levent. "I know how much you want this man. I was afraid you might decide to pursue him on your own."

"No chance of that," he said, moving back to the captain. "This is your territory. I'm the amateur here."

"Everything will work out," said Levent. "We might even recover the money that belongs to the company."

"That would be a bonus."

"He has it, you know."

"Really?" Wilding's voice was as lazy as a yawn. That was the best indication of his keen interest and his desire to be away quickly.

"That's why Tekel came here," said Levent. "And that's why he killed. He likes blood, especially the blood of someone he thinks wronged him, but he was always after the money. We have his accomplices, and they're telling everything they know at full volume. If there's anything to clean up, we'll find that, too."

"I'm sure you will, Inspector. I have full confidence. I'll say goodbye now. And good hunting."

Wilding snapped the phone shut and began to talk to the captain, using his hands like a native as Rasfar translated the sounds. If Levent had ever seen a man in a hurry, it was Ayla Acheson's uncle now. Something like panic had set in.

The Poyraz was ready to put to sea quickly. The captain cast off from the dock, tossing the line onto the deck and moving back to the wheel. No sailors, the other four sat down on cushioned seats to wait out a passive watch. Were they—like Rasfar—men from landlocked Moldavia?

On an outing for the day. It might seem suspicious with the day so close to ending, but no one asked questions. Stranger things happened every hour on the hour along this coast with stranger passengers and cargo.

Levent turned his back to the Poyraz and called Baran over. "Do you know the harbormaster here?"

"We're not blood brothers. He's a first-class tyrant, but I can talk to him."

"Find out what shipping left the harbor in the last hour," said Levent. "The harbormaster will know all the vessels, and not many should have gone out lately. And ask if he knows anything about Gurman or his cousin, and if either keeps a boat here. If they do, get what information you can. And ask about the Poyraz, too."

Levent began to walk toward the end of the jetty as the Poyraz backed out from the dock in a rumble of engines. Its horsepower might be greater than Levent thought, but the vessel showed no real speed as it nosed toward the open sea through the gap between the jetty and the land.

Levent almost kept pace with the cruiser as it churned from the harbor. The late light was nearly flat on the horizon, spreading bands of pastel color across the water. In an hour, visibility would be poor. The sea would turn black except for the lights from the ships in the Marmara waiting their chance to enter the Bosporus. It was a busy day with fifty freighters backed up in loose formation all the way to the Princess Islands.

When the Poyraz kicked in its engines, Levent accelerated his pace short of a run, moving behind a small waterside cafe where his movements were shielded. Ferhan and her partner had already taken up positions near the end of the jetty with their backs turned to the harbor, as if they had fishing lines in the water. Although they shouldn't have been able to see Levent coming, they got to their feet as he drew near.

"That must be the Coast Guard vessel approaching along the shore," said Ferhan. "Nothing else leaves a wake like that."

Levent followed the boat that moved parallel to the shore a hundred meters from it. Yes, the colors were right. And the speed. Nothing else moved like that on the water but a cigarette or a zodiac.

They would arrive soon after the Poyraz left the harbor. Good. Levent did not want his only lead frightened off by a faster, heavily armed boat. The Poyraz had begun to pass the jetty, engines at full throttle now, its stern digging the water. Even so, its advantage should not be much more than five minutes.

Levent turned his back to the Poyraz because the vessel was close. A pistol shot could reach them. He was startled when his cep rang at the same time.

"You won't need a pencil for this," said Inspector Baran. "The harbormaster says the Poyraz works out of this port. The captain will hire by the day but usually not longer. Nothing he won't do, of course, but he has no criminal record we're aware of. He's from one of the islands originally, but lives around here now."

It was good to know the range of the Poyraz usually did not extend far from port. Unless the captain changed his pattern, that meant the destination was somewhere in the local area.

"What does he have on Gurman?"

"You'll like this," said Baran. "Gurman keeps a boat here. It's a small one-berth powerboat called Gone with the Wind. She has blue blaze on her side, and she left the harbor about forty-five minutes ago."

"Did the harbormaster watch her move out?"

"Not for long," said Baran. "He didn't see anything. Gurman likes to go out on trips in the Marmara. In summer, he drops down to Finike to party with the rest of the *rakici*. But that should be much later."

"Thanks very much, Inspector. Tell your men to move in on the car now. I don't think they'll find our man ashore, but be careful. If they find anything, report at once."

"You sound like you're leaving us."

"As soon as my ship comes in."

Levent hoped his luck kept on a bit longer. He was sure Gurman had taken a dangerous passenger on board. Tekel might have kept him alive less for his expertise in banking than his knowledge of local waters. The Marmara was a placid sea when poyraz blew, but it rose up unpredictably when the squalls of lodos came on.

It was too bad Gurman knew his way around well enough to cruise the Marmara and the Aegean. What Levent thought he could count on was that Wilding had not chartered his boat for a long cruise. But money in large amounts had been known to turn a ship captain's head.

This one had set his Poyraz on a southerly course if it held. The vessel was not heading toward the Bosporus and the Black

Sea. To the west lay the Dardanelles and a swift run out of the country. To the south was the Asian side of Istanbul, and the islands of the Marmara Sea.

Levent did not have time to worry about a change of course as the Coast Guard vessel ran in the far side of the jetty on Ferhan's signal. The captain reversed engines and settled next to the biggest breakwater rock. Two of his men had already scrambled over the side to help their passengers aboard while the boat bobbed heavily in its own wake.

Levent had lived most of his forty-four years on the sea but never liked putting on it. He barely kept his legs as he boarded, and he hit the side of the vessel hard as it rose suddenly to meet him. When he found his balance again, he found himself looking at a short man with a huge chest who had extended his hand in greeting.

"Captain Zahir of the Istinye," he said. "Inspector Levent, I hear."

He twisted his handshake to grip Levent's thumb, giving him good purchase for the first time. Zahir's hands were as hard as shell, and he had no trouble with his balance or his smile, showing teeth that were barely lighter than the deep tan of his skin.

"We usually have drinks and *meze* for our visitors, but I was told to leave all the good things behind."

"We're in a hurry," said Levent. "We have to keep that cabin cruiser in sight but not crowd him."

Zahir looked ahead, where the Poyraz was still visible around the end of the jetty. She had a good five minutes lead and did not seem to have slackened speed. Levent felt the oncoming dusk in his eyes like a descending pressure from his brain.

"The stern chase can be a long one," said Zahir. "But I think we'll manage this time. Be sure to fasten your seat belt."

There were no seat belts.

CHAPTER 31

The Chase

Twenty minutes later, the light went out of the sea as if the Istinye was inside a container. The moon was in its first phase and the sky dark except for a haze of light from the west that would be hard to detect within seconds. The Poyraz would have been lost if not for Captain Zahir's night glasses. She had put out her lights in violation of the law, and was even careful of the glow of cigarettes.

For the first part of her night cruise, the Poyraz seemed to be on course for Buyukada, the Big Island in the necklace of the Princess Islands, until she corrected and began to slide for the open sea. Zahir did not know where the vessel was headed after she altered course. He said they would have to move closer to have any chance of keeping her in sight.

Levent did not argue, though he was afraid the Poyraz would find a quiet place to put in on one of the islands and wait out the Coast Guard. He did not know if Wilding had a schedule to meet, but he had obviously found someone to give him a look into Tekel's movements.

Levent remembered something else as they moved nearer to the Poyraz. Sibel Burgaz said Acheson had thrown her pistol into the Sea of Marmara while they were on the water with one of her cousins. Which cousin? How many did she have who owned pleasure boats? Had they been cruising, or did they have a destination? Levent used his phone and dialed Sibel's office number, but got no response.

She might be out to dinner, but ceps often did not relay well over the water, so Levent was not sure. He was surprised when the phone rang in his hand, and he was more surprised to learn the caller with interference around her voice was Berna Taner from Luna Bank.

"Inspector, I thought you should know. Someone just tried to access the account in Amsterdam."

"From here?"

"I can't be sure of that," she said. "But whoever it is knows what they're doing. They went in with the proper codes and passwords. They probably wanted to move the money to another account."

"Tell me your safeguards worked."

"Perfectly, Inspector. There will be no funds transferred today."

Levent rang off satisfied. Tekel had gotten where he was going and tried to access the account. It would be a place with a reliable computer.

That meant he had not gone far. He must have put in at another town along the shore or at one of the islands. He had no other choice unless he had gone directly across to Asia. And Wilding was not on his way there.

Levent did not know why the money had remained this long in the account in Amsterdam, but there would be a reason. It might have to do with the five hundred thousand dollar limit. To stay under it, several transfers had to be made in smaller amounts. And that meant more time spent doing it.

Tekel's instinct for survival was more like a method. He knew his chances diminished the longer he stayed in one place. He had left the Gurman apartment soon after transferring the money to Amsterdam. He could not know the police were close on his trail, but the question of dimensions came into play at that point. The man's antenna was good.

The reason he had not left two more bodies behind might be simple. He needed one of them to make the money move again, and the other as leverage for good behavior. It was his money now, and he would not like being told he could not have it.

That should keep the cousins alive. Tekel would try to siphon off the money again. He knew his access was blocked, but he would not necessarily know he had been tracked. Gurman might, but it was in his interest not to let on.

Imagine trying to talk that maniac down. Give me another chance, John. What do you have to lose? The flights to Mars run on the hour.

The cousins also might have cooperated, working with Tekel for a share of the money, but persuasion did not seem to be the killer's style. He had brutalized everyone to this point, which Levent was beginning to call the end.

That point seemed to come closer when Zahir stepped from the wheel, thrusting his face next to Levent, who was hunched down against the wind.

"He's made up his mind," said Zahir. "No turn signal, but he's headed for the Big Island the back way."

"The boat's captain is from one of the islands."

"He'd have to be," said Zahir with a smile. "Or he'll end up making a hole in the shore at night."

"So he wants to slip ashore quietly instead of making the harbor," said Levent. "Is there much around the back of the island?"

"There's high-priced charm everywhere," said Zahir. "Several docks, but not much in the way of sheltered coves. Some have collision barrels set up in case you miscalculate."

"Let's not."

Zahir laughed and clapped Levent's shoulder hard. "Are you saying it's time to move in?"

"It's time to do it fast."

* * *

Levent found out what happened when Zahir had a chance to reach for glory. His usual work consisted of tracking contraband in coastal waters, collecting waterproofed parcels of cigarettes, drugs and sundries that freighters threw over the side to be picked up by smaller craft. A mission that promised action and a close chase was like giving a child a credit card.

It did not seem possible for a vessel of the Istinye's size to rise out of the water and begin to plane, throwing so much sea-spray that it penetrated their weatherproofed gear. The engines roared so loud it seemed even a captain of great skill could find a bad answer on the dark water. The lights of the island were not many in the off-season, but that made them more ominous as they came closer, like lights in a tunnel. Oncoming. On course to collide.

Suddenly, out of the steady gloom, two vessels that had anchored off the rocks, protected by barrels around a small dock, appeared dead ahead. There were no others in the water.

Wilding's captain stood in the stern of his cruiser, waiting for his passengers to find their way back to him. He had been surprised and perhaps not for the first time by the Coast Guard. A second vessel promised to be Gurman's, though Levent could not read the writing on her stern until Zahir reversed engines and brought the Istinye alongside. Gone with the Wind. But not quite.

"Secure those boats, Captain. I'd like one of your men ashore if you can spare him."

"Go with them, Hakan," he said, tapping a short well-built man on the shoulder. "You're under the Inspector's orders now."

That made four guns, but the Tacs could be counted twice. Ferhan was already out of the boat, her long black hair gathered under her helmet, skimming the tops of the barrels while she carried a heavy line. Her partner, Kemal, jumped close behind her with the machine pistols. Hakan stayed on board the Istinye until Levent managed to grapple ashore as the vessel heaved.

When Levent stepped onto the dock, he saw two houses sixty meters up the hill. They stood fifteen meters apart, veer left, veer right, but only the one to the right had a light—two lights from two rooms—on the first floor. That was the approach.

"Hakan, you take the rear of the house. Contain anything that comes out the back door."

"Contain?"

"Shoot to kill."

Hakan, with a pistol in his belt and an automatic rifle on his arm, made for the back of the house at a run.

"They haven't come here to talk," said Levent to the Tacs. "We'll find at least two men armed, and one killer. Tell me if you have an objection to getting off the first shot and making it good."

"Do we knock?" asked Ferhan.

"We do whatever it takes to close."

The Tacs moved out along the stone path from the dock, flanking Levent on either side. He did not see how this would lay out. Tekel had two hostages whose status would not be honored by Wilding or his men. Levent could not afford to honor them either, though he would try.

They reached the broad terrace that fronted the house quickly, but it was slower going after Levent took the steps. The evening cold and age made the boards creak like something lodged inside his body. The lights from the windows fell over the boards in widening arcs that were hard to get outside. Levent used the light to guide his approach, feeling as if he was timing his steps to a hidden clock.

He peered through the first window, moving into the shadows surrounding the puddles of light. The first thing he saw was a middle-aged woman. She sat like a study in brown, her hands folded in her lap on the middle cushion of a divan. That should be Emel Demir. Levent thought he saw fear in her eyes, but she should have been past that point. Her eyes moved from the figure standing on her right—Samuel Wilding—to second man who occupied the central point of the room.

He sat in a chair with a high back as if nothing around him could touch him. Levent would have known him on the street or in a car passing in a blur. Tekel. The eyes that everyone remembered reduced the rest of his features to anonymity. He might be handsome, but the well-formed nose and sturdy chin hardly mattered. This was a man of will, concentrated, manufactured, and all one-way. He exchanged nothing with the things he saw. And everything was a thing.

He spoke. Levent could not make out the words, but he sensed they were defiant. Tekel was telling his audience he did not abide by its ways, and that included the broad-shouldered man who stood directly behind him. Levent could not be sure, since his view was obscured, but something in the man's posture said he held a gun.

Levent could have given the signal to break in the door, but he waited, thinking he could locate Gurman, the banker, Rasfar, the fixer, and Wilding's second man, who would certainly be armed, too.

Slowly, Levent moved from shadow into still light. If anyone in the room turned their eyes to the front of the house, they would see him. But no one did. Their focus was intense. Levent saw now that the first man had a gun close to Tekel's head. The end of the barrel was just visible, like an extension of his hand.

Where was the other man of the oversized pair? Levent scanned the room but still did not see him.

If Wilding had his choice, he would kill the man who had killed his niece. Why hadn't he?

The money, of course. After Wilding found out where Tekel put the money, he would put Tekel back on the boat and move him to a better place offshore where bank accounts and bodies were hard to find.

Now they talked. Had Tekel told Wilding the money in the account was blocked? Possibly. Was there any chance Wilding believed him? None.

Levent saw a flash of movement that came from the next room. A stout man with a large nose and no natural color in his hair came through the doorway. He had his hands raised just past his waist, a parody of a man under guard. Not a gun hand, this was Ibrahim Gurman.

He was followed by two men. The first was Delir Rasfar by the scar on his cheek. A Moldavian by way of Iran, he was the connection to Trip Cs.

Trailing him closely was a second big man—this one with blond hair. He was so broad he turned slightly sideways as he moved through the doorway into the room. Levent did not know where Wilding found these two, but there was a stockpile somewhere for those who knew how to look. It was not the usual places and it might be Moldavia.

Levent guessed that Gurman had been taken to a computer where he was told to access the Amsterdam account, and that he had failed a second time under more difficult conditions. Failure was clear in his posture and face.

The blonde man moved forward, prodding Gurman with a finger to his shoulder. Gurman lurched at that small touch, almost stumbling to the couch. He sat on the cushion that was nearest Tekel. As he did, Levent saw the weapon, a nine-millimeter with a laser sight, in the man's hand.

All the big men and the small were accounted for. Levent turned to Ferhan and Kemal, who crouched on both sides of the front door. Ferhan pointed to the knob and mouthed one word: "Open."

Levent moved to the door carefully. "We have two men with pistols," he said softly, pointing to their positions on the other side of the door and hoping they had not moved. "One blond, one with brown hair, both large. Four other men and one woman, but I don't think they should be a problem. They're probably not armed, but I could be wrong."

Levent did not say Wilding or Rasfar were problems, thinking they wouldn't be. He did not mention Tekel, because that was Levent's problem. Whatever happened, that man was his.

"Let's move."

The Tacs nodded at the same time. "Come in behind us," said Ferhan. "Don't disturb our line of fire."

Kemal reached to the brass doorknob, turning it slowly to release the lock, and when it clicked in, he nodded again.

They blew through the door. Levent knew he would never be able to write a reasoned report of what happened in the next seconds, which were less than a few and filled with tumbling noise.

Ferhan was first through the door, screaming "POLICE!" Kemal covered her from the doorjamb, screaming "DON'T

MOVE!" He put his machine pistol on the first big man who stood to the left.

The man fired. It was probably just a reflex, but it was the one that killed him. His bullet struck the doorjamb, throwing chips of wood like a spray of water as Levent heard multiple answers from Ferhan's weapon. The man slammed back across the room as if on wheels, smashing down on the glass-topped table before the divan, the glass and the legs collapsing over him.

When he hit the floor, the women in the chair screamed as if she had been hit. Levent heard himself scream at the second big man: "EVERYONE DOWN! DROP YOUR WEAPONS NOW!"

The blond man hesitated. He looked at the weapons pointed at his chest until they passed from the element of surprise into a region of fate. He put one hand up as if surrendering, looking at the other that still held the weapon. Finally, he shook the pistol from his hand onto the floor in front of the divan.

That should have been the end—all weapons down. Levent had stepped through the doorway, his eyes on Tekel. He thought the killer smiled when their eyes met, and perhaps he did.

Tekel put up his hands as if surrendering, grasping the high back of the chair. It seemed like a neutral movement until suddenly he lurched in the chair. Throwing all his weight backward, he upended it. No one moved or fired their weapons as he disappeared into the black bottom of the chair, tumbling, his body visible as he turned the somersault, and then quickly hidden behind it.

Levent moved fast, crossing the room in three steps. He knew he should not look to the place Tekel had been but where he was going. The dining room lay behind the divan and the chair. As Levent passed them, he saw the door leading out the back. He put his pistol on that point and focused until he heard the loud crash of glass to his left.

Tekel hurtled through the window into another medium. It was a tall window reaching nearly to the floor, and did not require much of a leap, but no sane man would have taken it. Tekel went headlong, his legs passing through the window last, raking loose a stubborn shard of glass. Levent fired one round at the legs as they vanished, not knowing if he had hit anything.

But Tekel was outside, and nothing he had done was less than animal quick. Levent heard a burst of automatic fire from the rear of the house. That would be Hakan answering.

Levent kicked the back door open. Flattening against it, he shouted into the darkness. "Where is he?"

"To the left," said Hakan. "He went into those bushes."

Levent looked left. A hill rose behind the house, growing steeper as it moved upward, and losing most of its ground cover as it climbed. Though his night vision was not good as he came from the light, he thought it was good enough to see movement on open ground.

The lower part of the hill had been cleared and replaced with ornamental plants and two trees of good size. The shadows thrown around the trees spread into a common gloom with the light of the waning moon.

"Did you hit him, Hakan?"

"I don't see how I could have missed," he said, stalking toward the bushes. "But the way he moved, I'm not sure."

Levent would have told Hakan to strip the bushes with live rounds, but he did not think Tekel lingered there. This man would move from shadow to shadow until he found a place where he could strike those coming for him. He would do it noiselessly, because he was always part of the shadows.

"Follow close behind me," said Levent to Hakan. "Put a burst into anything that moves."

Levent walked as quickly up the hill as he could in the dim light. Although his eyes were growing used to the darkness, and he could see every clump of vegetation as a distinct piece of night, he knew he saw things that were not there. A shadow that moved. A flower that swayed. And the low branch of the first tree that was anything but a hallucination.

Levent cursed when he hit his head, but not loud enough to show his anger. And when he was angry, he talked.

"John! This is Inspector Levent! Your pen pal from ICQ. We understand each other now. You want me to believe you're a maniac, but I know you're a tortured man who tortures to feel the blood moving through his body. You knew it would come to this from the beginning. That's why you wanted to talk with someone who could understand. You have a problem you can't solve, and we both know it has little to do with money. You're a thief, John, but not a common one. You proved you're uncommon, but you can't prove you're invisible. I found you here, and I'll find you everywhere you go. And believe me, you're not going far."

Levent stopped on the margin of a small path he had been following but had never seen. Ahead stood a thick patch of underbrush that began at the end of the space the second tree had claimed.

He heard a sound that seemed to come from the brush. Hakan heard it, too. He squeezed a burst that caused the foliage to jump as it ripped through the light cover and again as it ripped through the leaves of the tree behind.

Levent moved quickly, almost within the burst, toward the brush. There had been no response to the fire. No sound. No movement.

He felt the pistol in his hand like a wand, and this, the last part of the chase, like calling up darkness. Tekel was not in the brush, but he was nearby. He knew his enemy was prepared to walk his ammunition to the target, searching for him in the most efficient way. He would have to move fast again—or die.

"You have to give up, John! You know that! The end is where you say it is! The man who loves his sister in all the wrong ways and wishes they were right knows in his heart that he's been looking for someone to end his pain. You despise everything about this life except its symbols. You despise the thought of leaving, too, but you find the decision complicated. I'm here to help you simplify."

Levent did not expect his taunts to draw Tekel out, but if he put hatred into that man without a soul, he might cause a reaction.

Tekel would not act without thinking, but he might do it without calculating.

Levent thought he heard a sound coming from a clump of white oleander that grew in a dense colony halfway up the hill. It grew to the size of trees here, fed by the sun and sea air. Blossoms with no smell, but long leaves and a lot of them. That would suit Tekel. When Hakan did not react to the sound, Levent moved forward, pointing to the oleander.

Hakan, damn him, did not wait to confirm. He squeezed, and the sound of the rapid fire was loud as it rattled through the bushes. The flowers jumped and began a slow cascade to the ground that was like snow in its silent beauty. Levent waited until his ears could distinguish sounds again, and while the air was still filled with shattered blossoms, Tekel struck.

Levent did not know it until Hakan dropped to his knees, his weapon pinned to the ground by his fall like a crutch. Behind him was Tekel, bringing the large branch down again on the back of Hakan's head. In a motion that followed the first like a continuation, Tekel kicked the weapon free.

He was quick. Dream quick. Tekel followed the weapon without seeming to move, catching it by its grip as it fell toward the oleander. The stock twisted into the crook of his arm and the barrel twisted toward its target.

And that was Levent. He looked up into those eyes streaming from the bed of night hypnotized by the speed—the speed that seemed to come from another dimension where everything was decided—but he knew he would settle for any shot and thought he could get off two. Pulling to the left in case he missed, Levent dropped to the ground as he fired.

The first shot and probably the second had gone high. Too high. He had not brought them down when bringing them down meant everything. Levent was still looking up at Tekel, knowing he had found the worst place under the stars, when all the orbits suddenly changed.

Tekel's forward movement stopped. He seemed to rise, but as if the ground beneath him had risen. He waved his left hand as if waving farewell. Levent wondered about that afterward, because the gesture was too elegiac.

The only answer he could give with the passage of time—the passage of years—was that Tekel had tried to wipe the blood from his eye. It was the left eye that imploded from the impact of a bullet—the same one that he had cored like the most tasteless part of a fruit from the face of Ayla Acheson.

CHAPTER 32

Timing

"So you made sense of everything."

"Most of it," said Akbay, taking his feet down from Levent's desk. "We can bet Duran's story will change when he gets close to his lawyer. I pity that bastard. Duran's mind is like a snake pit with a glass bottom. It's impossible to get a straight answer when everything has to pass through his asshole first. If he gets the go ahead from the source, it comes out his mouth with the shit still clinging."

Akbay lit another cigarette as the last smoldered in the ashtray, daintily holding the stub of his finger aside. "It's hard to think so, but Duran was the one who brought all the things together into a nice chaos. I think he'd known Tekel for a while—from England or Turkey, or maybe ICQ—but he's smart enough to know if he admits that, he's in trouble he'll never get out of. So it's Atilla with all the bloody holes in him who did the evil things."

"What do we have from the hospital on his condition?"

"No change," said Akbay, who was seriously hoping for some. "They don't know how he's hanging on, but he's just this side of his maker. They transferred him to Memorial as soon as they could, and those people are good with chest wounds. But he's taking up half the Intensive Care Unit."

"As long as he's still alive."

"It's a good thing we don't need him to make our case," said Akbay. "If he recovers, he'll tell his own set of lies. Those two would sell out each other for a song, and a cheap Arabesque at that. I'm not sure they ever got along, but for a while it was cozy. In the end, Duran realized Atilla was just looking out for himself. He had no problem peddling his ass, and for the soul we'll ever know even if they pulled it out of his chest. Duran decided to cover his bets in both directions then. It happened after our street boy refused to come up to the standards of a first-class lover. That's how I got Duran going—when he admitted Atilla wasn't putting out properly. It was an emotional moment, I tell you. We both got down and cried."

"I wish I'd been there," said Levent. "I appreciate genius."

"I'd like a medal," said Akbay. "From the department or the dramatic guild, I don't give a damn. I was actually living that sorry thing he calls a love life. It was the only way to penetrate him, so to speak. After we went through a box of tissues, Duran admitted he was the one who put Atilla—and Tekel—onto Gurman. And the money. But then out of the bushes, Wilding comes along and applies his own pressure—the consulting kind. He promises the business will be shut down and Duran with it. He tells him some big men will be coming to his door very soon— and he doesn't mean the police. The only thing Duran has to do to change the future is cooperate. That's all Duran knows how to do is please people, anyway. He goes where he's pushed. With Atilla pushing, and Wilding pushing, what could he do but try to please everyone? So he tells the uncle about Gurman. And Duran knows a lot about Gurman. Everything it's possible to know, I'd say. Those two used to cruise together—with and without a boat."

"It's lucky he's incompetent," said Levent. "We never would have been able to track down Tekel except for Wilding."

Akbay blew several smoke rings, all obscene. "Duran came to regret it, though. Atilla found out the plan had been shared. Betrayed is probably too big a word, but things got bigger pretty fast. All that business with the gun at Duran's head was real. It had gone on for a bit before we got to the apartment. Atilla was mad and just about had the whole story from Duran when we showed up. If we'd been ten minutes later, Atilla would have been able to warn Tekel."

"Timing," said Levent. "It's the secret of life if there is one."

"There is one," said Akbay.

* * *

"It comes of suiting the man to the job," said the Chief, drawing on his Cartier and then as deeply on his cup of Turkish coffee. "The science of management. Personnel deployment. I take credit for that."

"As you should, sir."

"I suppose another man could have done the job," said the Chief, amending his virtues. "But to do it in a way that the body politic was not disturbed, yes, we owe you our thanks, Inspector. A foreigner couldn't be a better catch. A greedy foreigner with a bloody mind is near perfection. Truly, it's better than a psychopath."

"I'll tell Emine how pleased you are," said Levent. "She was worried about the political effects."

"A sensible woman as well as a Turkish beauty," said the Chief. "I don't know how you managed to talk her into your marriage bed."

Levent knew what was coming and he did not mind. Finding the right lie was the problem. "I had another man speak for me, sir. He had a better feeling for those kinds of things."

"A more direct man."

"Direct and honest," said Levent, using the two words the Chief had no use for. "In the same vein, I was thinking you would want to be at the press conference, sir. You might even consider a solo appearance."

"I've thought about it certainly," said the Chief, smiling his pleasure. "And I've come to the conclusion that I should be able to manage those howling dogs on my own. But don't worry, Onur, your participation in the case will be noted."

"Thank you very much, sir." Levent paused and took a long drink of his cup of filtered coffee. "Have you decided how to present the participation of the others in this affair? Rasfar will do almost anything to avoid being sent back to Iran. All we have to do is squeeze him."

"Will he tell the truth?"

"I wouldn't go that far," said Levent. "What he says will depend on what Samuel Wilding says. They're business partners, after all. I believe the towers off TEM are just one of their ventures."

The Chief cocked his sculpted head as if all the ghosts of Byzantium whispered in his ear. "I must say I'm disappointed in Mister Wilding. We extend him the hospitality of our city, and he does his best to abuse it. Responsible for the deaths of two men, though perhaps not directly."

"We're saying it was indirect, sir?"

"We will be, yes. That's one thing we can safely leave to the politicians. I imagine that even an inept man will be able to broker meaningful consideration from the British. It should be a good bargain that's struck in the end."

"Then the parties have already been in contact."

"Absolutely," he said. "Samuel Wilding seems to be a more important man than we imagined. The word I received is that not only the British government but the Americans have been pleading his case."

"The transportation firm he works with does work for the Americans," said Levent. "It's possible they do more than I was told."

"Was that in your report?"

"No, sir. Incidental information from a private source."

The Chief sat on Levent's answer as if it was an egg. "Do you think there's a chance I'll be asked about it?"

"I'd be surprised if that happened, sir. My source is deeply embedded and very discreet."

"I suppose he's the same man who told you where the money came from?"

"That's a good guess, sir. In fact, I received another call from him this morning. It seems the Americans have decided that discretion is the better part of embarrassment. They're unlikely to look closely at the origin of the money. At least, not as long as they need an Iraqi puppet government. That's where the funds originate."

"Corruption," said the Chief, caressing the word.

"On a large scale. With the price of oil, the disposition of the funds must be a problem for them. Nor will the shipments stop as long as the Americans need people foolish enough to fly to and from a dangerous country. They pretend not to know any-thing about Rasfar, by the way. Officially, they don't speak to Iranians."

The Chief mooed like a young girl. "I'd consider it a favor if I could speak with this source of yours. He must have the ear of God."

"I'd find it difficult sharing him," said Levent. "If I betrayed his trust, he'd never act on my requests again."

The Chief did not like that answer, but strangely, he turned his disapproval into a smile. "Discretion, Inspector. Your forte."

"Indeed, sir."

"I'm glad we agree," said the Chief, as if he had sprung a trap. He opened the first drawer of his desk and took out a paper with a face he was careful not to show. "I've just had word from a different quarter. It seems we've had an incident on the Other Side. Not much for mayhem—and certainly nothing like the last—but still a problem. It involves the son of a member of the Assembly. I don't have all the details, but you'll be wanting to get to the scene as soon as possible."

"I was planning on dinner at home, sir. Emine—"

"Understands," he said. "That's why you married her. Blood lines, Inspector. What are we here for if not to match up our glorious heritage with our promising future?"

From time to time, and certainly by accident, the slick bastard said something that was morally defensible. And he always said it well. Levent took the slim paper from the Chief's hand—a fax from Ankara bearing the seal of the General Assembly—and excused himself from the room. As he left the building by the back door, the legions of the press came rioting in the front.

Did you enjoy this book?

Visit ForemostPress.com to share

your comments or a review.